The Glass House

House

Jody Cooksley

LEAF BY LEAF

Published by Leaf by Leaf
an imprint of Cinnamon Press
Meirion House
Tanygrisiau
Blaenau Ffestiniog
Gwynedd, LL41 3SU
www.cinnamonpress.com

The right of Jody Cooksley to be identified as author of this work
has been asserted by her in accordance with the Copyright, Designs
and Patent Act, 1988. Copyright © 2020 Jody Cooksley

ISBN: 978-1-78864-911-7

Designed and typeset in Palatino by Cinnamon Press.

Cover design by Adam Craig © Adam Craig.

Cinnamon Press is represented in the UK by Inpress Ltd and in
Wales by the Books Council of Wales.

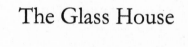

The Glass House

For my brother, David

Part I
The Artist's Death

Oh, mystery of Beauty! Who can tell
  Thy mighty influence? Who can best descry
How secret, swift and subtle is the spell
  Wherein the music of thy voice doth lie?
                    Julia Margaret Cameron, On a Portrait

1861 Freshwater Bay

Their words still rang in Julia's ears as she ran to the shore. Stumbling on a pile of tide-strewn pebbles, she put out a hand to steady herself against the breakwater and howled at the stars. How could she ever speak to the islanders again? All her plans had dissolved like dreams, leaving her defenceless. A silly, middle-aged woman, filled with the impotent rage of ambition. Only now could she see it clearly.

Moonlight bathed the damp sand along Freshwater Bay: a sweeping horseshoe curve that calmed the waves in the worst weather. A place of peace. The scene of her first encounter with the Society. How could she have trusted them? And the Signor; he had encouraged her all along, knowing she would be exposed. How had she been so foolish? All the visions in her head were nonsense. All her claims to Art, lies.

Placing her boots beside her, Julia sat to rest on the low wall behind the lighthouse and stared at the shimmering river reflecting from shore to horizon. Reckless of her to seek recognition in the first place; hadn't she always been told it wasn't natural for women to crave attention? Weary with sadness, she pushed her bare toes into the wet sand and raised them, watching the wells pool with water and merge again with the rest of the beach. Where was the footprint she had promised to leave on the world? She had carried the promise like a sword for most of her life and yet left nothing. No paintings, no words of any use, no brave new Art. Her only footprint would be transient, would fill with water and sand and simply disappear.

The calm sea beckoned her forward and Julia stood, stretched, began to walk towards it. A smooth surface prettily reflected with stars. It was much less cold than she'd expected and lapped gently around her ankles, welcome and comforting. Julia watched as the dark water swallowed her feet, then her calves. Still she walked, vaguely aware of the drag and swell of her skirts. Overhead stretched the low web of stars that wrapped her island, reminding her suddenly of India, the brightness of long hot nights and the yearning to capture the colour of skies. The sense of destiny she felt and the secrets she uncovered. It was a lifetime ago. A lifetime of making wings only to discover that she was never meant to fly.

Something flapped against her neck and she lifted her hand, touched the silk of her bonnet. Why had she felt the need to impress those fools with a ridiculous hat? Fumbling for the ribbons, she shook them free and threw the hateful thing behind her onto the sand. The tumble of her hair, long and loose, made her a child again. Mama's Indian sunbird, soaring high above the world to see what others could not. A hopeful princess at a vicious party, with a long pink bow at her waist. They had laughed at her then, and laughed at her now. She was tired of trying to please. All she wanted was to sleep, to forget. Scenes from her life flashed past, too fast to catch and hold.

Julia walked as far as she could. When the water reached her waist, she leaned forward and gave herself to the sea, wanting only to be taken, imagining herself floating forever like Ophelia in her bed of reeds.

1822 Calcutta

'Tell me what it means.' Julia traced her finger around the outline of a pink circle, studded with dark blue marks.

'It's not for children, ma chère. One day you will understand.'

Julia stuck out her lip; Mama was the only grown up who thought she was too small to understand things. Papa answered her questions. He was fun, striding like a king in his crisp military dress and swinging her in the air. She flounced away from the wall and caught the edge of the table, knocking a silver-backed mirror and hairbrush to the ground. Mama flew across the room to scold her.

'Seven years bad luck!'

'It isn't broken.'

'Lucky for you. Seven years is a long time to be punished for mistakes.'

'Two years more than Sarah.'

Mama's eyebrows closed in the middle when she frowned. Like monkeys before they attacked. 'Sarah would never be so naughty.'

She was using her distracted voice, starting to move away. It was important to know. Scrolls and parchments covered the walls of their stilted house, as hard to understand as Mama's mood. Julia tried again, tugging at her bangles. 'Why are they painted like that?'

Mama stroked the thick paper, her fingers dragging over the curled edge, eyes focussed on something Julia couldn't see. 'It's a science, ma chère. The stars hold your destiny.'

'When I'm seven, will you tell me what it means?' When Adeline was seven Papa had given her a pony he'd won in a game of cards. Seven was special, and it was soon. It was too exciting wondering what seven would bring. Mama shook her head slowly. 'But I want to understand! Papa says I'll only understand if I ask questions, but what's the point if no-one will answer them?' Mama didn't like the way he always laughed at her charts. Julia gave her a sly look. 'Shall I ask Papa then? Does he have signs too?'

'Very well,' she replied, rolling up the chart with a snap. 'But you must have your own. I'll ask the scribe at Pahor.'

The chart was delivered with a flourish by the scribe's young apprentice, curled in a thick bundle of parchment and tied with grass. If only Mama would look at her so attentively. Whatever it meant it was pretty. Each of the symbols was painted in double colours, surrounded by a pattern of silver stars on a background of swirling lilac and indigo clouds. How wonderful to make such pictures. She would ask for paints for her seven present. Julia turned to the scribe's boy, waiting patiently, and asked him in Hindustani what it meant.

'Master says you will live two lives. One will be taken by waves,' he replied in English, intoning in a flat voice as though reading from a script, his head bowed. 'One will be broken by mirrors and glass. You must watch for them both.' The boy raised his head, briefly catching Julia's puzzled gaze before casting his eyes back to the floor.

With a stony expression, Mama took the chart, gave him a parcel wrapped in cloth and a wad of paper rupiah to deliver to the scribe. Then she ushered him out to the door, before retiring to bed with a headache. Was Mama somehow displeased? Paintings usually made her happy.

Julia searched all over, finally discovering the chart in her mother's dressing room. It was inside a drawer, lying on top of a frayed yellow envelope containing two small white cotton caps and two dry locks of hair tied at each end with pale green string. Perhaps Mama was planning to make a doll for the special seven present? A doll with old dried hair? A horse would be better. Even one with thundering feet and a head that jerked on its reins like Adeline's.

She brought her finds down to supper. But, as she held them up for inspection, a swift hand struck everything to the ground. What had she done to make Mama so angry today? Sudden tears blurred everything but the sight of the pear-shaped diamond on her right ring finger as it flew back towards her face. Fine-cut edges left a weal across Julia's cheek the size and shape of a rosemallow flower. It still smarted the following week, when she and Sarah were taken to be schooled in Paris.

1827 Versailles

Julia's birthday fell in high summer, when the scent of lavender in Grandmamma's garden was strong enough to draw tears. A feast was spread on long tables, under the shade of the willow. Girls in muslin brought cards pressed with wild flowers. The number twelve was iced in sugar roses on a tall, white cake. She walked across the lawn to lunch feeling like a princess, hair loose at the back, a secret smile, a wide pink sash around her waist.

Afterwards, she hid in the washroom and wept. To think that she had spoiled such a perfect day by listening to the grown-ups! That coven of old women in jet-black lace and beads, always talking, crouched like spiders over their iced tea and four o'clock gin, crumbling madeleines between their pointing fingers. Yet, crawling along under the table to catch one of the kitchen cat's new silver-striped kittens, she'd heard her name and stopped to listen.

'I'm afraid it's no use pretending we're waiting to see how she turns out. Julia's certainly not like her sisters.'

Her ears strained to hear the second, quieter voice.

'Poor thing. So unlike her own mother too. Sarah's the very image of her, but Julia…'

She stayed crouched below the table, breathing in tense, shallow gasps with the effort of remaining silent. A light breeze lifted the tablecloth's edge, briefly exposing her left knee. Don't let them notice. A sudden vision of Grandmamma's fierce face brought the acid-sharp taste of tomatoes to her throat. Sarah had warned that too many slices of tart would make her sick.

'You must admit that, given her heritage, Julia is something of a surprise.'

Another pause. The sound of glasses being filled. Then Grandmamma spoke. 'She's young. Young ladies do change. And she's still quite the garçon manqué.'

'She's of age today. There's nothing about her looks that will improve from here.'

'And that figure! She's as dumpy as a sow.'

Hot tears pricked the edges of Julia's eyes. She would not cry. Not here, where Sarah would demand to know the reason and delight in sharing it among the guests. Grandmamma must surely contradict them? Dry grass prickled unbearably at her ankles.

'Julia's bright and intelligent. She will make a good wife,' the old woman spoke slowly, precisely.

'She's unlikely to make a good mistress…' the voice paused to accommodate a burst of laughter. 'But perhaps she doesn't care.'

Did she care? She didn't want to. But her eyes were wet, her stomach churning. A scraping of chairs as the old women rose sent Julia scuttling along the grass to the other side of the table, where she stood and brushed the debris from her pinafore, glancing around to see if anyone had spotted her, before running into the house and upstairs.

Music carried from the garden, rising and falling in jarring snatches. It would serve them right if she threw a bucket of water from the window. They weren't friends anyway, just boring little girls Grandmamma had gathered from neighbouring chateaux to fill out the day, just as she collected adults for her salon. Peering into the worn glass above the washstand, Julia examined her features with interest for the first time in her life. How had she never noticed she looked nothing like Sarah and Adeline, with their rose cheeks and delicate brows? Staring from the murk of the antique mirror was the colourless face of a peasant, with broad, rough features. Only the eyes sparkled, as though refusing to know their place. Slowly she turned her head from left to right, admiring her eyes with their heavy lids and deep amber-brown. From their depths flared tiny orange lights, like flames.

Noises mixed with the music—clattering hooves, the crunch of gravel under carriage wheels—signalling that the guests must be leaving. If they hadn't missed her before, they would surely be looking now. Grandmamma would never forgive such inhospitable behaviour. Julia, embarrassed and ashamed, jumped up so quickly the wooden stool fell backwards onto the floorboards with a smack that echoed in the bare room. Hiding for so long, she'd missed everything: the dancing, the cutting of that wonderful cake, the girls singing her name as they crowned her with a headdress of gold paper. Such a wasted day. She set the stool straight and peered through the window. At the gates by the front of the house stood perfect Sarah, handing paper twists of sweets to the guests, holding their hands and bobbing down in a theatrical curtsey. Something glinted in the early evening sunlight. A crown: the crown of a birthday girl worn with the confidence of a real princess. For a brief moment she felt nothing but hatred for them all.

Grandmamma put it down to excitement, even after the fight for the crown. Patronising in that special way of elders and betters, no questions asked and the children sent off for an early bedtime. Julia hugged the lumpen body of her doll, Amina, dressed in a thin white handkerchief and sharp-tufted wings made from magpie feathers. Moonlight slanted across her sisters' faces, lighting the delicate curves of their cheeks. Adeline still looked peaceful and kind, her mouth soft. Sarah's lips were flatter, giving her smile a sarcastic edge, even in sleep. Her own neat wooden doll lay by her head. Cake crumbs stuck at the corners of her mouth and the sight brought another spike of anger. The birthday girl should know how the cake tasted. She would go down at once to see if any was left. Wrapping herself in Adeline's silk gown she tiptoed to the door and felt her way along the corridor. No one would follow her even if they woke; Adeline wouldn't want to be told off and that baby Sarah was still scared of the dark. Who would want to be like them anyway?

She should have confronted them when she had the chance. So what if she looked different to her family? The lights in her eyes were fierce as fire. This was how she should be. Strong. Beautiful as the flames in her eyes. Because beauty could be found everywhere, it could be captured and discovered, she could feel it. She could create it. And it was part of her, whatever those old women might say.

Ideas formed in her mind. Visions of the walls in the Louvre; the frescoes in the church at San Sebastian; the portraits in the Long Hall at school. Pictures of ordinary people, made beautiful with bright colours, threaded with light and tipped with gold. She would learn to paint! Already her head was filled with ideas. No one could prevent her from becoming an Artist. As an Artist she would have more beauty at her fingertips than her sisters could imagine, and such beauty would never grow old and fat like Grandmamma's.

Forgetting the cake, Julia half-ran to the study and seized her short quill from the pot. Thank-you cards were stacked in the pile she had been made to start. Those that were finished were stamped roughly with the family seal and bright red beads of wax scattered the desk like a blood trail. Drawing the newly sharpened nib across the soft pad of her left hand she scoured a cut and squeezed it quickly onto the pages of her letter book, scratching thin red lines of script.

Until her twelfth birthday she had neither imagined growing up, nor considered what her future life might bring. Now she knew she would be an Artist. When she'd finished writing, she dried the ink, threw the blotting paper onto the embers of the fire and hid the promise in her reticule, drawing the strings up tightly.

Stories from the Glass House:
Henry Taylor

A wholly natural scientist: inquisitive, determined. Always
wanted to get to the bottom of things, to understand them
properly. Very unlike a woman in that regard. Such a
fascination for collecting the natural world, for sorting it
into piles and putting it into boxes that she could label. If
she'd been in possession of any kind of masculine patience,
she may well have discovered something astonishing about
the order of things. But she possessed nothing of the sort.
She was impetuous, impatient and she only ever wanted to
be an artist anyway. Of that she was certain, although one
could see how very unhappy it made her.

My wife, Alice, always claimed that the camera was her
saviour, and photography really the perfect thing for her. It
was creative science and she made sure she understood the
chemistry behind it, even if she did break all the rules. Such
a feminine approach, quite mad really. But then someone
like Julia Margaret could never have done anything ordinary.

We were all in thrall to her once she was on the throne
in her Glass House. I've no idea how she persuaded me to
wear that hat for my portrait. It wasn't mine, probably
belonged to her husband. She dragged the hat, and a cloak
too, from her costume box. A dreadful floppy velvet hat,
the kind a wandering minstrel might wear. It gave me a
soppy look, quite at odds with my work. Alice said it made
me look romantic, but I regretted it afterwards. I'd needed a
photograph I could use for my playbills and it simply wasn't
serious enough. Though I did refuse to wear the cloak,
which she'd covered in stars like the robes of a wizard. So
perhaps I got away rather lightly. A great many of her poor
subjects were bullied into the wearing of such costumes.

Julia Margaret loved the very idea of magic, and
superstition was rife in the whole family. Been in India too

long I should say. The mother was half mad with it, even when I was there, and what happened to those poor drowned babies was enough to send anyone screaming. I don't think Julia Margaret knew. She was so young she would have missed the worst of it. It affected all the sisters though, in their own ways. Adeline was dreadfully melancholy. Virginia was terrified of everything. Sarah was the only one of those Pattle girls with her feet on the ground; she knew what she wanted in life and woe betide anyone if they stood in her way, even her own sister.

Julia Margaret pretended superstition was all nonsense, but for her there was magic everywhere, not just fairies in the trees but a sense of the mystical about everything. She was filled with these romantic notions about the world, always expecting something to happen. In the end I suppose it did, though she waited long enough for it to come.

1832 Paris

'Don't make such a cross face Sarah. It's a wife's duty to be with her husband.' Mama looked across to where Julia sat, wearing a riot of colourful silk roughly sewn into a dress. A muddled heap of brushes and a little wooden easel lay at her feet. 'Julia understands why I must go back, don't you darling?'

Julia didn't wish to understand; she would far rather her handsome father was sitting before her, scented with cigar-smoke and whiskey, the promise of parties. Mama was no easier to talk to than Grandmamma, sitting straight-backed in formal lace while her daughters lounged on the grass. A light dusting of chalky powder lit her cheeks. The pear-shaped diamond sparkled on her finger. In the two years since her last visit, Julia had painted tirelessly; Adeline was the only person to have commented on her work. Approval from her elder sister was not worth having, she liked everything. If only Mama would show some sign of pleasure in her efforts.

'Little Virginia won't settle until I leave this time. You sisters will need time to get to know each other.'

'She seems terribly shy.' Julia tossed her head. That baby had done nothing but cling to Mama's skirts since she'd arrived. Worse than Sarah for her constant hovering by the looking glass, always swishing her skirts and dressing her hair. As if she wanted people to notice her. As if they wouldn't anyway. Already it was plain to see that Virginia would be the most beautiful in the family.

'Do you like my robe? Adeline says it's enchanting.' Julia performed a theatrical twirl that flared out her silks in a small coloured dome, like an Indian parasol. She was proud of the clothes she made, never using patterns but forcing the fabric into shape with heavy stitches that Madame sadly remarked could have fixed a fisherman's net. There were bright silks and satins for warm weather and evenings, velvet for the colder months and everything was liberally trimmed with ribbon and glittering paste jewels.

'It's certainly interesting.' Mama smoothed back her curls and patted a tortoiseshell hair-comb into place. Perhaps I will ask Madame to arrange some dressmaking lessons.'

Sarah scrubbed at the paint smear on the shoulder of her pale blue dress. 'If these marks don't come out, I shall need someone to make me a new dress,' she said, frowning. 'Don't you ever clean those filthy brushes of yours?'

'Delacroix never cleaned his brushes. He said it filled his work with the ghosts of his other paintings. I rather like the idea, as though looking at one painting might mean looking at them all.' Julia picked up a brush and swept it through the air. She'd been making a special study of paintings in the churches that dominated every street near their school in St Germain. Graphic depictions of martyrdom in bright jewel tones. Such paintings generated questions Madame found it difficult to answer, but Julia kept a list in her notebook, promising herself that, one day, she would be able to order as many books as she wanted, about whichever subjects she chose.

'You're not an artist, and I very much doubt you ever will be.' Sarah aimed her words with a sibling's affectionate spite. 'Grandmamma says you are wasting your time.'

It was a secret Julia wished she'd never shared. Sarah had a nasty habit of storing information to use unkindly. And she fawned all over Grandmamma, dutifully rubbing her swollen ankles, brushing her thinning hair. Did they think she didn't know about the wigs? Soon the old woman would fade away entirely, like her legendary beauty, and she would leave nothing: no legacy of great works, no lasting kindness on another's life. Such an end was everything Julia dreaded. She held up another brush and made as if to throw it at Sarah, narrowing her eyes.

'Do stop that Julia, you're much too old to engage in such silly behaviour. Let me see.' Mama retrieved the canvas from the grass, holding it in front of her and turning it from side to side to consider the unfinished image. Proportionally the figure was strange, the perspective of the background skewed, the wild brush strokes clearly visible. Julia was pleased to recognise the shock on Mama's face.

'It is a likeness. Of a kind,' she said at last, gingerly replacing it to rest against the legs of the garden seat.

Julia scowled.

Why on earth should a painting need to be a likeness? People should care how it made them feel. 'It's an image from my head! How do you know what it is supposed to look like?' She jumped to her bare feet and Mama gave a tiny cry.

'Julia! You're almost a woman, I should not need to remind you that it's unladylike to go about the place without shoes.' Mama threw up her hands and Sarah smirked, stretching out her own legs, the ends of which were neatly buttoned in high kid boots. They knocked against the edge of the painting and it tumbled face down onto the wet grass.

'Look what you've done!' Julia had worked for days on the canvas, each stroke a labour of love as she tried to capture the beauty of the colours she saw inside her head. It was ruined. Wet colours streaked the canvas, giving the impression of a world beginning to melt. If Sarah thought she would paint her portrait now, she was mistaken.

1861 Freshwater Bay

Perhaps, if she had learned to paint properly, like the scribes, she would have understood Mama. With such talent she could have travelled the world, not followed Sarah back to London like a tail. She would never have met Emily, never found this island, never met those water-colourists and their silly Society. Imagine the imperious Lady Caroline trying to paint their Calcutta house with its stilted legs, the gardens of mango, neem and banyan spreading below. Imagine her trying to catch the flashing colour of sunbirds, or the long limbs of monkeys as they streaked through the canopy. She would faint clean away. If that woman had ever done anything half as interesting, she would eat one of her ridiculous bonnets. Little wonder they couldn't understand her work. Julia leaned back further, and water filled her ears with a rushing roar that sounded like laughter.

Perhaps she should have stayed in India. She'd never felt alone there, even as a child. The house teemed with gardeners, bhisti, the men tending chickens and cows; she would follow them everywhere, sitting cross-legged in the dust to watch how they cut and pushed and dug every day to keep an elegant country house in the wild of the jungle. In the shade of the basement there was always someone to listen, to reward her efforts at Hindustani with hard boiled-milk sweets. But they were servants, paid to smile at children.

Of course she was alone. She had always been apart from the rest; nowhere more than at school in Paris, hiding from Sarah in their attic bedroom with its walls as grey as the city. Every balcony and apartment stained with the same peeling paint. The malevolent spires of the cathedral, the broad stone buildings with windows shuttered in hostile pairs. Even the flagstones were square. How could she have hoped to be inspired there? All those commercial painters with their works hung on railings, depicting the same depressing scenes—the banks of the Seine with a swirled grey sky above black bridges in decreasing lines; blood-red geraniums studding iron stairs. Why would anyone want to hang them in their houses? They were the very opposite of what Art should be, ugly.

Her chart was the only colour she saw in those years. Her promise was the only thing that got her through school at all. She had carried it her whole life. Now it would be soaked and ruined, ink running into cloth as her reticule floated away, out of reach.

1835 Calcutta

'I'm eternally in your debt, Miss Pattle. I'm not entirely sure how I can express the extent of my gratitude for the time and care that you've taken over my... affairs.'

The young man's eyelashes were remarkably long, his cheeks unmarked by sunlight. Such fresh blood was usually a good bet. If she could get to them before Papa, they were so much likelier to work for good, rather than dissolve into dissipation. This one had, unfortunately, slipped through Julia's net for several weeks. As a result, he had been persuaded to buy horses, dogs and all the trappings of a life he could not afford and then been introduced to the pleasures of native whiskey and card tables to make amends.

'Without your tea and kindness, I may very well be ruined.'

'Ruination is something my father bothers very little about.' Julia smiled as she spoke, but her words were heartfelt; she was deeply sorry for those newcomers to India that suffered at Papa's hands, the so-called griffins that he led astray.

'I have only myself to blame, and your kindness to thank for saving me.'

'Just remember to speak kindly of him, should anyone ask.'

Returning to Calcutta had been a bittersweet homecoming for Julia. Most things were as wonderful as she remembered: indulgent servants, the stilted house, wild animals in the courtyard. Mama was still difficult—fierce, superstitious and challenging. Papa was as powerful as ever. But salon-worldly Julia saw Major James Pattle quite clearly for what he was—a charming rogue.

'He's a very great man, he doesn't realise that not all of us can manage the lifestyle he prefers. I'm sure I would've very much enjoyed it,' the young man replied.

Julia noted his wistful tone. 'It's not a life to desire, Mr Carlyle. You'd do better to spend your time working to stop these dreadful crop pests. Do you wish to spend your evenings drinking and gambling when you could be changing lives? Did you know that they leave girl babies out in the jungle for the tigers to take because they're too poor to pay dowries?'

Now he looked as though he might cry. Really, what on earth did these silly young men think they were doing out here? This country was a playground for them, and Papa certainly didn't help. Yesterday he pocketed such a large bribe for settling a land dispute that he'd promised jewellery when the stone-sellers came from Kashmir. Sarah was already having designs drawn. Aquamarine, she'd said, to match her eyes. She'd do better to give it to the poor. Julia had seen the woman who stood behind the eager farmer with his outstretched fist of rupiah; she'd seen the way the woman watched the dusty floor, a cloth-wrapped baby perched on one hip, two silent, skinny children pulling at the yellow wrap of her sari. If she could do anything to help, then she would. It was too late for Papa, but there was no reason for them all to follow him. There would be time enough for painting when she'd put things right.

'I'm forever in your gratitude.' The rattan chair creaked as he rose and gave a deep bow. A flush crossed his neck as he straightened, twisting the straw hat he held in his hands as though he meant to destroy it. 'I... if I... I mean, I don't have the means to ask... not now... but perhaps if you'd wait, if I speak with your father I can...'

Julia gave a sudden, sharp laugh. 'Don't flatter yourself. Though I care what happens to you, it's only because you have the potential to do some good in this country if you apply yourself. I don't wish to see that potential wasted. I try to make myself useful to anyone who might suffer at my father's hands... and I'm more than content without a husband.'

The relief on his face as he left was clear. He was the second man to have confused her charity with ambition. Did the future hold nothing but an unappealing choice between the life of an endlessly dutiful daughter and a marriage of pity?

Calcutta had grown, and it was brighter than the city Julia remembered. Buff-white buildings, flanked by tall masts at the harbour, the markets in the redbrick bustle of Chowringee, all edged with the vivid splendour of the jungle. Possibilities unfolded. Julia was no longer a child, she was a young woman, allowed to ride, take up shooting and frequent the city's many ballrooms. Glittering with gold braid and self-importance, the parties were glamorous and brash, full of pale civil service daughters, keen to fulfil their duty and find a match.

Julia soon regained her fluency in Hindustani, seeking out servants for conversation while the others took naps—such a waste to lie under nets all afternoon! If she was ever to discover her purpose, she must push herself as hard as she could. A deep satisfaction came from simply looking at the spines of all the books that filled her rooms from the daily packages and deliveries. Finally, she had her dream library of philosophy, essays and scientific thought. All that remained was to read and understand it all.

'I find that I've missed you, Julia. You're still as curious as you were when you were small and your energy for life matches only your father's.'

Julia swallowed. Mama was not usually complimentary unless she was about to deliver a blow; she hypnotised her prey like a cobra. Still she had been working hard to gain Mama's approval, helping with the dinners and parties, the picnics, games and outings; scattering seeds of discussion from the theories she learned while the rest of Calcutta slept in the afternoons.

'I'm surprised to hear you say so. I'd always thought Virginia was your pet.' And everyone else's. Her little sister was tall and elegant, with a slender figure and a graceful neck. On the day she arrived in the city, crowds followed the carriage all the way to the house and Julia, perfectly invisible by her side, had spent the journey ignoring them, her nose in a book.

'Of course she's my pet! But I don't know how I managed without all the things you do. Perhaps I'm weary of parties, as your father suggests, perhaps I am old...' she paused, obviously waiting protestation, but Julia was not in the mood to flatter and, really, agreed with him. Papa boasted the constitution of an ox and his dissipation had done little to dull his looks, which still drew women and men to his side. But while the heat burnished his complexion and streaked his hair, the years of children and travel were causing Mama's famous colour to fade. She spent more time than ever with the scribes and astrologers that frequented Chowringhee, and her superstitions worsened by the week. 'I find I can't bear the thought of any husband taking you away from me.'

'I don't think we need worry about that, Mama.'

For a moment Julia thought she would cry, a reaction she'd tried hard to train herself out of in the wakeful dark of Paris nights. She had yearned so long for a sign that Mama found any pleasure in her company.

'Why ever not? You're a catch here, my dear, and quite wonderfully engaging. You have these men eating out of your hands. I saw the look Mr Carlyle gave you.'

Should she confide her fears? Knowing Mama, it could very well be a test. Julia willed herself not to break. 'Perhaps I'm quite satisfied as I am.'

1836 The Cape of Good Hope

'May I see?'

Julia looked up, surprised, to see a man of advancing age bending his neck sideways as he attempted to read the name on her volume of poems. She held it out for him to take and gave him an appraising look. A writer, or a scientist, perhaps. Certainly someone of great interest to an Artist, such as herself. He was a walking story. His dress was neat, but his hair stuck out around his head as though he need not bother with such mortal trouble as a hairbrush; his eyebrows were wild and his eyes shone curious with what she recognised as the joy of knowledge.

'Ah, Keats. A worthy accompaniment to such a fine afternoon.' The stranger continued to stand, turning the pages of the little volume as though searching for something.

'Are you a guest here?' He certainly hadn't been at table in the last week; she would have remembered such an appearance in this dreary hotel. Mama had insisted on the Cape for recuperation from a serious chest infection, but it felt like the ends of the earth, as though her family had decided India's chaos and charm were simply too much for her. She had been wandering the corridors for a week, learning the formal routines of recovery, the steam baths and bland food; silently acknowledging the other guests with their pallor and quietude. Perhaps life here was about to become more interesting.

'I arrived today, from Feldhausen. Quite a journey in this heat.'

'Perhaps you'd care to join me for some refreshment Mr…'

'John Herschel. And may I know the name of such an erudite reader?'

'Julia Margaret Pattle. And I'm not sure that the reading of Keats would mark me as erudite.'

'Indeed?' he raised a wayward eyebrow. 'You're not enjoying his words?'

'Truthfully, it's the third time I've tried,' Julia sighed. She'd brought dozens of volumes of poetry, determined to put her convalescence to good use. By now she should be old enough to write such verse and she was far from home, what could be more conducive? Perhaps words were to be her vocation. She'd thought it would be easy to write. Poetry was, after all, of the emotional realm. Some of the best of the Romantics were women, though she could remember none of their names. They were always just someone's wife, someone's sister. Her own poems would change the way feminine poetry was viewed; raise it to a new height. If only she could understand it. 'It's one of those volumes that everybody tells me to read and, when I do, I can't help feeling I've somehow missed the point. I don't find it difficult to disagree with popular opinion, but there's always a nagging doubt, when others are so sure, that if one disagrees then it's oneself who's missed the point. Please, can I offer you something?'

The waiter had arrived and was standing by Julia's chair with an air of expectancy and a supercilious glance at Herschel, who had made himself quite at home; his long legs, clad in bold broad-striped morning trousers, rested on the free chair by his side.

'I rather hope you'll join me in some champagne,' he said, pulling a serious face that didn't suit him. 'After all, it's my first of afternoons, and you're discovering Keats. There's much for us to celebrate.'

Julia rarely drank before six, but she had her father's head for it and, besides, her intuition was indicating that here might be an element of destiny. She took a deep drink, enjoying the light, cool then warming sensation of the bubbles as she swallowed. She was always quick to mark

28

out friends, enemies and those who were worth the trouble of neither. Time had shown her that her first instincts were generally correct. As she watched Herschel's eyes darting across the lines, she already felt a fondness growing, a sense of many long, enjoyable conversations to come.

'Aha! I knew it would be here. Now close your eyes and think, really think, about what this might mean to the reader.' He held the book before him and intoned in a beautiful, halting style quite perfect for the words. 'Bright star, would I were steadfast as thou art—

Not in lone splendour hung aloft the night, And watching, with eternal lids apart,

Like Nature's patient, sleepless Eremite, The moving waters at their priestlike task

Of pure ablution round earth's human shores, Or gazing on the new soft-fallen mask

Of snow upon the mountains and the moors—No—yet still steadfast, still unchangeable,

Pillow'd upon my fair love's ripening breast, To feel for ever its soft fall and swell,

Awake for ever in a sweet unrest, Still, still to hear her tender-taken breath,

And so live ever—or else swoon to death.'

'It is utterly beautiful!' she exclaimed. The more so because it made her feel, with all the strength of her youth, that her destiny was not to be loved like that, but to be a bright star. She had only to get away from home. If her sisters were here no one would be reading her poetry. Mr Herschel would be fawning over Virginia, or allowing himself to be bossed by Sarah, and she would be sat in the shadows, watching them. Perhaps her worries that she would be abandoned as they got married were unfounded. It would be easy to exist apart from the Pattles, in this charm of independence.

'A toast to Mr Keats!' He raised his glass and grinned. 'He writes, I think, about the Polaris, the North Star. It's the brightest in the firmament and the star around which all others move.'

How had she not known that? She had watched the stars without any thought to discover their secrets. Tomorrow she would spend the afternoon in the hotel library and begin to learn astronomy. It would not do to feel ignorant. 'I detect a hint of bias to the subject.'

'His poem isn't really about stars.'

'Of course not! It's about his one true love.' A youthful thrill shook Julia's voice. How daring she was to sit here, drinking alone with a man she had only just met and talking airily of love as though she did so often.

'The stars themselves may well be my one true love.'

Julia at once determined they should become great friends. Didn't she love the stars? And now she loved champagne too. So much common ground.

'The new observatory at Feldhausen is to my father's design, the biggest telescope ever built. I call it the Gateway to Heaven. I came back to check on it, make some more observations, collect data charts from the records. Now I plan to spend some weeks figuring out what is beyond what we can see.'

'How can you see further than the stars?'

'Mirrors, my dear girl. Very powerful ones. With the right magnitude and the right series of mirrors the heavens themselves become visible to the human eye.' Herschel took a small silver pencil from his breast pocket and drew inside her book of poems a series of ovoid shapes increasing in size.

Julia tried to imagine life spent peering up through a small lens at the night sky. Glasses and mirrors; it was surely no coincidence the fates had brought her this extraordinary man. Could she be an astronomer? It seemed a solitary sort of life. Not quite the cultural storm she'd intended to create. But it was romantic. To see beyond the stars, beyond the sight of sunbirds. Seeing what humans could not see. That would be wonderful.

'I understand that the stars are really suns. I imagine planets like ours for each of them.'

Herschel raised his glass. 'Your imagination is admirable.'

Julia flushed with the pleasure of praise from such a man. 'It's late Mr Herschel, and I must go to dress. But I'd very much like to learn more about the stars and your mirrors. Do you have a dinner companion this evening?'

'Indeed I do, but he'll be as delighted to make your acquaintance as myself.'

Julia nodded, and Herschel watched her disappear, deep in concentration. Her face, though plain, was delightful in its earnest animation and she cut a striking figure in her flowing garments as she walked, her head bent in thought as though she did not expect a single eye to appraise her and would not notice if it did.

'Since I appear to be the only person who's not here for the sake of my health, I believe it must be down to me to lead the charge.' Herschel raised a hand for another bottle and beamed at his guests.

'My health already feels quite restored and there is clearly little lacking in Miss Pattle.' Charles Hay Cameron, Herschel's friend of many years, leaned back in his chair and smiled at Julia. Although twice her age, he cut an imposing figure with his elegant clothes and long, fine-flowing hair and beard.

'Might I enquire after your health?' she asked anxiously. 'You know why I'm here, but you seem never to have lived anywhere except hot climates for any length of time, so I must assume, for you, that India isn't the problem?' Julia had already discovered that Cameron, a widowed lawyer, was the son of the Governor of The Bahamas. He had travelled to India in the firm belief that the country required expert legal assistance and had instantly fallen in love with the place and its people, all of which combined to win Julia's approval. She was exhilarated by the conversation, not least because she was alone in a foreign land. For the very first time she was meeting people, interesting people, away from her family and their preconceived assessments. More importantly, she was meeting interesting people away from her sisters; if Sarah and Virginia had been there, these men wouldn't have said twenty words to her, she was sure of it.

'Alas, India is the problem. I've just completed my work on the Penal Code. It's taken many, many years, and I've been told that I'm quite exhausted. I find I must be tired, since I acquiesced to rest at all.'

'Your diligence is to be commended! In such a country there must hitherto have been merely local say so.' Herschel leaned in intently.

'Well it's not entirely my own work but, yes… an immense undertaking. A double tour of the country, interviews with more local regulators than any man should have to see in his lifetime, and the learning of three dialects of Hindustani.'

'A wonderful language,' said Julia, in the dialect of Calcutta. 'Your work will undoubtedly change the country for the good.'

'I've begun to wonder just what's needed for the good of India,' he replied in the same language, 'For a moment I lost my faith in progress, and I am yet to be convinced of the ability of the English to govern there. So, I'm here, for the time being, to rest and gather my wits.'

'I don't think it will take you long to gather them,' said Julia, returning the conversation to English with a sense that Herschel was beginning to feel a little left out of his own party. 'But don't give up on India in this hour of her need. There are few enough good men willing to create the stability she needs.' Julia thought of Papa, his superficial politics and pocket lining, and became vaguely embarrassed. 'I could lend you some poetry to soothe your mind. Mr Herschel has quite changed my opinion of Keats with his reading of Bright Star.'

'You've never struck me as the romantic type, Herschel?'

The scientist gave a rueful smile. 'Indeed, I'm not. I feel it keenly as the one great failure of my life that I've never known romantic love.'

'I've heard that it's never too late to find love,' said Julia, carried away with her own sense of romance and oblivious to the effect of her words. 'But if you spend too long looking up at the heavens, or gazing into books of law, I'm sure neither of you will ever find your happiness on this earth.'

Julia extended a hand, loathe to leave her new friends, although Cameron would eventually return to Calcutta, and Herschel had been promised a weekly letter. In their few weeks together she had learned more than in all her years at school, grown in confidence and poise and loved them for it. They had both come to see the carriage leave, and the three stood watching the drivers throw trunks onto its roof, shinning across and through the windows to tie them down with lengths of thin rope that they held between their teeth.

'I'm certain you'll help me discover something wonderful! You seem to know the answer to every matter of science, and yet you're perfectly willing to listen to my foolish observations.'

'All science is merely observation and testing, and your thoughts are far from foolish Miss Pattle. There seems to be nothing about which you're not passionate. I believe that's the key to all success.' Herschel brought forth from his pocket a telescope, around a foot long, with a polished brass case and leather bag in which to keep it.

A pocket instrument with which to see the stars! She must learn to use this splendid object as soon as possible.

Imagine showing Mama the stars close up. Destiny beckoned. 'I can't thank you enough for opening my eyes to the wonder of the millions and millions of little suns above our heads.' She shielded her eyes to look up at the sky.

'Does such vastness not terrify you?' asked Cameron. 'If I can be truthful here with friends, I find I'm quite easily overwhelmed by the contemplation of such ancient endless space.'

'The idea excites me.' Julia laughed to cover her embarrassment; it would not do to make it obvious she felt the need to impress this man. She barely understood it herself. Yet there was no denying the thrill of conversation, the way he made her feel she must compete on every level. 'What is this world in the wake of such light? It gives us infinite possibility. Herschel's gateway will help us climb closer and closer to the stars in their firmament.'

Cameron bowed with a low flourish, 'If anyone could, Miss Pattle, I believe it would be you.'

1861 Freshwater Bay

Stars hung low over the dark water, spread in a tangle like a fisherman's net. They were as clear over the ocean as they had been at the Cape. It was one of the reasons she fell in love with the island. The clarity of light, the clear view of the heavens. Julia raised her head slightly, her hair snaking out in a rush of water. She could no longer see the shore.

Charles had loved her then, in her youth, on those walks across the umber earth while she grew stronger under the gaze of a man who found her interesting and spoke to her as an equal. What deep peace she had felt as he listened to her ideas; her plans for her Art. What a surprise it had been to realise such a grown-up lawyer and academic took so little of life seriously. He was good for her, so everyone said. But he always laughed at the very worst moments, when their conversation was, to her, at its most intense. Perhaps he had never taken her seriously at all.

Where was he now? He had faded into the backdrop of their family life until he all but disappeared. Once he'd encouraged her Art, all of it. Or was she fooling herself about that, too? He wasn't even there at the exhibition. Perhaps he knew. Perhaps he hadn't wanted to watch her humiliation. Or, perhaps, she had pushed him away. She hadn't been the best of wives. He'd always just been expected to go along with her, with what she needed. When it seemed that her Art would succeed... That should have been enough, it would have justified the sacrifice of anything, but it wasn't sufficient. She had failed Charles too. When had she last done something to make him happy?

As the years of her life unfolded, full of adult cares and disappointments, she'd often yearned for the Cape; a simple time when the three of them sat peaceably and watched the stars, listening to Herschel's theories. She was so fascinated by those lenses, so eager to know the names of the stars, the shapes of their constellations. It was hard to use the original instrument he'd given her, the gauge of the lenses too precise for her patience. She'd bought bigger telescopes then, spent hours looking through them in all the places of her life. Yet, as she drifted away from her island, underneath the bright night sky, she could not recall the names of the stars at all.

Stories from the Glass House:
Annie Philpot

It was awfully cold in the scullery and I kept my new, smart coat buttoned all the way up to the chin, even though the stiff wool collar scratched my neck. It was very similar to the one Mummy wore, which made me feel terribly grown up. I absolutely refused to take it off to dress up in the costume she had ready, which made Aunt Julia furiously cross for some reason. I particularly remember that, because she was usually so kind. We always looked forward to visiting. Her house was by the beach and there were so many dogs to play with. Aunt Julia could be full of fun. But she was different that day, sort of excited and cross at the same time, and I wasn't sure what I'd done to make her so.

A huge wooden box stood in the middle of the room. I'd never seen a camera before, not many of us had, and it frightened me a little. It was enormous, perhaps the size of a kitchen table and I honestly thought she was going to ask me to get inside it. Aunt Julia must have realised I was scared because she gave me a doll to hold, a lumpy one with sharp feathers sewed to its shoulders and a head that was quite flat on one side, which made it look awfully sad. She looked at it for a long time before she handed it to me, as though she didn't really want me to have it.

I sat on the hard chair on the other side of the box and Aunt Julia told me I mustn't play with it because, if I moved, I might spoil the photograph. I was used to being told to keep quiet; Mummy found children terribly annoying, still does. But I wasn't used to keeping still. I didn't really like the doll, so I put it in my pocket where I didn't have to look at it. All the while I tried not to move, I imagined what fun Henry and Arthur must be having with the dogs on the back lawn.

Strange things hung from the scullery ceiling on one of those pulley contraptions that usually store pots and pans— a mothy fox tippet with horrible yellow eyes, a little wooden bucket, one of her old rain hats, and a pair of goose wings, spread flat like shoulder blades. I wondered if Aunt Julia was practising magic, whether I would just disappear if she asked me to get into the box. I got spooked then, fancying that she looked a little like a witch. She looked, not at me, but almost through me, as though I wasn't a person at all but a wooden bucket or a pair of wings; and then she marched across and snatched the slides out of my hair, rubbing at it hard until tufts stuck out. I knew I'd be scolded for such messy hair, but I didn't dare to tell her Mummy wouldn't like it.

I don't know how long I sat there. Afterwards, it was hard to walk because my legs had become quite stiff with the cold. When I got home, I realised that the sad-faced doll was still in my pocket.

1838 Calcutta

'I can't abide the sight of white cotton gloves. If there's one thing that will send me screaming from civil service, it'll be those accursed things.' Charles never spoke in anything other than a pleasant mild and even tone. It gave his stronger statements a satirical air that Julia found herself drawn towards in a country where most people took themselves too seriously.

'They're everywhere, Mr Cameron. It's like saying one can't stand cows. But I do confess that I rather agree.'

'They're worn primarily to give the impression that one's hands are clean, when, in fact, the very people who wear them are likely to have extremely dirty hands indeed.'

Julia quickly pushed to the back of her mind an image of Papa, in crisp white dress clothes and white cotton gloves. 'Unlike cows then, which, in this country at least, are highly unlikely to be driven by anyone with any kind of dirty hands.' She smiled. 'Mr Cameron, I've sincerely missed your humour. For purely selfish reasons I'm delighted to see you in Calcutta, but I hope your health is sufficiently recovered for you to be working?'

'I don't believe I'll ever work on anything quite as exhausting again... which certainly doesn't mean I'm past the age where I may try, simply that I'll know better the next time.'

'For all our sakes I hope you don't.' Though she would have spoken to any guest in the same way, Julia sometimes felt as though this could be flirting in a manner that her conversation with others was not; a confusion she didn't enjoy and yet could not leave alone.

Mama had noticed quickly. On first meeting she had ear-marked Cameron and hadn't missed an opportunity to remind Julia she shouldn't be fussy, that girls with limited options would do well to remember their place. It wasn't a line of thinking that tempted. Why should she set her cap at someone just because Mama said so? Besides, a spinster life appealed more. Why would she ever want to be told what to do, to read, when to go out?

'We're enjoying your arrival and your contribution to our little gatherings. It would seem a shame for work to claim you quite so soon.'

'There's so much to be done. The Code itself isn't enough. Only in its implementation without corruption will the work have been worthwhile. And that means several years of travel throughout the regions, once I've found some regulators I can trust.'

Here, at last someone who agreed with her ideas! If only he could work with Papa to change his mind. The idea of losing her wonderful new friend so soon brought a rising panic that Julia fought to dispel. She affected a light-hearted tone, 'Where will you find them?'

'Where indeed?' He made a show of looking keenly around the ballroom before pulling a comic disappointed face that made Julia giggle.

'You'll find whoever you need if you look hard enough. Every single person on this earth is individual, according to our scientists. Like the unique patterns of our fingerprints or the bumps on our heads. So, there must be someone for every role, and someone for everyone else.' What on earth was she thinking, spouting such notions, and why was it only Charles who made her talk like that? Mama, wearing a particularly annoying knowing look, was staring hard at them across the ballroom as though she'd heard every word.

'I do believe there is,' Charles affected a mock serious tone. 'And since we've been invited here to dance, should we not dance? There'll be time enough for such theories when we retire.'

Julia adored the life Cameron brought to a party, the way she felt free when they danced, the possibility that, in the

40

light of his admiration, she would grow the wings she so badly desired. His humour was infectious. He made her feel like a sunbird, hovering over the ballroom, smug with understanding of the entirety of the scene. Above all, though, what drew her to him was his knowledge and his boundless generosity with sharing it.

Each ship from England brought new volumes for Julia to devour under the nets of her bed in the heat of the afternoon. Since meeting Herschel, she was more inclined to read scientific treatise and she ordered them indiscriminately, sometimes adding equipment to the delivery instructions. The microscope she purchased was a great success with her nephews, who brought her new objects to see the way they were transformed and made new when she pressed them onto her glass plates. Skin shed from a cobra, the petal of a lotus flower, the joined front legs of a female praying mantis. Everywhere they sought the unusual to examine. How typically male! They did not understand that what mattered was the microscope's utter transformation of the ordinary, the things she would have walked past every day if she had not procured it. Such a sense of joy and wonder dwelled within the magic box— the perfect craft of the brass instrument, the precision of its glass and mirrors, the lenses and plates that fitted neatly into the little mahogany compartments—that her destiny felt within reach.

My Dear Herschel,

I feel almost foolish in writing of my excitement over these wonderful glasses, which you recommended to me and have probably been using for many years. Perhaps you've even made your own extraordinary lenses. I'm quite certain that you have, and that you'll find my small amusements just that in comparison with your gateways to heaven. Nevertheless, my little microscopic laboratory has been causing much excitement among the family in Calcutta.

Each day I'm brought new wonders to dry and press between the plates and I realise that almost the whole of the natural world is covered in magic, that every small leaf, each petal, scale or speck, is covered in a miniature enchanted world of its own devising. Even the mould on a piece of orange peel teems with its own fairy forms. I can't see the natural world in anything like the same light again. When I walk along the edges of the jungle, I'm alive to the possibility that on every tree, every stem, every part of every leaf!— exists a wonderful microscopic world that I've yet to see.

I'm enormously grateful for the slides that you sent, which arrived safely last week. The diatoms were remarkable. Such extraordinary patterns. Surely living proof of the existence of divinity. Creatures that I've discovered in the water of the Chowringhee become minuscule monsters under the lens; even strands of hair have the most extraordinary patterns. Already my dressing room contains so many boxes of slides that I'm bound to remove my dresses and rename it my study, something I know you will find amusing. Cameron has seemed to find it so, though he has yet to visit us here.

I've begun to classify my collection twice now and yet both times have been so confounded by a sample that does not fit my system that I've found myself destroying that particular attempt and having to develop a new way of grouping together my finds. I begin to see, in some way, the angst of a Scientist in a world that's so rapidly being discovered. I hope your stars won't give you quite so much trouble. Write soon and let me know more of your discoveries, you're keeping me quite the centre of attention for my scientific knowledge in our little society.

Your ever-affectionate Julia,

1838 Calcutta

'Have you ever noticed how Rohit looks at you?' asked Cameron. 'He's been watching our every move.'

The young boy who had delivered the chart to Julia before her journey to Paris was now a grown man and a permanent member of the Pattle household. When he spoke, he no longer stared at his feet, but his hair was still wayward, springing from his forehead in a great wave he continually swept back. Julia glanced over to where he sat, absorbed in his books, a pile of scrolls at his feet.

'I only ever see him looking like that, so studious that I feel guilty for my frivolous pastimes,' said Julia.

They'd been firm friends since her return—she'd remembered him at once—and Rohit was now the only person who knew her thoughts on her birth chart, her sense of destiny. Latterly he'd become part of Mama's more trusted entourage and was generally to be found within the house. He was handsome and scholarly, and only a few years older than Julia, a fact that seemed to annoy Cameron.

'I don't believe you ever had a frivolous pastime in your life.'

'I have many. I like to think of them as work, but they are pastimes really.' A nonsense, of course, nothing was more important than being an Artist. Even this work with the microscope could be considered a step on the path.

'He's a very good-looking young man. I assume he's studying astrology as a trade?' Julia looked up. Why on earth was Cameron so interested in Rohit? It was his first formal visit to her home, a few miles from the centre of Calcutta, where they usually met at dinners and events, and, although he said he found it peaceful, the discovery that she might be enjoying such company daily seemed to fill him with jealousy, the strength of which took Julia by surprise.

43

'Astrology? I suppose so, but he'll hardly need to seek trade. Mama could keep a pet scribe in business all on her own.' Indeed, she grew worse, barely daring to leave the house without consulting the movements of the stars.

'Perhaps I will ask him to draw one for me.'

'I would very much advise against it,' she said, fixing him with an intent stare.

With her pale-green silk robe, dark trailing hair parted in the middle and the shards of sunlight streaking through the green blinds behind her, she made a striking image and Cameron listened in silence.

'If you have one birth chart made, and it isn't good, you won't want to believe it. You'll have another made and, perhaps, it will be good, but even if it is you won't know which to believe. Or you may never be able to find someone to interpret your chart correctly, in which case you will always be wondering.'

'It sounds as though you are quite an expert? Perhaps you share your mother's interest?'

Mama would doubtless be hovering on the veranda, listening hopefully for any evidence that her burdensome daughter may finally catch a man. This one had already piqued her interest, despite his age. She had her beady eye on his prestigious position, looking at the way it would help Papa.

'Not at all. I would never be so foolish.'

Cameron nodded and shifted his attention to the slides, peering at the miniature inscriptions. 'I think your collection is becoming quite magnificent,' he said, adjusting the brass dials of the microscope. 'It's certainly not frivolous work.'

Hours spent collecting began to seem worth the effort. A sharp thrill brought colour to her cheeks. 'I'm glad you consented to visit, I was beginning to think we may never tempt you from the city.' Really, his fingers were quite remarkably elegant.

'Had I fully understood the tranquillity of your haven, you wouldn't have found me so slow to abandon my work.'

'At any rate you're here now, and we're pleased to see you.' Julia fussed with the slides in her second box; it was a haphazard way to store them compared to the splendid high cabinets in the museums of Paris. She would design something similar, made from mango wood or mahogany. It was vital he should see she wasn't a silly amateur, but deadly serious about these mirrors and glasses.

'All the slides on this side of the box are wings, from flying insects. Butterflies, beetles, even tiny fruit flies. They were the first of the slides I labelled myself. When I ran into difficulty over my taxonomic system, for storing them, I came back to these slides and it fell into place.'

'Impressive. So, if I wanted to look at a moth's wing I would look here.' He pulled out the correct slide and smiled broadly. 'My housekeeper found a moth the size of a woman's hand last week, in the pantry. She knocked it with a broom, and it fell straight onto her face. I'm sure you must have heard the screams from here.'

'I've never seen one quite as large as that. I'm sure I wouldn't like it either.'

'If you've ever seen a cobra dance, you'll understand me when I say that beauty and terror go hand in glove here.' He selected another slide, noticed the label of cobra skin, and held it up for her to notice.

'The fearful symmetry.'

'Exactly so.'

'And do you agree with Blake?' asked Julia. 'That it's incontrovertible proof of deity?' If she'd ever enjoyed conversing with anyone so much, she could not remember. It was as if he had the answers to almost everything. Moreover, conversation with him inspired her, made her feel as though her thoughts were worth hearing.

Cameron rose from the table and walked over to the window, pulling aside the blinds to peer through at the garden. 'I think it is evidence of divinity,' he said finally. 'But I don't think any of us yet understands what that divinity may be.'

Though Julia believed the pair of them had quite made up their minds that afternoon, she refused to be drawn into speculative conversations with Mama, desperate for the match and infuriated by her daughter's calm dismissal. Once she was certain it could happen, as far as she was concerned it could wait. There was much to be done. Society would not reform itself. Better by far to keep going with her campaigns and to develop her Art and Science as thoroughly as possible before having to answer to a man, even such a man as Mr Cameron.

'Oh, Charles, don't! You're ruining your clothes.' Julia pulled at his hands, but he stayed steadfastly on one knee, spattered by dusty puddles. Why hadn't she seen it coming? One moment they sat in companionable silence, hiding from the last of the rain, listening to the slow beat of water dropping from the broad curved leaves of the banana plants by the veranda; the next he had dropped to the floor and disarmed her with a proposal. What was she supposed to say? Never mind his beautiful trousers, what about the stain of the Pattle tribe? How could her dissipated father be any good for Charles's career? Not to mention her sisters, swarming in silks like a troop from the Arabian Nights. 'There are so many lovely young women in Calcutta, women who would be able to give you the quiet life you deserve!'

'Why would someone like you wish a quiet life on anyone? I'm quite hurt you believe it to be what I deserve.' Charles dropped his head in mock approbation.

Julia knew he enjoyed her company, her conversation, yet she worried he confused her youth with beauty, that he may not really love her for herself. And what of her calling? Something he found endearing now may be burdensome in a wife, would he tolerate her campaigning, understand her desperate need for Beauty and Art above all? 'I am flattered Charles, and very pleased that you have asked me. But I need to be sure that you understand fully what you will take on with my family. You're aware, I presume, that my father... I love him dearly, of course, you mustn't think me disloyal... but my father doesn't run straight.' Julia watched his face so anxiously Cameron began to laugh.

'I fail to see why you might find that so amusing.' Was nothing sacred? Here they were discussing something that could change their lives and he couldn't keep a straight face.

'Dear Julia, everything is amusing. Most especially you when you're cross. I know your father doesn't run straight, but why would anyone want to? That's when the crocodiles will catch you.'

Julia smiled behind her hand, feigning offence. At least he wasn't put off by Papa's reputation, despite his firm moral convictions. 'Perhaps you simply wish to marry me so that I can amuse you?'

Cameron caught her chin in his hand and held her gaze in a way that stopped her breath. 'You're asking for my reasons? I want to spend my life with you because I don't think we'd ever run out of conversation. Because you have a beauty, in all your movements and deeds, that's like warmth on my tired bones. Because you light a room full of people. Because your lovely eyes hold all the light of intellect. And because, to me, you are like a painting.'

An image of the garden at Versailles sprang to mind. The Pattles and their reputation became slightly less important. Someone found her beautiful; and Grandmamma's spiteful friends had been wrong. The marriage would be a good one. It would make Mama happy. And if Mr Cameron's shining words were to be believed it would certainly not be loveless. She would accept. There was plenty of time yet to worry about Art.

1861 Freshwater Bay

Even the shine on the paint as it dried had felt original. A new texture. A far cry from the dulled ridges of oils and a wonderful way to throw light into her works. It felt like discovery. For the first time in years she had allowed herself to believe that she would be an Artist, revered and welcomed. She'd painted the island landscapes the Society wanted. But her beaches were full of her elegant sisters, imagined as sirens and goddesses; creatures of myth and magic, with fluid gowns and long limbs flowing together. Arabian days and nights.

It was all so clear when she closed her eyes. Scenes of fairy-tale wonder came tumbling, one after the other; scenes collectors would swoon over, that could hang on the walls of Parisian galleries. They could have made her famous. When she walked into the exhibition, she had expected applause. She'd succeeded in capturing Beauty; all that remained was to show the world.

How could she have been so wrong? And why had Charles not stepped in? He had been her saviour once and she had expected him to carry on, to always be there. Would life have been different if she'd never married? Would she have been an Artist without the chains of a husband and children?

Even on their wedding she'd worried that they married quickly to satisfy convention. Had her head been turned by the thought no one would want her? Had marriage taken away her chance to shine? There were many advantages to spinsterhood that could outweigh conventional life. The ability to think and discuss freely, to wear whatever one chose, to write books or paint, to select one's friends and spend as much time as one wanted with them. In the end she realised that, of course, her fairy-tale sisters would marry, her parents would age and fade like Grandmamma, and she would be left alone. She never wanted to be alone. It had made the decision for her.

Papa was drunk and happy, Mama triumphant, her sisters tearful. Julia had allowed them no interference in her dress. They would have chosen robes to flatter prettiness, the fussy frills favoured by Sarah or Adeline's high lace collars. Instead she'd based her costume on a classical heroine and people were overheard saying that she looked like a painting in her long flowing shift of white silk, her hair loose and unadorned, a thin gold filigree band around her forehead to match the one at her throat and those that jangled on her wrists. Dainty white meadow flowers and deep green leaves twisted trails around her hair, around her waist and arms.

She had felt like a princess. No one could take her crown that day. When she came to cut the cake, it was covered in spun sugar roses, like a child's birthday cake, and as their hands pressed down on the knife together, their fingers knitted over the handle, her most fervent wish was that her late grandmother could see it.

What had it brought her, such fear of being abandoned? She had thought her marriage happy once. What did she know of anything? She was better off alone, and they were better off without her.

Stories from the Glass House:
Charles Hay Cameron

I didn't realise, until I looked at all her portraits together, that she only took one photograph of me where I was myself, and it was the only one I kept. I was always made to dress as a wizard or king, once as some sort of archangel. She said it was because I couldn't be serious about sitting, but I would have rather liked to be treated like one of her 'great men.' I think I would have liked how that felt.

Many of her first experiments were tested on me, along with other, much fairer, faces from the house. I like to think I was the first of her theatrical subjects. Usually she'd cast me in character, or sometimes just in the most eccentric of the clothes I brought back from India. Those were early days with the camera, when I enjoyed the effect it had on her, before it all became life and death. It was wonderful, to me, to see how absolutely alive she became once she was behind her lenses.

In the photograph I kept I'm half-sitting, half-standing by the plum tree in Sarah's garden, dressed rather smartly for me, with a buttoned waistcoat and a neat little hat. My eyes are closed, but I'm leaning back on a garden seat, walking stick in one hand, and the impression is one of energy, as though I'm about to leap up and move. The effect is probably caused by the movement of the leaves, blurred by the wind and the length of the exposure, but I like to think that's how she saw me. Benign, but ready to act. It's clearly what I was to her; and I'm happy to have been that because, although she would always deny it, such support was exactly what she needed.

It's true that Julia changed in the Glass House, though not as much as some people would have us believe. Always, even before the camera, she wanted so much to be taken seriously for her Art that she took it too far. By the time anyone noticed it was too late. She was really quite wild. As wild as her father but without his inclinations. Most of society thought it was my job to tame her, but I would no more have tried than I would cage a bird. To me she was full of life itself. All her youth and intellectual curiosity breathed new vitality into my old thoughts. She drew from me the very best in myself and I liked it. I don't think I ever saw until afterwards that she made everyone feel the same; we fed on her energy. I don't think anyone understood that except Sarah, and Sarah, of course, didn't care. Sarah took it anyway.

1839 Calcutta

Julia set her mother's shopping basket on top of the low crockery cupboard in the dining room and drew out a small package, wrapped in thin paper and scraps of bright sari-silk. Inside was a turtle, perfectly carved in pale soapstone, its ancient face turned slightly to the right, listening to something unseen, its body arched up on oversized flippers. She held it up to the window, admiring its translucence, before placing it carefully on her shrine.

She should have unwrapped it before their argument; should have shown Mama the shrine as well. It would have pleased her in such a simple way. Why could she not just do that, like a dutiful daughter? Because Mama would assume she was pleading with Kali to give her a child, when all she wanted from the gods was her destiny. Marriage had brought her freedom, of a kind, why would she want to rush into motherhood and deny herself opportunities? Her Art was still nowhere near ready. Children would, inevitably, delay it further. Beauty and purpose remained frustratingly ephemeral. If only Mama would understand.

'It will happen when the time is right.' Julia spoke with a defensive tone.

'What harm can it do?' Mama raised an eyebrow and began to unwrap some of the things she had brought. A moonstone ring, a block of rose quartz.

Julia gripped the sofa back and forced herself to breathe deeply. 'Please assure everyone that I'm perfectly fine.'

Charles, whose first marriage had been childless, was as desperate for babies as Mama. Perhaps it was possible that he could not become a father, such things were not unknown. Life could deal worse hands. In any case, it was important not to rush things.

'You remember what I said on your wedding day?' Mama seized Julia's right hand and slipped the ring onto her middle finger, twisting her hand slightly for the large moonstone to catch the light. It gleamed iridescent green, like an opal. 'Babies won't make themselves Julia. With an older husband you have to work quickly.'

'Charles is not so much older than Thoby.' Sarah's husband was barely two years younger than Charles, though he didn't look it. His skin was baby pink, his whiskers still a robust chestnut brown. Charles himself had an ethereal beauty, to Julia, with his long hair and beard. He looked as she had always imagined King Arthur, or his wizard. And yet, of the two men, Charles was easily the youngest at heart.

'You know what I mean to say.'

'Yes, I know exactly. Every week you bring me more trinkets to remind me!' Julia pointed accusingly at the six wooden elephants stood in a line on the shelf above the fireplace, trunks and tails linked, their faces turned to the window to welcome in the baby, their backs padded with silk cushions to carry its spirit.

'What harm can it do to ask the universe for kindness?' She spoke in the soothing voice Julia could not trust.

'You can't make bargains with the gods. If such behaviour worked, you would not still be making exactly the same request of them every time father stays away from home.' Instantly she wished she could take it back, but there it was, hanging between them like a malevolent presence, like a rosemallow mark.

Julia sighed, remembering how the colour had drained from Mama's face before she disappeared, rendering her fragile and translucent in the thin late afternoon light. For all his terrible behaviour, she understood Papa more. At least he had fight and life in him.

Removing a pot of coloured rice and cardamom seeds from the offering plate, Julia knocked it out on the window-ledge, stopping to watch the finches swoop backwards and forwards to peck at the grains with their orange-pink beaks.

53

When the birds had finished and moved to the shutters of the house along the street, she turned from the window and picked up the soapstone turtle, placing it carefully on the wooden ledge of the shrine.

Perhaps it was the turtle. Perhaps it was the kindness of Kali, or just the right time. Either way, once Julia's belly grew, she still made offerings daily, begging her life not to be subsumed by parenthood, cursing herself for adhering to the superstitions that were ruining Mama. Indiscriminately, she gave thanks for the new life she bore; to the pantheon of Indian deities and their amulets, to the Christian god she came close to forsaking whenever she read Herschel's letters of new discoveries and to the unnamed goddess she felt watching through the leaves whenever she walked along the edges of the jungle. If she were blessed with children, would she still deserve the chance to be an Artist? Could she love a child that she resented arriving before she had found her purpose? She tried to think of female artists that had married, been mothers, but could not.

Juliette was born two months after her cousin Vanessa, healthy and perfectly formed, with the lustrous hair of her mother already abundant. A wizened old goddess in a bundle of fierce new life, with a heart-wrenching cry and a beauty Julia could never have foreseen. Dark eyes, soft skin, the scent of fresh dew. A scent to breathe in forever. Each tiny finger was a blessing from gods that had not forsaken them; the curves and lines of the skin on her feet more precious than jewels. For days and nights Julia stared at the face of her daughter, marvelling at the way her features moved in sleep. How could such a tiny life stir such feeling? A life entirely dependent. A life to love and be loved in turn. A daughter to see what others could not. Kali the mother had stayed, she had watched over them. To be a mother was surely all Julia needed.

54

1847 Calcutta

'I must extend my warmest congratulations on your advancement Charles.' Major Pattle, already slightly unsteady on his feet, held out a gloved hand to his son-in-law and clapped him on the back with a heartiness Julia knew was not shared. She stiffened, hoping the evening wouldn't end in another disagreement.

'Thank you.' Charles had confessed earlier he never quite knew what to call Papa, first names felt too informal and familiar for someone so different. 'I hope I shall be able to repay the ministry's faith in me.'

'Hopefully you'll be able to repay me in some ways too, plenty of mouths to feed as always.' James surveyed the room with the self-satisfied air of a man with many children, all married well. With Sarah and Thoby gone, he was hosting a dinner to say farewell to Maria and Eliza, leaving the next week with their respective husbands, an earl and a well-known doctor.

'Whilst I can always be counted upon to do my duty to our family, I shall of course continue to govern with the diligence for which I've been kindly rewarded. Besides, with this new role we have now the power and the potential to do some real good here.'

Why did Papa always make Charles behave in a way that was stuffy and pompous? Quite unlike his usual self.

'You think so?' James threw back his head and laughed long and hard before signalling at a servant passing with an enormous silver salver of chilled claret. He took one and drank it down, replacing it empty onto the tray before handing one each to Charles and Julia and then choosing another. Before the boy could drift into the crowd, he made a circling motion with his right forefinger to indicate that he should hover. 'New staff. No idea. You know, you've been in India long enough, Charles, to understand that whatever you want to do to change things it isn't going to work.'

The proximity of the serving boy made Julia uncomfortable, she had no wish for the staff to think that her or Charles shared such views. 'This is a party, Papa, for Maria, perhaps we had better continue this discussion another time.'

James took another glass and waved the servant away. 'There, he's gone. Is that better? Probably wouldn't understand anyway. You can carry on talking about education for the natives; you know my daughter will throw herself into almost anything you wish. But nothing will change.'

'Papa! That's most unfair.'

'If we educate adequately then they'll be able to govern themselves. Don't you think you've drunk enough for a while? Let me get you some water.'

James pushed away Charles's hand roughly, half stumbling and spilling claret in two red drops on the front of his white jacket where they rested like neat bullet holes. 'They will not. And if you think they'll listen to us you're mistaken. Look at the maharajah there, talking to Taylor, do you see his manservant hovering next to him with a bowl of water?' Angry spittle flew from his mouth as he talked. 'He must wash his hands in that every time he shakes hands. When he goes home he'll have his priest purify him because he's been forced to spend the evening with us.'

Julia watched their conversation anxiously. If Papa was right, then what was the point of their attempts at reform? They would never change anything. The idea that all this effort might be as useless as her painting was almost too much to bear.

'The Brahmins don't need educating. It's the other castes who are denied learning. We need them to understand how to govern themselves; we can't bring someone from England for every job there is to do here.' It was a practised speech, one Charles found himself using more regularly than he would like.

'Why not? Plenty of opportunity out here yet.'

'And you think none of us should work to change what's wrong?' asked Julia.

James puffed out his stomach and waved his empty glass at another waiter. 'Stop your protests. Women are a burden on the family everywhere. Even in Dorset unmarried daughters are paraded in front of rectors like slaves at market.'

'I'm not sure how you can bring yourself to speak like that when you have seven wonderful daughters!'

'So I do. And I love every one of them. But I can afford them. Or at least I could afford to show them off until I married them off.'

'Is that really how you feel?' Julia tried to ask, but the two men were locked in, ignoring the very thing they argued over.

'You've benefitted, have you not? My clever daughter's half the reason for your promotion. You'd do well to remember that if you want to keep her happy. Stop sloping off to bed early and leaving her to business.'

'It seems everyone considers entertaining to be the most important part of my job.'

'You need to live a little, before it's too late. Neither of us has long enough left and woe betide you if you bore my daughter. She's as wild as her father and that's saying something.' James grabbed Julia's hand and swung her around to face him, claiming her next dance.

'Your husband's been telling me that you would like to disappear to England with your sisters,' he said. 'Is it true?'

Dressed in a long flowing gown of pale blue silk, flushed from dancing and with her lustrous hair long and loose, Julia knew she looked her best. She shook her head in what she imagined a coquettish gesture. 'I'm more dutiful Papa, something I must have learned from Mama. If

I left, he'd lose his job in an instant, he's hopeless at small talk.'

'I had noticed.' Major Pattle spoke with derision.

'Besides, what would we do? Charles's work is here, completely bound in the legal system, he'd never find work in England and we would starve.'

'You should think about buying some land here, before it's too late.'

'You know very well we may not do that. Charles's code prohibits investment in any region of India for those that work here.'

'Not India, Ceylon. Different country. Hill plantations, far more fertile than here. I'd be tempted myself. Take the old chap on a holiday; he never stops working. He'll be too dull to talk to before long.'

1848 Calcutta

My Dearest Julia,

I write in haste as I mean to get this parcel to the post in time. I trust that you are all quite well? I can imagine the children flourishing like little milkweeds in the wilds of Calcutta. Do express my warmest congratulations to Charles on his promotion. One is so used to his great and worthy deeds that I very nearly forgot to write it, he will find that amusing I'm sure. And your new plantations in Ceylon sound wonderful, I should like to visit them.

After your uncommon interest in the slides for microscopes, I wanted to share with you the enclosed plates, made by my friend Henry Talbot. He calls them Talbotypes, but I've assured him that the name will never hold. I believe the term 'photography' captures it best, after the Greek for 'light writing', for that's exactly how these extraordinary images are made.

He coats his paper with silver chloride, a substance that will darken and keep darkening depending on how long it's exposed to light. So, he is literally writing or drawing with light. Talbot calls it 'salted paper', which is misleading. He's developed a series of lenses to hold the plates through their exposure. The paper on them stays in the lens box until he can start to see the image clearly, which can take up to an hour, so it must be a landscape or a still life as no living thing could be expected to sit for so long and any slight movement would simply blur the picture. He is, I believe, working on a different process of developing the picture, which uses very strong sunlight on the lens and enables the image in the box to be produced in just a few minutes, after which it can be removed in a protected way, shielded from light, and developed with other chemicals to be finished. He's a long way off from perfecting the technique, but, I am sure you will agree, the possibilities are very exciting.

I hope you enjoy the plates. As I know you'll want to learn more than I have time to write, I'm also enclosing two papers,

which Talbot submitted to the Royal Society. They'll tell you much
more about this exciting new science.
With warmest wishes to yourself and dear Charles,
J Herschel

Writing with light. What possibility! Though the images
themselves were hard to make out. Julia read the papers
avidly, twice to herself, and twice aloud, first to Charles and
then to Rohit, who listened more patiently. Such exacting
science was an extraordinary way to create Art. It might be
just what she needed. No need for brush strokes or pallet
knives. Although, as Herschel pointed out, nothing living
could sit for so long while the light performed its trick. If
the only possible images were inanimate objects it would
soon lose her interest.

Julia searched fruitlessly for more examples to
demonstrate the effects of light on salted paper, but in
India there was nothing. Even English relatives and French
bookshops could not uncover anything more to send. After
a time, she folded the letter, and the papers, back into their
parchment envelope. There was so much else to discover,
and so much responsibility with young children. The boys
were no trouble, they were never happier than when they
were chasing animals in the yard; but Juliette made her
increasingly anxious, not least because she didn't seem to
need her at all.

'I like it better than your canvas of me as an old wizard.
You should concentrate on painting the children and stop
asking me to sit for you.'

Charles leaned in to kiss her cheek and Julia wiped the
flat blade of her knife against the easel, cleaning off the
thick stripes of brown with which she'd failed to match the
colour of her daughter's hair. All the love she tried to pour
into the canvas made no difference, she had yet to produce
a decent painting of any member of her family. Juliette

herself showed some talent, yet she seemed content with copying flowers from books. The child lacked any kind of imagination.

'They're much more difficult. They can't stop moving. How can one paint something that never stops moving?' They sat, side by side, on the veranda, watching Juliette play with her little brother, Henry, in a wooden box filled with sand.

'I'd be rather worried if they did,' said Charles. Henry banged himself against the wooden box and howled until his sister scooped him up in her arms and set him to sieving the sand again. 'Don't you think it's time for her to start at school?' he added lightly.

Julia's stomach tightened; she lifted her head from his shoulder, straightened her posture and folded her hands into her lap in preparation for a fight.

'She's almost nine years old. She needs an education, and some space to be allowed to grow in her own way.'

Julia could hardly bear to listen. She watched as her daughter patiently rescued a wooden scoop, passed it to her brother and helped him pat the sand into shapes. Poor thing, her plainness was heart-breaking. Already she had developed a squarish figure, with a broad nose and forehead that marked her out against the delicate features of her cousins. And she was still in blissful ignorance of how she would be judged. It was kinder to keep her here.

'Henry would miss her,' she said, trying to keep emotion from her voice.

'Henry has lots of other people to play with. Eugene will be old enough for him soon, then he can be the big sibling. That's what happens, Julia, children grow up.'

'It's so unbearably sad!' She took up a silk-covered cushion and cradled it against her as though it were a child. 'Even thinking of those children who have no mothers, or of the babies they choose to destroy, I can't help but cry for them, all of them.'

He patted her hand. 'It's not fitting for you to grow so emotional. Or to throw yourself across the streets in protest.'

Was he really thinking of her or just concerned that she might be seen? Last week she and two weeping civil service wives had been escorted home by the chaprasis, dressed in their red coats and gold sashes, bright enough for the whole city to have noticed. Such an over-zealous response to a handful of women peacefully protesting about female infanticide

'Not fitting! Your position has gone to your head. What is fitting? You sound like Lady Macbeth.'

'In this instance Lady McCauley is right. Don't look at me like that; she's right about what doesn't work in India. You can march all you like and no one will notice. Things must change, yes, but they won't change overnight. Only a radical reshaping of the economy will ever get rid of the heavy burden of a daughter on a man who is not rich enough to pay her dowry. And if you continue to behave like that, you'll undermine my authority to do anything about it.'

'You are too infuriating! Juliette is looking over at us so smile and wave now please. I don't wish her to understand any of this and grow up believing wives may not hold opinions. Or that little girls don't deserve the life that god has given them.'

They both dutifully waved as she lifted her younger brother's podgy fist and waggled it in the air for him. Not for the first time Julia wondered whether her own family would have got rid of her if they could. If a daughter was a bind, then an unattractive daughter was worse; the bride price escalated wildly in accordance with the looks of the girl.

'Then she needs a European education,' said Charles, with a disarming smile. 'How else will she grow up exactly like her wonderfully fierce mother?'

Julia gathered her paints and arranged them on the tray of the easel. 'You haven't won, but you're right. And if I allow her to go away, and stop any kind of protest, you must absolutely promise that you'll build as many dedicated schoolhouses as this city needs.' He nodded. 'And the schools must educate boys and girls together. And natives with colonials.'

'That may very well stop the parents allowing their children to come.'

'Then we must educate them too.'

'It's really a very good thing that you're not in politics, Julia, you'd turn the world clean upside down within days.'

Squeezing oils in several shades of brown onto her palette, she mixed them together, narrowing her eyes to better see the colour of Juliette's hair. Brown with a glossy sheen of burnished red, like the conkers that grew on the trees by the town hall in Versailles. Beautiful, for those with eyes to see—like everything else. Wherever she went to school Juliette would not be made to spend her childhood looking for colour and comfort in those freezing grey cities. She would see by the painting how much her mother adored her.

Charles watched the movement of her arms as she swept the paint in clumsy strokes, her face set with intense determination. 'You'll be doing the right thing for her.'

'I forbid her to go to France.' Grandmamma was long gone, but there would be other witches in her place, elegant aunts and beautiful cousins. There would be the inevitable fall for Juliette, when her relatives realised her looks did not live up to their standards. If she must go at all, she must be protected from such judgement. 'Sarah and Thoby will move to London in six months. She can live with them and be schooled in England. It will be worth the wait for a decent education.'

1861 Freshwater Bay

What had happened to that perfect vision of family? Children who played by her side, small hands clasped tightly in her own? She might as well admit it to herself; she was a terrible mother. Even from the start. In every confinement she had hated, resented resting for the benefit of the baby. Being made to lie on sweating bed cushions in the afternoon heat, swathed in nets and clouded with incense to ward off the biting insects that brought illness and death. Too weary to read anything academic. Kept apart from their most interesting guests in case she might become over stimulated. Often, having lain still for hours in the daytime, she was too restless to stay in bed at night and dear Charles would find her wandering in the small courtyard garden, calling to the servants as they tried to sleep under the house.

Was it her own foolish fault that her daughter didn't need her? Had she tried to protect her so much that she had scared her away? Juliette was always terribly independent. She would wriggle away from embraces and edge right to her knees when made to sit upon Julia's lap, arching her back away as though she wished to jump off. From the moment she could walk she ran several steps ahead, never holding hands. And when she grew, she refused to have fun at all, never wishing to climb trees, chase animals or dress in jewels or costumes. Juliette liked nothing more than playing quietly, in the peace of the kitchen garden, dressed in plain, conventional clothes. She made Adeline look exciting. Babies, it seemed, were not bound to do as their parents wished. Where was the child of her imagination, fascinated by Beauty, talented at drawing and clamouring for her to teach it everything it wished to know?

Motherhood was not all that the poets would have you believe. A vast amount of thankless time could be expended on running to fulfil a child's every whim, time that could be spent on Art, on writing poetry, or writing to Herschel for the latest scientific discoveries. Equally time that could be spent on setting up schools or protesting injustice. Useful occupations. Once the boys arrived, one after the other, she was forced to hide from them to find any time at all. Little Henry, so sweet, so fond of his mother! And she had actually covered her ears to block out his cries while she stood before her easel. How she wished for that time again. She missed them desperately once they went to England, if only they could have gone all at the same time. There, a good mother would never think such a thing. Had Juliette felt sent away? Had she grown up to resent the loss of India in her childhood? Julia had felt it herself. All those years of thin grey rain, trying to remember the colours of the market or the shape of elephants.

Charles always thought it was the children that brought her back to England. And she did miss them, of course; once Ewen had joined the others there seemed little meaning to a family split apart by so much ocean. She never wanted to be like Mama, ignoring whole years of their upbringing. But it wasn't just the children. The real seeds of doubt about India came mostly from the call of Sarah's salon. Every other letter from her sister read like a roll of honour. It was hard to keep pace with the names, especially when their shipped magazines were always three months behind date. At the time, removed from it all, it had seemed everyone in England was a creative genius. Why not her? For years she had imagined taking Sarah's salon by storm. What had happened to that rage? She had lost all the colour of her early life. And she had been so convinced she had found it again at Freshwater. Why had no one told her just how foolish she appeared?

Stories from the Glass House:
Christina Fraser-Tyler
(The Rosebud Garden of Girls)

It was Mummy who wanted our photograph taken, all four
sisters together. She'd bought us new capes, trimmed with
fur, and I think she'd imagined that we were all to sit in a
row, looking pretty and respectable, so she could give the
prints to the family, or even use them to find suitors—
knowing Mummy that wouldn't have surprised me. It was
in the week that Nelly was betrothed. Rather shockingly,
because she was seven whole years younger than Ethel,
who'd never been asked herself, poor thing, and wore a
look of terrible disappointment for the whole of our
holiday.

Mrs Cameron wouldn't allow Mummy inside the Glass
House, though she kept us there for half the day. First, she
despatched the gardener to bring in tubs of tall shrubs,
which then wouldn't do because they didn't have flowers on
them. Flowers were what she wanted. She marched outside
with scissors to take blooms from elsewhere and threaded
them between the leaves. Someone else was summoned to
make us posies to hold, her sister perhaps, though they
looked different, and she eventually agreed, tying up some
beautiful bouquets but grumbling all the while as though
she'd never been so insulted.

We hadn't expected to be asked to change our clothes
and we worried about what Mummy might say, especially
when we saw the dresses Mrs Cameron had chosen. Simple,
flowing robes with no structure underneath, just loose and
embroidered with leaves and medieval knot work. They
were lovely, but they made us feel as though we wore
nothing at all. Mrs Cameron took off her own dress and
worked in her petticoats, to put us at ease, which made

Mary giggle so much we thought she might not stop. She brushed our hair loose and read us some lines from a poem, by Tennyson I think, about a rosebud garden of girls. We were all, she said, Queen Lily and Rose in one; and we felt beautiful after that, even Ethel.

It was a shame we weren't allowed to keep the print. I would've liked to have one, but I knew better than to plead with Mummy. Mrs Cameron didn't. The pair of them broke into such a dreadful rage, Mummy was furious about the waste of the capes and shocked by the clothes she made us wear. Mrs Cameron just kept telling her that she had no soul and she didn't deserve to have such beauty in her family if she didn't know how to treat it. She said everyone was responsible for creating the cult of beauty and, since it was with us, we ought to worship it. She seemed equally angry, especially when her print was ripped.

Mummy was ignorant about photography and didn't know other prints could be made. But we did, and we were glad when it appeared at the Academy's summer show, especially when it sold to a private collector. We liked to imagine that whoever bought it would get pleasure from the way we looked when we were together, just as Mrs Cameron did.

1848 Calcutta

'Sarah writes that Juliette is developing a talent for painting and her poetry is already superior to mine.' Julia held out the letter with a cross expression.

'That's not exactly difficult, Julia, you're not proud of your poetry yourself. How is Henry?'

'Quite well. Still obsessed with cricket and loves to be out in the fresh air. Thoby says he'll make a fine academic if he can keep up concentration on his books.'

Such updates were reminders of all the children's little triumphs and changes, which she missed while they were away. Episodes in their young lives in which she wasn't included. When she next saw them, they would be grown, no longer need her or, worse, would be calling Sarah mother.

'What else does she say?' Charles prompted.

'There's nothing more about the children.' Julia turned the pages in her hands, scanning both sides for their names. 'The rest of it consists entirely of what can only be described as boasting. It appears my sister is developing an enviable literary and artistic salon at her new home, for which she obviously expects us to be impressed.' How typical of Sarah to show off in such a fashion. There must have been seven new names listed, any one of which would be a catch to most households. Grandmamma had evidently taught her well.

'I'm surprised you're not impressed, Julia. You've always enjoyed meeting artists.' Julia didn't smile and he relented. 'I know it's hard to read about the lives of loved ones. And England now seems so much different to our lives that it's almost unimaginable.'

Really, how could Charles remain so calm? High society had engulfed the rest of their family and that was all he could say? Such fame, and the way Sarah worshipped it, was a new phenomenon and there was something in these descriptions that felt uneasy. Things were changing. Society revolved around discoveries of all kinds, making and collecting men of letters and culture, women of beauty. And something about it made Julia nervous and fascinated, all at once.

'I can imagine it well. My sister seems to have launched forth into fashionable London life at an alarming rate.' It would be hard for the rest of the family to follow. Particularly hard if those people were currently on the other side of the world. Or not blessed with the requisite physical and social graces.

'It sounds exhausting,' said Charles, wrinkling his nose. 'I wonder how poor Thoby is enjoying a constant houseful of socialites?'

'Sarah won't be giving him much choice. Though I fear she's mistaking real happiness for that which seems at best its semblance and which, to me, has not even that to recommend it. She speaks so gleefully of the trophy names she has in her salon that I wonder whether she has realised they're living people!' It was so hard to know whether she felt jealous or disapproving that it was easier to just feel angry. The scene was at once dangerous and compelling. Yet what was the point in wishing herself there if there was no part for her to play? Not an Artist, a genius, a beauty or a host. Just a plain sister. Perhaps, after all, Juliette was better off without her.

Charles took the letters from his wife's hands. 'If you won't read these out properly then at least allow me to see them.' He skimmed through the pages with an amused expression. 'She doesn't seem to be particularly changed… she says quite plainly here that her one ambition is to have the best salon in London,' he looked at Julia as though attempting to gauge her reaction, 'And we all know that she's quite as determined as yourself when she sets her mind on something.'

My Dear Herschel,

It seems, over the last few years, that our splendid intellectual trinity has been reduced to two. Try as I might I'm unable to coax a letter from my beloved husband. He works all day until late in the evening, returning only for dinner. I know he wishes to do good here, but he can't see, and I can't tell him, that his position is neither comfortable nor fair. While his friends implore him to stay in Calcutta and work out his reforms to completion, they don't realise he's utterly powerless without the support and help of the rest of the service. So, while he sacrifices the best years of his life in this climate, devoting his best intellect and energies to the service, he's really doing no good at all.

I find there's little to occupy my soul's yearning for culture here. I miss my sisters almost as much as I miss my children, and in many ways am pining for the interesting people they seem to meet in London. I can hardly keep my mind from imagining the way they live, surrounded by Scientists and Artists of all kinds.

It's still my dearest wish to create beautiful Art, but I've quite abandoned oil paints, the layers are too painstaking for my temperament and I confess I become easily frustrated.

I do wish you would write to Charles and enquire about his plans. I know he's tired. With so much taste for literary leisure and a retired life he would be much happier in England. But I may not ever discuss it and Charles remains convinced that retirement might waste his capacity for doing public good, he is so desperate for his career to have been worthwhile. Please do write and help me to remind him that it already has.
Your ever-appreciative,
Julia

Papa had seemed immortal, although his friends rightly agreed he had lived to outdrink the time he should have had by a good ten years of dissipation that would have killed off a lesser man in an instant. While a hundred glasses raised a toast to the infamy of 'the biggest liar in

India' his widow sat quietly in the shade of her bedroom and told her daughter that she absolutely would not stay in the country without him.

'Please think about it for a while, Mama,' Julia pleaded. 'You're in shock, grieving. It's the worst of times to make such an important change.' Julia had rushed to the house on hearing the news, dismayed not to have the chance to say goodbye. Their last conversation had been another of her lectures on his treatment of the weaker men around him and she cursed herself for it. For all her disapproval of his cheating, she had loved her father and there were many things she wished she could have asked, so many conversations left unsaid. Worse still if Mama was to rush after him. Then she would never be truly reconciled with either of them. She couldn't let them both disappear before she had a chance to understand them.

'There's no colour left in India for me,' said Mama, draping herself across the day bed with a dramatic flourish.

'Colour is here wherever you look for it,' Julia replied. But Mama was not a lover of nature and, besides, it was hard to console someone you didn't understand. It had felt like the chance to bond, but already their bereavements seemed poles apart. They were such different things to each other. Major James Pattle was the glamorous and dashing love of Mama's life and everything else—everything—had played second fiddle to his virtuoso.

'He's here!' she wailed. 'Whatever I look at he will always be here. I must go to England. To take him to his family crypt in Westminster. Our final journey together. For what is my place without him? What will I be?'

Julia had no answer. It was hard for her to imagine their lives apart too. Like a mirror without a reflection. Like one of Herschel's double stars, cut-off from its twin and condemned to circle a pointless orbit in the night sky. It would be impossible, after such a life, for Mama to merely lodge with one of her daughters, divorced from the means

71

to run society as she had always done. Julia took a deep breath. 'Mama give yourself time. Please. Calcutta has been your home for over fifty years.'

'There is nothing to wait for. Your sisters will need husbands before long and where better to find them?' She paused, 'You could come with us, for a while?'

'You know I can't leave Charles, not the way things are here. He relies absolutely on my support.' It would have been nice to feel that the offer had been genuine, but the hesitation was clear. She had said 'us' though; did that mean she would be taking the younger girls? How could she? Not only had Sarah been with Juliette for years, now she was to get Mama too, and Virginia and Sophia who were still unmarried. Imagine the stir their looks would cause among the fashionable set. It was too much to bear. Sarah would have everyone and her letters would become as insufferable as their author in the company of celebrity.

With no time to get used to the idea, Julia was distraught when they left. She was further devastated by the news from the ship that Mama, already weak, had never quite recovered from the fright of seeing what she remained convinced was her husband's ghost and had subsequently suffered a heart attack whilst sailing through a storm. It was hard to grieve for Papa; he'd lived his best life, died painlessly in his cups as he would have wanted; he had also given true love and affection that she could carry always. He, of all people, had loved her for who she was. But her chance to be reconciled with her mother was lost. After all the promises, neither parent had reached England. The Captain, with a sailor's caution, was unwilling to carry such bad luck any further and insisted on a double burial at sea. Sophia and Virginia, orphaned, frightened and barely of age, already possessed of a beauty equally dangerous to themselves and others, were forced to finish the journey alone.

'What will become of my sisters?' Julia sobbed into the letter as she read their news.

'Your sisters will thrive my dear,' said Charles, 'As the Governor always said, mankind is divided into men, women and Pattles. And, one way or another, Pattles will find their dominion over the rest.'

1848 Calcutta

My Dear Sister,

I hope you and Charles are well and surviving the heat? I know you'll be missing the peace of the river and that Charles will be refusing to leave his work in the city. Your trip to Ceylon sounds wonderful. How clever of you both to invest there; I hope you'll be able to visit your new estates often. You both work so hard.

You'll be heartened to know that Juliette, Henry, Ewen and Eugene are all here again for the holidays; they're growing so fast and are as charming as ever. Juliette is developing her painting and shows real talent, you would be proud of her. We're quite the houseful most of the time. Sarah is tireless in her entertaining. The Taylors are always here and Henry's poetry is making him famous, but he doesn't seem it to us. He hasn't changed. Mr Thackeray visits often, you'll remember him from Grandmamma's house, and even Mr Tennyson came to call once. He's serious and has a beard as long as Charles's, though not so silky. He looks as though he needs someone to care for him.

George Frederic Watts, who has a studio near to our house, is practically become one of the family. His studio is remarkable, a jumble of half-finished paintings and vast sculptures he makes in clay and then transports all the way to Limehouse for dipping in bronze. He has shown his sketches of me at the Royal Academy. I do wish you could see them. I wanted to post you a catalogue, but they were very heavy indeed. I've saved you one. Instead I enclose the review of his exhibition in the Art Journal. It is all true. He possesses an incredible talent. I don't know how he works in such chaotic surroundings as his studio. It's all painted the whitest of whites and the windows stretch to the floor, so even in the winter it seems to be bright and light. There are drapes and props strewn across every surface and huge, silk cushions, on which he makes his visitors sit. He always sits on them cross-legged, which gives him the air of a schoolboy. You would wish to look after him. Sometimes

he makes his visitors wear pieces of costume that he has collected
just so he can think about compositions for paintings while he talks
to them. He is a true bohemian and I think you would adore him.
Yours,
Virginia

'His portrait of Virginia Pattle holds a rare, elevated sentiment... She stands like a pilgrim on the stone terrace, her hair simply braided and a long grey coat of nun-like simplicity falling round her... She has no curls, frills or furbelows, no jewels; she is as God made her; a perfectly beautiful woman...' Julia read aloud from the review in a disapproving tone, snapping the pages at Charles who seemed about to slip into a doze. 'Did you hear any of that?'

Virginia's descriptions did nothing to allay her fear that her sisters, vulnerable in their grief, would become shallow and pretentious if they stayed with Sarah.

'Yes, a perfectly beautiful woman and so on, what's wrong with it? She is beautiful, and she said herself he was a talented painter,' Charles spoke without opening his eyes, leaning comfortably against the pillows of the broad-backed rattan chair.

Julia pushed her foot against his footstool, causing him to jerk upright. 'And this is exactly what she doesn't need. She's little more than a child.' The least Charles could do was listen, she'd only just lost both her parents. The poor thing was weak and vulnerable.

'She's older than you were when we met at the Cape.'

'An age when she should be developing her tastes and intellect. She should be charming people with her conversation not gathering idiots to moon over her looks.' It was all well for vain married Sarah to court and prize the public gaze, but what would it bring Virginia? She'd already had a poem in her honour published in the Literary Review, been subjected to a public mob on Regent Street and had

75

dozens of offers of marriage from gentlemen she'd never met.

Charles eyed his wife. 'She's not you, Julia. Not everyone can charm with words. And she's been given little choice in anything else.'

Well who did get a choice? Was he trying to say that Beauty was a curse? Perhaps it was. Virginia sounded worried. Worried for herself, for Sarah, for her younger sisters. London was a madhouse and now Virginia had a famous artist falling over himself to sketch and paint her all the time. It must be hard for her, and yet, something in it must be wonderful. She glared at the way Charles's head had nodded back onto the pillow. 'You're so tired all the time, you can hardly keep awake to speak with me.'

'My dear, you married an old man, I can't be expected to dance all night long.' He smiled and patted the seat next to him, taking her hand as she settled and pressing it to his lips.

'You could very well dance all night if you wanted. It's not your age but your weariness that concerns me.' He was not usually so morose. This was the point at which he generally spotted her need for assurance and made her feel better about her sisters. 'What's the matter, Charles, what's happened today?'

'It is, rather, what has not happened. I met with the committee today.' He shook his head. 'Only one of the schoolhouses is finished... one... we had planned to have sixty up and running by now. Even that one has no staff yet.' Charles let out a long sigh and dropped his hands heavily back on to the covers.

'Did they explain why?' He was too soft on these men; he should expect more.

'It doesn't really matter why it hasn't happened this time, does it? There are always excuses here. There always will be. Reasons why the schools won't be built, why the changes won't be implemented. I am weary, you're right, weary of men who expect to collect payment for work they're not inclined to carry out, men who have no pride beyond the collection of their service pensions.'

He looked suddenly old, the flesh on his cheeks and neck hung loose. India was ageing him and keeping them away from family. If she didn't act, he would change his mind in a few days and they would be stuck in this cycle forever.

'If you truly feel like this... and won't forgive it all tomorrow... then, there's nothing to keep us here, Charles.' Julia held her breath; if she could have done so without detection, she would have crossed her fingers too.

'Perhaps,' he said finally, 'you are right.'

'I am always right!' Julia jumped up, sensing victory, and made hurried lists of what the move would entail, what she could bear to leave and what she must ensure she took to remind her sisters of what was important in life, above and beyond looks and fame.

1849 Kensington

'Julia's decorations are rather less peaceful.' Charles admired the tranquil greens and painted wallpapers at Little Holland House, where Sarah and Thoby had moved to accommodate their growing salon. 'She has covered all of the wall space with prints and photographs. Even in the bedroom. It feels as though we share the place with a hundred ghosts.'

'Luckily you are only next door. You must feel free to escape from Julia whenever you like, dear Charles.' Sarah beamed across the table, laden with strawberries, cream and scones in piles and dishes, with mismatched bowls and spoons for guests to help themselves.

Too perfectly beautiful, thought Julia. Little Holland House never seemed messy or crowded, despite Sarah's very best efforts at bohemia. The rooms were wide, bright and spacious and painted with splendid, sweeping frescoes by Watts, whom Thoby now supported financially, and who so loved to spend time near to Virginia that Julia feared he may be running out of walls to paint and turn to their own crowded cottage. She half suspected that the only reason her sister had married poor Thoby was the money he was able to use for artistic patronage. It was rather like purchasing a cultural colony. It was also convenient Sarah had managed to find them a place so close to her house, and even more so that their tiny place made her own salon appear even more sumptuous. One day she would find a place that was truly original for her and Charles, which reflected their natures, her creativity. London may not hold them for long.

'We are grateful to you, and Thoby, for finding us the cottage, and for your endless hospitality. This lovely house is full of graceful women and gifted men.' If Charles was less smitten with the artists than his in-laws, he was far too polite to say.

'I've had enough of the gifted men, it makes one think one shouldn't bother,' grumbled Thoby as he wandered in and helped himself to a bowl of fruit. 'Are you hiding in here Charles? I think I may join you. The croquet is getting rather malicious.'

'I miss the climate,' said Julia. 'Here the rain seems to come every week, winter or summer. Such thin rain. I don't think I'll ever get used to that.'

Sarah tossed her head. 'In Calcutta one never knew if anyone worth inviting would be in the country from one party to the next. All those dull dinners and boring civil service wives.'

'Better to be dull and work hard than swan around all day with nothing to do but dress for dinner.' Julia's eyes narrowed dangerously and Charles straightened on his chair. 'I seem to have met dozens of people in the last few months who have nothing to offer the world but their own petty celebrity.'

'I assume you're not referring to any guests of mine?' Sarah set her cups and saucers on the table with slow, deliberate care. 'I would defy you to claim even one boring evening in this house.'

'I'm sure Julia does not mean any offence.' Charles patted Sarah's arm and Julia glared at him.

'On the contrary, it's often I who am offended... by the fact it's possible to be so very famous for doing so very little.'

Sarah gave a short and humourless laugh. 'Your own sister is the best-known person in London, the city waits with bated breath to see what she will wear as she walks along Regent Street.'

'Then you agree with me?'

'Not with your offence. Is it not delightful that Virginia has reached such accolades? Would you have her deny the pleasure?'

Julia's eye was drawn to the portrait of Virginia hung on Sarah's salon wall, next to a framed copy of the ode to her beauty. 'It's a shallow and hateful thing to be judged and adored on the turn of your cheek or the colour of your dress. I would have thought better of you, Sarah, than to throw yourself at fame for its own sake. It should only be awarded to those with talent and creativity, or those who gain great status as politicians and thinkers, or scientists. And you can stop drawing Virginia in; the fame you seek is undoubtedly your own. The admiration of all those social climbers.'

'Well, since our family boasts neither creativity nor talent in art or politics, I find that our sisters and myself must use our social gifts to excel. You will find my parties as desirable an invitation as any in London. Perhaps you should enjoy the chance to be a part of them?'

Julia seethed. Sarah knew only too well how she laboured at her easel, pleading with the knife to do her bidding, drawing comfort only from the colours of the paint. Yesterday, Sarah had walked in on a brief lesson from Watts and delighted in her embarrassment. There had been scant improvement. She might as well admit it. Perhaps she should give up and enjoy the parties in close contact with true talents instead. It didn't seem to bother anyone else. Yet she could not shake the feeling that she had a true creative purpose, something that eluded her and danced just from her grasp whenever she got close.

Charles cleared his throat. 'Well I don't miss the weather, or the dull parties. In fact, I miss little about my former gainful employment except that I was generally allowed to skip dinner and retire to bed with my newspaper whenever I liked. Here that's apparently bad form.'

'Why on earth would Sarah let you go to bed when someone more famous may appear at any moment? I'm usually forced to stay awake for several hours after my preferred time to retire. Thankfully we may find refuge in each other now.' Thoby seemed relieved that the sisters had been steered from their argument.

'But you at least count as one of the creative geniuses?' said Charles, who was writing a treatise on the social economics of tea plantation. 'I often feel as though I'm the only person in London not engaged in beautiful artistic endeavour.'

Thoby gave one of his barking laughs. 'I'm afraid, between my lack of published novels and of physical beauty, I rest on a very low branch of the great tree of genius. A fact for which I'm grateful every day. I couldn't bear to race through life being fashionably erudite and witty every time I opened my mouth.'

'But you are always wise.' Charles held up his teacup and chinked the rim of Thoby's glass.

'If you two have quite finished congratulating each other,' said Julia, 'perhaps you can explain why creative genius seems only ever to apply to men?' The two looked at her as though astonished by the question. 'When you speak of genius, why is it only male? Women are never included. You should know better, both of you.'

Thoby opened his mouth, but Charles gave him a warning look before interrupting. 'You're quite right, we shouldn't. There are many gifted members of the fairer type, they just don't feature in your sister's salon.'

'That is unfair, Charles! My salon is always full of the best-known society beauties.'

'That's all you care for, I half believe you are responsible for this ridiculous cult of beauty,' Julia glowered.

Sarah looked pleased. 'You cared very much for beauty yourself once. And we had a lady novelist here last week, oh and Elizabeth Browning of course.'

'Not painters though,' said Thoby, stroking his smooth, pink chin. 'In fact, I can't think of any at all.'

'Gentileschi!' cried Julia. 'Artemesia Gentileschi was one of the most gifted painters who ever lived.'

'Quite a tragic start as I recall,' said Thoby. 'Wasn't she the one who was…'

'Yes,' said Julia. 'She was. And it doesn't surprise me at all that you know nothing else about her.'

Sarah smiled as she pushed her bassinet along the street, chattering with excitement. 'He plans to exhibit his works of you, all of them, even the first sketches. They'll let him do as he pleases, it's his third showing at the Academy, Thoby says he can barely put a foot wrong there.'

'I heard you talking about it at dinner,' Virginia bowed her head, 'but, actually, I believe he said there would only be three of me, and I'm sure they'll be very small in comparison with his real portraits.'

Julia gave her a look of concern. George Frederic Watts was fast becoming known for his paintings of society women, all full length, richly coloured and flattering to their subject. It wouldn't do for these drawings to bring Virginia any more unwanted attention. She'd been spending more and more time with her in sittings, trying to learn the painter's techniques as well as chaperone her sister, and the sketches were certainly sensual. Virginia was far too young. If she'd felt it was in her power to do so, she would have asked him not to show them to the public at all.

'He seems to finish at least one portrait a week. His output rivals Julia's, although his is all exceptionally talented. I really don't know where he finds the time, when so much of his focus is you.' Sarah threw a sly glance at Virginia, who blushed a deep and flattering shade of pink and released the hand of her nephew, Thomas, who ran ahead and began to jump on and off the bottom step of each tall house.

'His studio's so close, perhaps we should ask him to stay?' Sarah considered.

Julia knew she was weighing up the size of his fame and reputation as a trade for their sister's beauty. It made her angry, although sometimes she felt she would sell her soul for a taste of either. 'Really, I think that's a terrible idea.' Watts was likeable with courteous manners and spent many hours carefully showing her how to mix paints, explaining his techniques as though he was talking to a fellow artist. What would become of him if he moved into that maelstrom at Little Holland House?

'I can't imagine sitting with him at breakfast each morning,' said Virginia.

'He never tires of drawing you,' said Sarah, 'One day you may have to get used to him at your breakfast table.'

'Perhaps he would if he saw me every day.' Virginia blushed as she realised, too late, what her sister implied.

'Don't worry, I won't ask him stay, not yet, although Thoby's fond of him and Thoby must always have someone to talk to... Do you like sitting for him?'

'I have nothing with which to compare the experience, I've never sat for anyone else. Thomas, do come back, you'll get lost!'

'He's quite alright, he knows the way to the studio now too. I believe he's in love with you Virginia.'

'All small boys should love their aunts,' said Julia.

'Not Thomas! George Watts. Do you love him, Virginia? You certainly do encourage him.' Thomas ran back and, prying the bassinet from his mother, jogged it up and down as he walked with it, eliciting happy gurgles from his baby sister.

'Sarah! That's most unkind,' interjected Julia. 'I've never seen Virginia interested in anything other than Mr Watt's art and that is hardly surprising. He's quite the most talented man I've met. And self-taught, too. His upbringing sounds quite austere.'

'That's just the problem.' Sarah sighed in that way Julia found deeply irritating. Why did she always have to feel the weight of responsibility without their parents, surely as the eldest here it was her job to marry her younger sisters well, and happily. Being stuck in India for so long had allowed Sarah to take charge. 'He's full of social conscience. And he'll never make money while he insists on giving his best work away to galleries and museums.'

'Artistic endeavour is not, first and foremost, about making money,' said Julia, quickly. 'That's why it's important for artists to have patrons, like Thoby and Henry.'

'He's not exactly a patron of Taylor's poetry. Although I suppose he's helping him with the rent on the house, while his play becomes established.'

Julia wasn't certain the play would ever be popular, if that was what her sister meant by established; she had struggled to stay awake when they'd taken a box. Must artistic endeavour always bring money? Sarah seemed to imply that it must, as though it was the recognition, and not the art, that was worthy.

Sarah turned sharply to face to Virginia, just as they reached the front door of Watts's studio. 'Would you consider him, if the money was there?'

'The money means nothing!' cried poor Virginia. 'I'm half inclined to accept the first proposal from someone who has done more than simply see my picture or read a poem another man has written about me!'

Julia saw Watts's pale face at the open first floor window and realised that he must have heard every word. From what she knew of him it would have wounded him deeply. Was he one of those men? The ones who saw nothing beyond Virginia's looks? Perhaps so. But he was an Artist of Unquestionable Talent, and, for Julia, that would have been enough. What did it matter if an Artist was poor? She would be delighted if Virginia accepted Watts, perhaps she should try to persuade her. 'He doesn't seem to be answering. Are you quite sure of the time?'

Watts ran down to the front door, throwing it open wide just as they had turned. 'Forgive me, dear ladies, I was engrossed in my work and I forget that here I've no housemaid to answer doors.' He bowed low.

'We know very well that you have no maid at all,' said Julia, 'and that, dear George, is why the place looks like this. Would you like us to keep house for you?'

'An artist should live a little wildly.' Virginia peeped up at him from underneath her low bonnet and Julia marvelled at how naturally the claws of charm drew from unmarried young ladies without them realising. Poor Watts was helpless. It would surely not be long before they wed and then, of course, he would allow her to be his studio devotee and teach her all his tricks of the trade. Days spent inside this peaceful treasure trove would give her the inspiration needed and the muse would draw down to embrace her.

1849 Kensington

'It's certainly me, and yet not me.' Julia stood before her portrait with her hands clasped tightly, her expressive eyes as wide as a child's. It was hard to breathe. The face reflecting from the canvas wore a wistful expression, as though half-remembering a beautiful dream. Her features were softened and slimmed, cheekbones high and mouth gently curved. Was this how Artists saw others, with all the light of life and intellect clear in their countenance? A reflection, not of true physiognomy, but the person within. It was recognisably her, but with the handsome features of her sisters. 'You've understood me quite as I appear to myself. It is magical, Signor... I am not sure what else to say.'

'You've silenced my sister!' Sarah threw her arms wide in a gesture of disbelief. 'Remarkable. A magician, as she says.'

Julia felt a slightly guilty triumph at the shade of bitterness. Sarah had always claimed Watts as hers, because of Thoby's patronage, though everyone knew he chased Virginia and it drove the poor thing mad that she'd been offered no portrait of her own. Julia had asked outright, but Sarah did not need to know that. Their younger sister, Sophia, fascinated by his stories of Italy and finding herself unable to call him George or Fred, had christened Watts 'The Signor' and talked so much during her sitting it had taken him almost twice as long as any other painting he had undertaken. He'd even painted Charles. Yet he'd never asked his own patron's wife. What a shame it was Sarah's lifelong ambition to be a muse.

'Another perfect portrait, dear Signor. You have made Julia look almost attractive.'

Julia ignored the slight. Far better to have this portrait than to be like Sarah, destined to the side-lines of Art, with no painted legacy to hang on her perfect white walls and no ambition to create anything more inspiring than a dinner menu. 'Sarah is right. It is a perfect portrait and I think it is simply wonderful. You must let me buy it for Charles's birthday.'

'I'm rather pleased with it too.' Watts took an oilcloth and rubbed at imaginary smears on the gilt frame. 'I thought it might make one of my presentations to the Academy, at the end of the summer show.'

'Absolutely not!' Julia pushed away his hand and straightened the picture on its temporary easel by the hearth. 'Why would you bring it to me only to take it away! I simply won't allow it to go out of this house! It would be as though my soul was ripped from within me.'

'My sister is rather prone to romantic fancy.' Sarah's eyes swept the room with a look of distaste. 'Is this really to be its final resting place? It's already a little cluttered, Julia, don't you think?'

The Camerons' house, wedged between the sprawling semi-rural idyll of Little Holland House and the Taylor's spacious Hall, was, by comparison, cosy. With lower ceilings and exposed beams, along with broad fireplaces and dark walls and curtains, it had the feel of a cottage, without the gardens. Each room was stuffed to the brim with artefacts from India and the general detritus of Julia's constantly evolving hobbies.

'A wall space must be cleared. I think this room will be best because I can't bear for it to go unnoticed, it's the first thing I'll share with my guests.' Julia surveyed the room. It wasn't so bad, the clutter was homely and comforting, and the colours wonderful. The Signor himself had said yesterday that it seemed to contain every shade of blue. It was like a puff of spring air or the ripple on a lake, with a beauty of its own spotted only by true Artists. 'Perhaps it could do with some reorganisation.'

'Indeed it could!' Sarah puffed her chest and straightened her back to show she was serious. Charles would imitate her after she left, he always did. 'You need a maid. It's not enough here to have a cook and a gardener, you need someone to help you keep things in order.'

'Perhaps,' agreed Julia. 'Though they're hard to come by in London, particularly if you require a decent conversation.' Scurrying servants, too frightened to talk, were the last thing she wanted overrunning the house. In India at least she had enjoyed speaking with her staff with some mutual interest and respect. They never minded her unconventional household management. It was quite a different story here.

'Most people don't want a good conversation with their maids,' said Sarah.

'Then their lives must be terribly dull. Tell me, Signor, how did you paint this? You can't have used mere oils. It's impossible. I've never seen flesh made so soft, so lifelike and yet so dreamlike. It's a portrait of a woman seen in a dream.' Watt's style seemed a manifestation of everything she'd tried to create in paint herself. She swelled with love for his ability to render the truth with such an overlay of Beauty. It was the ultimate expression of artistic integrity, fashionable and beyond fashion. No matter how many hours she spent at the easel, she would never create something so meaningful.

'What is your next commission Signor? Or do you have leisure to choose a sitter?' enquired Sarah with an unsubtle hint. 'If you don't wish to paint... another of us then perhaps you're hiding a famous name?'

'As a matter of fact, I'm bound to paint Mr Alfred Tennyson, perhaps you've met him before? I can paint in my studio, of course, but if this weather remains I would prefer to use your gardens.'

Julia had taken it on herself to invite Watts to stay with the Prinseps for the duration of her sitting and he showed no inclination to move now it was finished. The previous day he had asked to be allowed to change the wallpaper in his bedroom.

'I would be delighted to see dear Alfred again,' said Sarah who had briefly met him, with Virginia, one evening at the Holland's. 'And a garden painting would be so much nicer for him. He is, I think, a man who spends too far much time indoors.'

'Do please remember that he's always Mr Tennyson,' reproached Watts. 'He very much dislikes first name terms, and he is, like most poets, inclined towards melancholy. Although his conversation is never dull, but always of the utmost interest.'

'Then we must cheer him up at once!' said Julia. 'Please do tell him he's welcome to stay with us.'

'Julia means my house, of course,' hurried Sarah. 'There's more space there and it will be far more convenient for his portrait. When is he expected first?'

'I believe we start tomorrow,' said Watts. 'There's simply no rest for a wicked artist.'

'Then we must ready a room for him.' Sarah began to gather her things. 'Do come and help me Julia, you have such an eye for these things.' She gave the portrait a final lingering glance. 'What are you thinking I wonder?'

'She's thinking of India,' said Watts.

Julia nodded, though all the while she had sat for him, she'd been thinking of Ruskin's essays on the nature of beauty, and wondering just how brutal the image would turn out to be.

1861 Freshwater Bay

It had been a mistake to leave Rohit behind in India. He would never have betrayed her like this, nor let her make such a fool of herself, and he always knew what to say to make everything feel better. But he'd refused to make the journey. As clothes, cushions, rugs and hangings were thrown into trunks, he sat quietly watching and painting out birth charts, one for each of the sisters and a secret one for Charles, who said he had no wish for the sky to tell him how he should live. Sarah's chart was filled with rising fire, a result of the strange alignment of the planets on the day of her birth, and Virginia's showed striking influence from water and tranquil moons. Somehow it was reassuring.

The new chart Rohit painted was almost identical to the one she had carried for years, except for one astral line, which he said he'd discovered was a mistake on the original. Now a lone bright star appeared in the central plane, with six smaller stars around it. It meant, he said, not exactly mirrors and glass but reflections, and expressed his delight at being able to give her a correct interpretation after so many years. It was all the same thing. Hadn't Mama said something similar when she first returned to Calcutta? That she reflected people, their true selves. It was nothing new. More interesting was the brightness of the central star and the number of smaller stars around it. Six stars. Six sisters. All looking to her bright star for their reflections. In England it was supposed to become clear. Secretly she felt it was a sign that her ambition would be realised. How wrong. How proud and foolish. Why hadn't she listened to Rohit more carefully?

She would have done better to concentrate on being a better mother. Why had she insisted on filling their house with other people's children? It had felt like the right thing. Sarah always said they made Juliette stay away. It was probably true. All those children kept her busy, made her feel less of a failure, but they drove her own daughter further from the house. Juliette quickly stopped coming home in the holidays, preferring instead to spend time with her school friend, Claudine, an only child with a large and peaceful country estate.

Sarah's own girls stuck to their mother like limpets, begging her to walk in the parks with them to show off their new gowns. So much like their mother. Prancing like little hobgoblins in their frills. What would she do with children like that anyway? But someone to walk with, to take to the galleries, that would have been nice.

Juliette should have become an Artist. Her talents were considerable, but she had no ambition other than to get away from her family. Where had it gone wrong? Had she simply repeated Mama's mistakes, placed a distance between them? Perhaps so, but not entirely the same. She'd spent her whole life trying to prove herself to Mama, but Juliette did not care for approval at all. None of them needed her. They would not miss her if the sea carried her off entirely. Perhaps their young lives would be more enriched, free of the embarrassment she caused.

Stories from the Glass House:
George Frederic Watts
(The Whisper of the Muse)

When they arrived in London, the divine sisters were like a wonderful travelling theatre in their flowing robes and cloaks. Except Virginia, who always wanted to seem more ordinary than she was. Unfortunately for her, at a time when the fashionable world favoured ostentation, the simplicity of her costume pushed her further into the limelight.

Only now she's gone can I realise that Julia, with her violent disregard for convention, was my true muse. At the time I had only eyes for her younger sister, making sketch after sketch in silverpoint, attempting to capture the elegant line of her brow, the sweep of her cheekbone. Studies of the fall of her soft cloak on her slender frame. Such extraordinary beauty was challenging to replicate on a cold canvas, and I knew, in the end, I was not worthy. Julia herself was easy to paint. Her noble plainness, like so many of my best portraits, required simple flattery. A slight softening of the features, a faraway look.

I was pleased that Julia, too, was unable to take a good photograph of Virginia, as though that proved something. She certainly managed to capture other souls. Her portrait of me was enchanting, shot through with the light and energy of the creative muse, something I would have been proud to paint. Adding the violin, another instrument I never learned to play, was a stroke of genius; bringing music and life to my pose as I held it above her young nieces, as though I had just played a wonderful tune and one could almost see the sparks fly from my fingers. It's how I felt when I painted and Julia knew that, because she listened. Listening was what Julia did best. She saw inside people, brought out their inner beauty. She called it 'greatness,' sometimes, but that wasn't it, not really, it was just more surprising to see such dreamlike portraits of all those heavily worthy men. They were quite remarkable. And Julia was quite remarkable for making them give themselves to her.

We spent hours talking about painting—she was so convinced that there was a trick, a foolproof technique, something I could teach her. But there is not. One can paint, or not paint, teaching is worthless. When she finally found her art, her passion, there was just no talking to her. We were happy for her, happy that she had what she wanted. But, in many ways, the change was unsettling. She had lost something, a softness and gentleness that were her beauty, her uniqueness. That's what I thought, privately, that she lost her real beauty when she found art.

1852 Putney Heath

Gentle sunlight warmed the skin of Julia's forearms where her shawl had fallen back. She inhaled the scent of spring. Dark shoots of daffodils burst through the banks of grass and loose balls of cloud skidded across the clearest sky. A perfect setting and a sense of calm before new beginnings. The very air tasted of wonder. It was good to be alive.

Julia sat and made herself comfortable, stretching her legs to take off her button boots. She placed them on the ground, next to her book, a purple velvet cloak and the wide-brimmed hat she had untied and removed as she shook her hair loose. Relaxing on the sun-speckled ground, she curled her bare toes with the sheer pleasure of existence. Mama would have been furious. Bad enough for a child to go barefoot and hatless, but unthinkable for a woman of middle age! Middle age; was that an apt description? Would she really live beyond seventy? Charles would be almost a century, though it was easier to imagine him as old and easy to think he could reach such an age with his long walks and daily yoga.

In the distance, she saw two figures approaching the small groups of people standing on the paths of the heath, conversing as they passed each other. Their arms were outstretched in supplication, as though begging for money. Checking her pockets, Julia saw that she had, by chance, remembered to bring her small purse and leaned back on her elbows to await their advance so she could share some luck. A legacy from India where gifting a coin or food to a mendicant was a matter, not just of helping them, but drawing auspicious events towards oneself.

They drew closer; a woman, of unrecognisable age, and a girl, perhaps twelve or thirteen. Both wore long red skirts, torn and patched, with thin, woollen shawls over white blouses; a pleasing peasant look that made her wish to paint. In her mind's eye she saw the composition, a band of bucolic women with faraway looks on their faces, gathering fruits into low baskets they carried on their arms. A clear pastoral scene; the Signor would have sketched it in an instant. Why could she visualise such paintings? It was too cruel. In her mind she could paint the scenes to perfection, but her hands could not give them life; her tools and easels remained stacked against the cellar wall.

Heads downcast, the picturesque beggars walked across the heath just before her. Julia called out and they stopped, glancing briefly at each other before the woman nodded and they approached.

'Didn't you spot me here?' she asked, smiling, and the pair exchanged another look.

'We did,' said the woman, in a broad Irish brogue, 'but we thought perhaps you were in similar straits to us.' Awkwardly she indicated the mess of belongings on the grass, the bare feet.

Julia was delighted. How very romantic to be considered a woman of the road. 'I am rather untidy! But quite comfortable, thank you, and I'd like to help you, if I can. You've travelled a long way to be walking here, Dublin perhaps?'

'We've come from Cork.' The woman coughed again, behind her hand, and Julia held out a handkerchief. It was silk, embroidered with Charles's initials, and the woman hesitated.

Julia insisted. 'I should have recognised your accent. I've met a lot of people from your fair country, in India and at my sister's house, though I've never visited myself. I'd like to, it sounds very beautiful.'

'It isn't very beautiful at the minute, ma'am.'

'No. I daresay it isn't.' Julia kicked herself. She knew that, only last week she'd helped Sarah arrange a famine fundraiser. Neither of the two women wore shoes that properly protected their feet; the uppers were bound to the

95

worn soles with strips of frayed leather, showing cracked skin between. 'Sit down, please. Don't worry, I'll give you something for your troubles.'

'Would you like us to give you a prayer ma'am?' They knelt carefully in front of Julia, resting back on their heels.

'Is that what people usually ask?'

The young girl nodded and Julia noticed she carried a small string of rosary beads wrapped around her right hand. 'I'm not that way inclined, I'm afraid, though I'm sure your prayers are lovely. I'm more interested to hear your story.'

'There isn't much to tell, ma'am. We're the same as all the others. Nothing to eat at home. No work. We were lucky we managed to get passage here without money.' Her face clouded at the memory and she put a protective arm around the young girl.

'Did you come alone? Is this your daughter?'

'Yes, it's just us two now. Mary, say hello to the lady.'

'Hello.'

The girl lifted her eyes briefly, before staring back at the grass and Julia was shocked to see a beauty that would rival Sophia's, if not Virginia's. With her red-brown, waved hair, haughty cheekbones and enormous hooded eyes, she had the fairytale face of a pre-Raphaelite heroine. Her mother, careworn and aged, with the rough red hands of a working woman, showed no sign of having possessed such looks. Mary's surely came from her father. It would be impossible not to paint her. Perhaps just the muse she needed.

'Where's the rest of your family?'

Mary put her hand out to rest on her mother's. It was a simple gesture, full of care and the daughterly love she had never known from Juliette, or felt for Mama.

The woman looked at her daughter and then coughed again, in long ragged gasps, before answering. 'Mary's Pa died a long time ago. He wouldn't have helped us much anyhow. When he was working, he spent all his money on anything other than his family. When he fell ill all the weans had to work to pay for his medicines. He didn't last long, thankfully, god rest his soul.'

Julia waited, full of questions, while the woman coughed again. 'The others... Mary had two older brothers. They came over to work on the railways as soon as their Pa was gone. Never heard from them again. All the money me and Mary could make wasn't enough after that and that's when we decided we'd do what we could to make a change.'

The woman stared ahead, over Julia's shoulder, and Julia wondered whether it had been good for her to talk. It sounded like the first time she had done so, perhaps the first time anyone had cared enough to ask. Too late now to take it back. She'd made her talk, and now it was there between them like an accusation. Now she was the one who felt she should be putting it right. Julia dug her fingers into the earth and pulled at the strands of grass. 'You haven't told me your own name.'

'Violetta.'

A lovely name for such a woman. Straight from a story. A name that could equally carry a curse or a blessing. 'I'm Julia. Where do you stay?'

'Anywhere we can shelter. Sometimes in the communes they've set up for the famine travellers, though they can be dangerous enough places for women and girls. Sometimes we sleep under the trees here.'

'What about when it's cold?'

Violetta looked across the park, her jaw set. In outbuildings maybe, she wouldn't want to get in trouble for that. Julia brooded a moment. She saw the woman's hands and the girl's beautiful, delicate features, she saw their silent determination and pride. Something drew her to them. What if these people somehow held her destiny?

'You must come home with me,' she said in a voice that brooked no dissent, and began to gather up her things, throwing her cloak over her shoulders. There was only

97

Charles to consider and he would not say no when she explained. He never did.

'We can't do that,' Violetta protested.

'What work did you do in Ireland?'

'Kept house, took in laundry. And Mary used to clean at the school house.'

'Then you'd be doing me a great favour. I'm in dire need of domestic help, you can ask my sister when you see her, no doubt she'll be delighted to share her opinions, in which case she'll tell you that I need help and have needed it for some time. I'd be very grateful and so would my husband and, no doubt, my children when they come home for the holidays. If you can clean and wash clothes, if you can give some order to a very disordered household, then you'll be perfect.'

'What about Mary?'

'She'll come with you, of course! She needn't work. But she can go to school with my daughter.' Would Juliette mind? Too late to consider it really. 'Juliette's not much older than you, perhaps one or two years. Have you been schooled before, Mary?'

The girl nodded, looking anxiously at her mother as though she suspected Julia to be mad.

'Then it's settled. Violetta, you'll be my domestic saviour and Mary will be educated until she's ready to choose for herself what she'll do with her life. You'll be fed. You'll have no more need to beg, or to sleep in the open, or to make up prayers for people who don't need them.'

They looked doubtful, as though such talk should not be believed.

Julia finished buttoning her boots and stood, hands on hips, waiting for an answer. 'Why do you hesitate? What worries you?'

'Would we work just for you, ma'am?'

'Only you, I think Mary should finish her schooling.'

'Not anyone else? Are there any men in the house?'

'There's my husband, but he's rarely there during the day, he won't give you any instructions.'

'Can we have your word? It's not instructions I'm worried about. If I can work for you, we'll come. But I don't want to... I don't want Mary to be...' once again she put her arm around Mary.

What has happened to you sweet things, wondered Julia, that you must have such a promise or remain sleeping outside?

She put her hands on the woman's shoulders and looked into her eyes. 'There's nothing in my home for you to fear. Neither you, nor Mary. It's as safe as can be, you have both my word and promise that you won't be harmed, and won't go hungry.'

Sarah tossed her head. 'I don't know what in heaven's name you were thinking, Julia, they could have been thieves or worse!'

When had she started to wear her hair down like that? An irritating copy of Julia's own style. Sarah's hair might be pretty, but it was nowhere near as thick as hers and it suited her better in the woven braids she fussed over having done in the mornings.

'Does that child look like a thief?' Of course she didn't. Mary was quiet, polite and charming. She was also beautiful. And that was the problem. Ever since she'd arrived, painting her was all Watts was interested in apart from Virginia, and it was plain Sarah did not approve.

'I never said they were thieves. I'm just saying that you should think before you bring strangers of that kind into my house.'

'I didn't bring them into your house, Sarah; I brought them into mine. Your pet artist brought them into your house. And I think you do not like that.' A violent coughing interrupted her. 'Do keep your voice down, Violetta is just on the other side of the door.'

Sarah pulled hard at the enormous camellia blooms she was arranging in a low bronze cooking pot, brought from India. 'That cough seems to worsen by the day. It'll do her no good to sit in the studio watching him work, he keeps the garden doors wide the whole day long.'

'I believe fresh air always does good,' said Julia in a firm voice. Really Sarah was becoming too fond of her fireside, no wonder she was getting fat. 'Violetta works far too hard. I wish she'd rest sometimes. It's as though she has something to prove.'

'She does. She must prove that her rescue was worth your while. And she isn't working much while she's constantly having to chaperone Mary with the wicked painter.' Sarah took a step back to admire the camellias and place them in the centre of her long refectory table. There were blooms and pots of all kinds still strewn over the sideboard. She passed two blue glass dishes to Julia. 'Take these, would you, and make the lilacs fit them? I want them for the table ends. We have Monsieur Hugo for supper later and he has always so admired English gardens.'

Julia took the dishes and pulled leaves from the lilac stalks. 'She doesn't trust men. Neither would you if you'd lived her life. And there are many painters who aren't quite as morally upright as the dear Signor. Anyway, I'm already certain it was worth my while, you must admit our house looks a hundred times better.'

Flower arranging was not Julia's forte, the more she teased the lilacs the worse they seemed to lie in the bowl.

'It's certainly more habitable. And what of Mary?'

'She'll join Juliette at school at the start of next term. Meanwhile I've given her some books. She reads every evening.' Juliette didn't seem too pleased that she was to be expected to look after someone from her mother's collection of waifs and strays, her last letter had been most particular on that. But she hadn't met her yet and Mary was such a sweet girl she was bound to love her when she did.

'She reads already?' Sarah's eyebrows raised in surprise. 'What in heaven's name are you doing to those poor flowers! Give them here.'

Sarah took every leaf and bloom from the pot and started the arrangement from scratch. Julia threw up her hands and walked over to the studio door, which Sarah had left deliberately half ajar.

'She reads very well. Poverty does not mean stupidity, Sarah.'

Peeping through the space in the doorway she saw Violetta sitting straight-backed in a hard, upright chair, watching closely as Watts painted her daughter. Mary sat immobile, her face in its habitual thoughtful expression, mouth slightly turned up at the corners. 'Like Patience on a monument', thought Julia, 'smiling at grief.' I must tell the Signor later, he'll like the idea he's painting something timeless and worthy. Perhaps he could add some columns and decorations. Or perhaps I should keep the idea for myself and try it out.

1853 Putney

'We were beginning to think that Mr Watts was inventing you.' Julia touched Mr Tennyson's arm playfully and heard Sarah give a sharp intake of breath. Really, why did everyone feel they had to tiptoe around this man? Watts had taken great pains to explain he was a serious poet, not given to familiarity and not particularly fond of women's company. Well, he could warn her as much as he liked, she was not going to pass the opportunity of getting closer to his extraordinary mind. Especially not when it annoyed Sarah so much.

'And yet here I am, in the flesh.' Mr Tennyson inclined his head and accepted a helping of mutton from Violetta, who had been brought in to help with the evening's unusually large dinner, arranged by Sarah to introduce the poet to the circle and, hopefully, charm him enough to stay. 'A thousand apologies for my delayed arrival, but I believe that a marriage is, perhaps, a good enough reason to explain some tardiness in my other plans.'

Julia glanced across at his new wife, Emily, who was talking to Thoby on the opposite side of the table. Pretty, in a childlike way, with blonde curls and delicate features, she was also pale and thin, with a waist so cinched she seemed likely to faint away at any moment.

'It is indeed, and we must drink to your happiness, both of you.' Julia nudged his glass of claret with hers and he raised it to his lips, although his face bore none of the warmth that might be expected from a husband discussing his recent bride, neither did his gaze stray to where she sat.

'The celebrations are quite finished now,' he said, replacing his glass on the table a little too firmly. 'And I find it's time to commence work. I've several commissions waiting.'

'I don't know how you can write poems to order.' Julia thought of all the hours she'd spent willing a visitation from the romantic muse. She had never succeeded. 'We've always been led to believe that the poetic force is one of pure emotion.'

'A poet must eat. And to write well he must eat well. He can't afford to choose his subject. Besides, a commission is only a poem's setting, the heart of it will always be the emotional journey; and that is something he carries within.' Having eaten steadfastly through their conversation Tennyson set down his knife and fork and dabbed at the corners of his mouth with a linen napkin.

She should be telling him off for such wild assumptions —as though women didn't write! As though she couldn't understand such a journey. If it was anyone else, she would. But he looked so sad, his lilac cravat so oddly touching next to the wild grizzle of his beard. 'Henry told me you were awarded the laureate. It seems your star's in a very bright firmament.'

'No doubt he also told you that he really deserved it himself.'

Julia gave what she hoped was an ambiguous smile, because that was exactly what Taylor had said.

Tennyson grunted. 'No doubt you also agree with him, but I'm sure that, in the fullness of time, I'll prove all of my critics to be wrong.'

It was just how she felt herself. She may not have uncovered her talent yet, but she would. 'Mr Watts will be disappointed if he loses his subject.'

'I can write perfectly well while he applies his daubs to canvas, I've asked to be painted whilst writing. Though he tells me his studio is something of an open house and that will, naturally, need to stop.'

Sitting to the left of the guest of honour, Sarah was listening to his conversation whilst pretending to be enthralled by the discussion next to her. Julia could see her face fall, disappointed to learn that she was not to be welcome after all the inconvenience of losing her breakfast room. She would have to turn her attentions to Emily, his bewildered bride, who would no doubt become bored during her stay. Already the poor girl looked as though she would rather be anywhere else.

'My sister's house is usually so full of the great and good I'm afraid you may not be able to stop them. But perhaps they'll inspire you and the intrusions will all be worthwhile.'

'I'm not generally inspired by greatness, though this house contains great beauty and that is never unwelcome to the artist.'

Julia felt a warm flush rise from the neck of her gown and travel to her cheeks. She followed his gaze, expecting it to fall on his young wife; instead, he still stared at Virginia. So, he was a typical Artist, waxing lyrical over Beauty that was unattainable, safely untouchable. He was quite as bad as the Signor. Poor Emily would need to be stronger than she looked.

'But none of us knows him at all!' Julia sat before the arched glass over her dressing table, glaring at her husband as he sat up in bed, a folded newspaper in front of him, looking as though he hadn't a care in the world when her baby sister was about to be taken away by a perfect stranger.

'I would say that's an excellent thing,' he said, pushing his pince nez further up his nose. 'We'll have no preconceived ideas of what he is and so we'll care only about whether he makes Virginia happy.'

'He must make her happy!' Julia took up the heavy silver brush and began to pull it down her hair vigorously.

'He won't have much choice my dear, the holy sisterhood will no doubt waste little time in commencing their offensive if he doesn't. Besides, she isn't happy now. I believe she feels she must do something to make a change.'

'I do wish you wouldn't call us that.'

'Everybody calls you that.'

'That is precisely why you shouldn't!' Julia dragged a comb across her brush to remove the loose hairs. 'I know she isn't happy now. I've been grieving for her happiness for months if you recall. She has simply not wanted to be involved in anything after that awful business on Vine Street.'

It was her own fault for having her head turned. Watts's last exhibition was so full of Virginia the poor girl could barely leave the house without some man asking for her hand and yet they had all been caught up in the attention. Sarah's salon became the most desirable invitation in London and they had all adored the people it attracted. She should have known better than to enjoy such shallow pursuits. Could anyone stand on the edges of fame and beauty without suffering their flames? Poor Virginia could not. For her it was a torment and Julia wished wholeheartedly that the poor girl had never been persuaded to sit before an easel at all.

'It frightened her, naturally.'

'It changed her. Only last week she told me that she would never consent to marry a man who knew her only from a painting and now here we are, planning a wedding to a man who saw her portrait in The Signor's studio!'

Charles tried to fold his paper to the next page silently. How could he sit there so calmly?

'You did especially give her the card, did you not? Despite the fact she asked you to burn them all?'

Julia pursed her lips. 'Yes. I did. I'd never seen such a card before, all edged in silver. I thought she would like to see it.'

'And you invited him here when she showed interest?'

'Yes. Because she said she'd made her up her mind. We had to meet him, didn't we? And he did turn out to be rather charming,' Julia admitted, though secretly she thought he was a little too like their late father, with his easy good looks and an overzealous approach to the claret jug that the sisters agreed to attribute to nerves.

'She'll be far better off when she's married, you'll see. It will afford her a shelter that, as an orphan, she simply doesn't have. And so long as her husband is halfway decent, she'll be fine. She certainly won't want for money.'

'You are always so confoundedly wise!' Julia gave her hair a final brush and joined her husband. 'Now tell me how you plan to get her to change her mind about the wedding party.'

'I hope you're not planning any surprises. Virginia won't enjoy attention,' warned Charles. 'Do remember the last time you interfered in another's matrimony.'

On the day of Maria's wedding, Julia had fixed a set of paper wings onto the backs of each of the young pages and bridesmaids, all Sophia's children along with Sarah's two youngest boys. They trotted along the centre aisle looking like cherubim fallen from heaven, earning the disapproval of the vicar and the adoration of the newspapers and sparking an instant trend for theatrical antics in churches.

'There was no need for everyone to have made such a fuss about it.'

'It's Virginia's day, not an excuse for dramatics. And it's her choice if she wants only family. Good heavens, Julia, with your lot that will be plenty. And I do believe that, after all this time, poor Virginia should finally get what she wants.'

1861 Freshwater Bay

Virginia's wedding had seemed like the end of their childhoods. The last girl to have been sent to her fate, reliant on a man for survival. She had looked so beautiful and young, hair flowing over her shoulders, her un-gloved hands carrying a trailing bouquet of lilies and ivy. It all felt final, one of Juliette's last visits home. And Violetta spent most of the ceremony coughing outside the church door, Mary standing with her and then refusing to return to school. The poor woman was dead within weeks. Hard to forget her words, or the surprisingly strong, rough grip of her fingers. 'You're a good woman, Mrs Cameron, the best of all women. Look after my girl. Keep her away from the painters… from all those kinds of people.'

At the time she had bridled at the slight, offended that Violetta did not consider her a painter. In any case she had known that she could promise nothing of the sort if Mary were to stay with them. Now it just seemed enough that someone considered her to have been a good woman. The memory was as soothing as the sound of the sea.

She should have done more to find their relatives in Ireland; she was a bad friend as well as a terrible wife and mother. No one outside their circle had paid their respects because she had assumed that it was pointless to place a notice in The Times, that working people weren't likely to buy newspapers or be able to read them. That must have been hard for Mary. What would happen to the girl if she stayed in the sea? Would Mary be better off without her? She had already lost everything. Was it kinder to leave her without a bad influence on her life?

So many of her favourite people seemed desperately unhappy and she had failed to do anything to help them. Sarah losing her soul. Mary distraught from the loss of all her family. Alfred and Emily circling each other, afraid to talk about the things that mattered. Alfred had confessed himself the worst husband, unable to comfort his wife in her needless fears. Didn't she understand how that felt? To watch someone reach out and know you could not help them? 'We may not always make the most difference to those closest to us.' She had soothed him even as he despaired. Words, all words; she herself was the worst of mothers, and daughters. Were people destined to keep making the same mistakes? Wouldn't it help everyone if she just stopped it all now?

She should have asked Sarah and Virginia to watch out for Emily, they were so much better with such women. Dear Emily, pretty and unassuming, scared of the world, made her feel slightly panicked, knowing she would run out of things to say that might be sure not to upset or offend her. In some ways she sympathised with the poet. But he had his work, his words, his adoring public; he had all those things that would ease his pain and passage through the world. All the things that should have made him happy. Even as he described the depths of his despair his words were beautiful. If she had a gift like that, her heart would sing.

Stories from the Glass House:
Mary Hillier

When Ma got asked for me to work up at the Lodge, she weren't sure at all. She'd heard about the looseness of that lot, all poets and painters and actors, and lord knew what else besides that she wouldn't let on to me. But we knew Louisa and Jones and his wife, and all three of 'em had nothing but good to tell of their life with the Camerons. Ma'd never actually been inside since they'd built that strange block up betwixt the old houses, so she come up wi' me that first day, just to get a look.

When we get there, Mrs Cameron's with Mary, and Mrs Tennyson, and dressed almost respectable like, wi' her hair brushed and a smart dress. After I started, I realised that were quite unusual for her. She 'ad tea ready, which we weren't expecting, so Ma were quite charmed and I started the next week. They were overners, like all the other artists, and I s'pose you could call them bohemian, but they weren't up to no good in there, not like the villagers said. Least I never saw any goings on.

I thought the other Mary were house-maiding too, but it turned out she didn't do a lot of work except with the photographs. Mrs Cameron had me in the studio a lot and I liked it, it was better'n housework. I could sit quietly for hours on end if I thought about how I weren't being asked to black the grates or scrub the flagstones. That were what she liked. The longer you just sat still, the more she liked it. She wound old cloths round our 'eads and made us hold babbies, or look into the distance like we wanted to be holding babbies.

It were Tommy Gilbert give me the nickname of The Island Madonna and it riled me and pleased me all at the same time. That didn't change any, even when I married 'im. He were wrong about the name though... it should of

109

been Mary Ryan's. When Mrs Cameron stopped all the things she used to do for the islanders, when she stopped doing anything but the photographs, Mary kept it all up. She'd visit all the families in need, take round baskets of food'n that. People used t'bring babbie clothes to the house and she'd sort 'em all out in the laundry room, then take them out where they were needed. She nearly got into trouble in the church rooms, taking lunches in for the pupils, because the curate thought she really meant to go and see 'im and he didn't like it when she wouldn't go out walking wi' 'im.

I know where Mary come from, and I think it were her way of being thankful. Mrs Cameron used to complain that Mary were never there when she needed her most. But I once heard Mr Cameron say that Mary were the only reason she were famous at all. It weren't far from the truth. Mary were fierce loyal, and she were obsessed with the pictures. And with Mrs Cameron herself. She wouldn't rest until everyone were admirin' them pictures.

1856 Putney

'I can't imagine why she's trying to torture us this way. She knows exactly what I've suffered.' Julia paced the drawing room, picking up and replacing objects on the small tables.

'She probably doesn't.' Charles closed his book with a sigh. 'Juliette's been away at school, and she's young... surely you remember what that's like? It's hard to see things from another's perspective until you have travelled the same road.'

'I've written to her almost every day!' Compelled to share her distress and confusion over the loss of Violetta, words poured from her pen. Alfred—a man!—was the only one who understood and Juliette herself had barely managed a response. How had she raised such an unfeeling child?

'It's not the same. Do be careful with that, Julia, it was a gift from my father, one of the few things I have left to remember him.'

Julia replaced the wooden ship forcefully and flounced to the windows. It was raining heavily, too wet to take the long walk to soothe her mind. 'We're not even to see her! She won't come home!'

'She's a sensible child and I'm afraid I agree that to pack trunks three times rather than go straight away makes little sense, particularly as she'd have no time here to do anything.'

Juliette, who took her studies seriously, had not only refused to leave school early, but had written to inform her parents she planned to tour Italy when school finished for the summer.

'We could visit her. We could stay a day or two to say goodbye. It may be pleasant to go to the country for a few days. She'll probably need some new clothes and it would make a nice trip. She'll think better of you, Julia, if you don't make such a fuss.'

Julia glared at her husband. Why was he always so sympathetic to others' opinions? In silence she watched the rain running down the long glass panes. 'Who are these people anyway?'

'Friends of The Signor. They've toured before and they have a daughter of Juliette's age, Claudine... you know all this, Juliette became friends with Claudine some time ago. She spent most of last summer holiday at their estate in Chester.'

'But we don't know them. Why don't we know them?'

'You've met them, at Sarah's, at least twice. As I recall you rather liked them, or at least we would all have remembered had you not.'

'That's not the same as knowing people.' Juliette knew how unhappy she had been since losing her friend, why was she choosing to spend the summer with strangers? Why spend time with anyone other than her family who missed her so badly while she was away?

'We can visit them too; if you like? We have time and I'm sure they'd understand. Although, I won't agree to visit them if you don't promise to behave. The last thing Juliette needs is to feel uncomfortable about things.'

'Behave?' Julia put a hand to her chest, protecting her heart. 'Perhaps it is not too much to expect that my own daughter might behave dutifully?'

'She's never given us any cause for upset, Julia, and she's been a wonderful sister to the boys.'

'Mary seems to care more for my feelings than my own flesh and blood.'

'Mary was home before,' said Charles gently, 'To care for her mother. And she has lost her. It's natural relationships should be more important to her and that the school room has lost its charm. The comfort of home is what Mary needs. Juliette is different.'

'She's abandoned me in my hour of need!' Julia seized a cushion and threw it into a chair on the other side of the room.

'My dear, it's exactly what you would have done yourself at her age. And the furnishings are tired as they are, do be careful.'

'I would have gone with my mother.' Julia had suggested she accompany Juliette and been told, rather firmly in her opinion, that she was needed with the rest of the family. It wouldn't have hurt her to invite her to go with them, even for a short while. It was a daughter's duty to be with her mother, just as she had stood by Mama when she needed her, even though she was distant and cold, something she had always tried not to be.

'Would you? You weren't so much older than her when we met at the Cape. You'd also spent little time with your mother before you were a young adult. In my half-considered opinion that time is when mothers and daughters work best. Give her time, you'll see. If you allow her some freedom now, she'll thank you for it when she returns.'

'Father is right,' said a quiet voice.

Julia whirled around as though she'd heard a ghost. In the doorway stood Juliette, holding the dripping hems of her wet skirts. Mary hovered slightly behind, twisting one hand in the other in a gesture reminiscent of Violetta. 'When did you... What in heaven's name did...' Julia covered her mouth with her hands.

'Do sit down everyone, you're making me feel quite anxious,' said Charles, ushering the girls onto the sofa. Julia flung herself at Juliette, who edged backwards.

'Please Mother. There's little need for this. I'm sorry if you feel it's the wrong time for me to go but I don't think I'll have another opportunity and I'll be back before you know it.'

Just look at her! Her own flesh and blood and she could hardly bring herself to make eye contact. 'We can go to Europe whenever you like!' Such desperation in her own voice, she should be ashamed.

'But I'd never have had the idea if Claudine hadn't asked. I can't decline now and leave her without company. It's only four months and then I'll be home for good.'

Julia studied her daughter's face, marvelling at her composure in the midst of such a crisis. If only she'd had the forethought to suggest such a trip herself, they could have taken Mary. An image of Paris came into her head.

'I would have liked to take you to France, to see where I spent my childhood.' Julia's voice was pleading.

'You didn't seem to enjoy the time you spent in France; you've never spoken of it so fondly as you speak of India. If we are to travel anywhere together, I'd like to go with you to Calcutta. I've almost forgotten what it's like.'

Julia smoothed her daughter's hair. Did she mean it? Such a journey would take months, a chance to get to know each other and put some of her other ghosts to rest. 'How did you get here today? You look as though you walked, we must ask Mrs Jones to fetch dry clothes and light a fire in your room.' She hesitated. 'You are staying, I assume?'

Juliette laughed at such fussing, but Julia had not missed the looks she had exchanged with her father. Of course, Charles had sent for her, she'd never have thought to come on her own. She'd been made to come.

1858 Kensington

'You promised her mother you would keep her away from painters.' Sarah peered into the small window of Watt's garden studio, shielding her eyes against the low thin sunlight. 'Surely he should be fed up of painting the peasant girl by now. Two exhibitions and another planned. She has simply replaced Virginia! It's not as though she's even all that young anymore.'

'I didn't exactly promise,' replied Julia, keeping half an eye on the game of croquet. 'What she really meant was keep her away from the worst sorts. And Watts isn't the worst of sorts, is he? Quite the opposite. If he ever got near enough anyone to behave badly, he'd probably faint clean away first.'

'Well you must be missing the help. Why you put her through school and support her just to sit in his studio is a mystery to me.' Sarah threw herself into the seat opposite, blocking Julia's eye-line.

'Why don't you just ask him to paint you?' Julia folded her hands into her lap and tried not to crane her neck to look at the man who held her daughter's attention.

'Really, Julia, I'm only commenting. If nothing else, you need to give her a different dress to sit in. She's been wearing that one in most of them.'

'I've tried, she's refused it all.'

'Who has refused you! I shall fight for your honour!' Charles burst from the French windows of the studio holding a large jug of lemonade. He was followed by Mary and Watts, both bearing trays of glasses and fruit.

'It's the first pleasant day for the garden, let's save the fighting for less clement weather.' Julia rose to help her husband, embracing him and then Mary in quick succession while Watts shuffled over to Sarah.

'How is your hundredth painting of Mary progressing?' Sarah's lips pursed, presumably in annoyance that Charles had been in the Signor's workspace when, since Tennyson's dictat, no one else was given licence.

'It's progressing nicely, Sarah,' said Charles, handing her a glass with a sweeping flourish, 'Though I do think he might try his hand at something more difficult than a beautiful woman at some point, a peacock perhaps or a house.'

'I don't paint merely things, my paintings are ideas.'

'A good idea then, to paint a portrait.' Charles raised his glass to Watts who looked as though he would like to dash it all over him.

'This series is the House of Life, an allegory of hope; it's based on this house, where so much life and love and art is created. It is a garden of Eden.' Sarah smiled as though she might burst with pride.

'It's true,' said Julia, momentarily kindly disposed towards her. 'This place is a creation.'

'That's the trouble with artists,' said Charles. 'Always so serious!'

Watts raised his spectacles to take a better view over the garden. 'Who is that with Juliette?' he asked.

Juliette had returned from Italy with even more quiet confidence than she had formerly possessed. Not quite a swan, but taller and more elegant than her mother. She moved gracefully, with a slow, considered purpose and wore a permanent half smile, a self-contained look Julia found infuriating as she tried to guess its meaning. Juliette's clothes, too, were subtly changed. Her dress was still simple, but the fabrics were richer, the colours more suited to her youth. Like her mother, she attracted the gaze of intelligent men, because she neither expected nor needed it.

'Perhaps we might be introduced?' Julia stood pointedly before the low seat in the white garden until the man talking so animatedly to her daughter rose and took her hand. She decided not to like the look of him.

'Mother, this is Edward McKenzie, a friend of the Hamiltons.' Juliette remained seated, unperturbed.

'A pleasure to meet the woman who brought such a lovely young lady into the world.' He bowed low with a little flourish, a theatrical gesture and sentiment Julia would usually have found charming. On this man it was simply irritating.

'May I join your little group? I've been intrigued by your topic of conversation, it seems to have kept you occupied for hours.' She fixed her daughter with a stern stare.

'We were talking about astronomy mother,' said Juliette, 'A subject very dear to you, I know.'

A subject also dear to those who wish to speak of love and other things they shouldn't touch. It wasn't so long since the poetry of the stars had opened her mind to the possibilities of romantic fancy and Juliette was far too young to see where that might lead. 'It is indeed a hobby of mine; if you're so inclined perhaps you might like to come and view my husband's telescopes? They were a present from our great friend Sir John Herschel.'

'Thank you, but Juliette has promised to show me the instruments later, when the skies are dark enough to show their full display.'

'Has she indeed.' Julia gave the man an appraising look; older than Juliette, certainly, perhaps as old as the Viscount. Serious-looking, tall, a neat set of whiskers and quite a beautiful suit of clothes. A large emerald pin fixed his cravat to the top of his waistcoat and the ring on his pinkie finger bore a family crest, the shape of which Julia could not discern. His appearance was difficult to disapprove. He was probably stuffy, as well as pompous. What on earth could Juliette find so fascinating?

'Edward tells me that the stars in the Highlands are more beautiful than anywhere on earth,' said Juliette.

117

'It would be difficult to find a more beautiful night sky than India's,' said Julia, struggling to stay polite. 'Juliette and I plan to visit soon, do we not my dear? She has not long finished school.'

'I've been hearing about the grand tour,' said Edward. 'It seems Juliette is quite the traveller. I'd very much like to invite you all to visit Scotland, when you're able.'

'Your invitation is most kind,' said Julia, 'Now you must excuse my daughter. The Robertsons are leaving and she'd never forgive herself if she didn't say goodbye.'

Julia peered over her daughter's shoulder as she worked patiently at a bush of white hydrangea in the Prinseps' garden, rendering pretty oils in muted colours. 'You should exhibit some of these.' Juliette's technique was skilful, her style consistent. From the tips of her tiny blunt knives she conjured garden scenes, full of elegantly dressed women walking lawns edged in detailed flowers. 'They're easily as good as the sets we saw in Regents' Park last week. You could join the Society. There can't be many female painters.'

'Why would I want to invite the criticism of strangers? There's no reason for anyone to want to look at my paintings. I just like making them.' Juliette's gaze flickered between the hydrangea and her canvas.

'I would be delighted to have your skill.' Julia was perplexed. Why would any artist want to hide their work away? If she could capture a scene with such skill, she would be covering the walls of the Academy, not sending them to school-friends as little presents. 'The Signor has said you have talent.' Perhaps she would listen to him.

'The Signor is just being kind.'

'He has framed your painting of Virginia by the apple tree.'

'Because it is a painting of Virginia.'

Julia sighed. Always such a difficult child! She began to set up her easel a few feet away, fussing over the tubes of paint and trying to clean her knives, which were thick with dried pigment. 'You should try to paint a visionary scene, something from inside your head no one else has imagined. Or a scene from a play, or a heroic legend.'

'You should try to paint something ordinary for a change. The garden bench, perhaps, without covering it in fairies.' Juliette smiled.

For once the differences between them were amusing and Julia relaxed. Easy company, both occupied, a shared understanding; it was what their relationship should be. Perhaps, as Charles predicted, they were destined to become closer as adults, and if Art could bring them closer, then all the better. It was wonderful to have her home. She must try not to rush their reconciliation, to spoil things with her eagerness as she always did.

'I'm glad you've joined me today, mother.' Juliette paused, wiping the smallest of knives on a neat square of clean cotton. 'I have something I wish to discuss with you.'

'India! Of course. I've been so busy with Maria's wedding, and Virginia's baby, and everything else, that I've quite stopped planning our trip and I know you're desperate to go. I'm so sorry. It won't take me long, I promise. We have plenty of friends there still who'll be pleased to arrange whatever we need. We must see Simla, it's quite the most beautiful place, Calcutta of course... and your father would never forgive us if we didn't visit Ceylon.' She looked at her daughter for encouragement, but Juliette stared fixedly at her painting.

'No. Not India. In fact, I'm not sure when I will be able to visit India now.'

'Are you ill? Has something happened?' Julia searched her daughter's face, but her expression gave nothing away.

'Something wonderful has happened.' Juliette put down her palette knife, making sure it wouldn't fall from the easel tray, then turned to face her mother. 'Mr McKenzie has asked me to marry him.'

Julia fell to her knees. Something wonderful! In heavens name the child didn't even look happy. What on earth was she thinking? She can only have met him a handful of times. 'You're a child! I forbid it.'

'I'm a woman of eighteen. And Edward asked father's permission before asking me,' said Juliette in a firm voice.

'He didn't ask for my opinion!'

'He doesn't need to. Father allowed him to ask me and has given his blessing if I'm happy. And I am happy. I had hoped you'd be pleased for me too.' Juliette stood, perfectly straight and still, her hands clasped in front of her. In her plain, white muslin dress she looked like a small girl at Sunday school.

'Am I to guess that you've accepted his offer? He's far too old for you, Juliette!' Damn Charles. Why must he always let the child have her own way? She was pig-headed and spoiled and it was her father's fault.

'He's thirty-two. It's a good age for a husband and he's well able to look after me. He's a wealthy man. In any case, father was twice your age when you married.'

'Your father was never boring!'

'Mother! Really. Do keep your voice down. You'll bring the house out here.'

'Does this Mr McKenzie know how to have fun? It doesn't seem so to me. Will he delight you? Will he sit by the fire for hours just to hear your thoughts on architecture?'

'He respects me, I find his conversation interesting.'

'Do you love him?'

Juliette coloured prettily. 'Yes, I do.'

Julia wasn't sure she knew what that was like. Had she loved Charles? She did now, of course, he'd proven himself to be such a good husband and father. But had she been quite so certain she was in love with him when they married?

'Then there's nothing left for me to say.' Julia hugged her daughter with a force that almost knocked her easel flying. 'We must begin to make plans.'

'Edward would like us to marry in Scotland.' Juliette took a step backwards and began to smooth the folds of her dress

Julia nodded. The girl's mind was set, little point in trying to influence her plans. 'If that's what you wish. We'll need to find somewhere for us all to stay.' She counted on her fingers. 'There are at least twenty of us who must come, perhaps we might rent a castle, that would be fun, wouldn't it? I've never been to the Highlands. Has he proposed a date? I suppose you'll stay there for a while afterwards?'

Juliette clasped her hands tightly and took a deep breath. 'We will live there,' she said. 'Edward has just inherited his family's estate and he's preparing to become the laird.'

Stories from the Glass House:
Alfred Lord Tennyson
(The Dirty Monk)

Julia could certainly be terrifying when engaged in the application of her craft in her house of glass, but only if you allowed her to be. Although she adored innocents, by no means would she suffer fools. Unfortunately, her sister's set contained many of them. Fame and fortune are no measure of intelligence and never were.

Neither did she shy from difficult conversations. Some of those who found her awkward were simply those who disliked such conversations. Myself, I found that there was no one else in the world prepared to talk of those difficult emotions that I felt such a deep and pressing need to understand; to help me to make sense of the world. Even my wife would brush aside such thoughts. Like most women she was mainly concerned that everything should be 'nice', as though humans and all their troubles could be reduced to the form of a floral teapot.

We were close friends long before she found her calling. Julia was possessed of a startling intellect, quite unusual for a woman, and was entirely self-taught. She read anything and everything and, once she had read it, wanted to ask endless questions until she was sure she knew it as well as yourself. If she liked you, she was not content to be friends, she wanted to truly understand you. My publisher was slightly shocked by her portrait of me, the one they called the dirty monk, and, at first, refused to use it. 'There's a difference,' he said, 'between brooding and murderous.' But the hollow way she made me look, as though I was sinking into myself, seemed to me to capture my soul; and I never used another portrait again.

Apart from Mary, the only person I saw her treat tenderly in the studio was Darwin. Equally unusual was her treatment of his family, whom she welcomed to the Glass House, taking plate after plate of them posing in groups about him, without use of props or costumes, causing everyone to wonder if she was having a change of heart. She was not. Both the costumes and the imperious treatment of her sitters reappeared soon after the Darwins returned to Kent. Even Charles was confused by the visit. But I could see that she loved him because he was troubled, because he was trying to make sense of the world. For her he seemed a kindred spirit, someone else searching for beauty, pattern and form in the world, searching for the truth and trying to reconcile it all. And she also loved him just because he was troubled and because his family cared that he was. She was drawn to Emily and I in much the same way; for that I was grateful.

1859 Isle of Wight

'Do you not feel it Alice?' asked Julia, 'A tiny hole in your happiness as you watch Henry with his work? He is permitted to create as he pleases, why do you not at least try to compose some of the music you play so beautifully?'

It was pointless to needle her. Alice was content to be the wife of a poet, but her own longing seemed to grow worse daily. From the descriptions in Juliette's infrequent letters she even envied her daughter's quiet sense of purpose as she helped her husband work his new estates, hidden in the Highlands. To have a true purpose would be something.

'You should be proud of creating your perfect healthy children,' said Emily quietly. 'A man, even a genius such as my husband, could never deliver such a perfect work of art, nor dream of such an accomplishment.'

Julia's heart wrenched to hear it. Emily had already lost three in the womb; the last delivered without breath, fully grown, its skin waxed white, its name to be Charles. Reaching for her stomach, Julia found the soft rounding, saw the fear in her eyes. 'Not this one,' she whispered. 'I promise not this one.'

'If it pleases God then he'll take it again.' She raised her hands in a helpless gesture.

'Not my god,' said Julia, anger rising. What kind of deity would punish a woman in such a way? Visions of the Shiva festival at Simla came to mind. She'd lived long enough in a place where women knew how to rid themselves of babies to understand what should be done to keep one. The girl needed rest, fresh air, gentle walking and kind conversation. She needed removing from Alfred who, half-sick with grief, would stoke her fears and suffocate her with his longing for this child. Emily needed to breathe. Above all she needed not to worry. 'Do you know how far along you are?'

'About four months.'

'Then you'll be safe to travel.'

Emily looked alarmed. 'Travel where?'

'To Alfred's house on the Isle of Wight; I've always longed to visit, but he never seemed to have the time.' It was ideal to nurse the poor girl back to health; walks in the fresh sea air, picnics in the countryside. Far away from the sickly parlours and stressful socialites of London. Emily would be glowing again in no time, Alfred would be free enough of the constant anxiety to concentrate on writing and she would feel the satisfaction of helping friends. Not to mention enjoy a holiday from the tireless social whirl. The trip would fulfil an important purpose and it felt so timely and right that she would accept no protest.

'But Alfred must be in London, he has so much to do!'

'Even better. Now what must we do to make the house ready?'

Exactly one week later they were disembarking the ferry at Freshwater, with Mary Ryan and Emily's maid, Rose. Emily looked slightly green, though the crossing had been calm as a millpond, and confessed to feeling confused as to how the move had happened so quickly. There was no arguing with Julia, Charles and Alfred both had tried to explain, once she decided what was good for you; usually she turned out to be right. Alfred had given the idea his blessing, making the arrangements and promising Emily that the next time they met he would have finished his epic poem and they could take as long as they needed to stay on the Isle of Wight. Unlike Julia, he could not bring himself to make promises about the baby.

Tennyson's housekeeper, Mrs Ruttle, had sent one of the local farmers down to collect them for the two-mile journey to the house. He had brought such a basic cart that Julia was forced to empty the clothes from her trunk and spread them out for Emily to sit on, cushioning her slight frame against the worst of the ruts in the roads. She and Mary clung to the tails of dresses and shawls as they threatened to fly off over the meadows and decorate the rows of cows that stared over low gates.

It was the prettiest of days to travel the narrow tracks through green meadows, seagulls wheeling and diving above the neat thatched cottages. As they neared the house, the sun lowered, throwing a pale gold light across the sky and studding the waters with sun-diamonds. Proud to share the view with these newcomers, the farmer stopped at the headland of Freshwater Bay. Fine white sand stretched around a wide curve of shore, littered with small stones and shells, lapped by foam-edged ripples.

'Beautiful,' breathed Julia. Before anyone could stop her, she had thrown off her boots, hitched her skirts and was dancing along the sand, whooping and calling for them all to leave the carriage and join her. Only Mary obeyed, walking gingerly along the little stone wall to speak with her mistress.

'Look at the sky Mary!' she whirled around, arms raised, the sleeves of her emerald green dress flying out from her sides like wings. 'The fields, the sea! This place is Beautiful!'

'So it is. It reminds me of home. But we can explore and celebrate tomorrow. I'll walk with you. I can see this place is going to do you as much good as it will Emily. For now, though, she's tired and in her condition we ought to make her comfortable quickly,' Mary spoke firmly, indicating at Emily who stared at them from the carriage as though she thought them both completely mad. Julia ran back, still barefoot and whooping. Mary walked carefully behind her, suppressing a smile.

Farringford was a sprawling country villa built from buff-coloured stone, Georgian in style but adorned with the Gothic touches Julia adored. Arched windows surrounded the second floor and the shapes of arches echoed over every internal doorway. Castellated parapets ran the length of the walls, but the building was welcoming, bending its wings towards them in a half circle of embrace. Mrs Ruttle sat on a bench by the front door in a neat white apron and jumped up ready to greet them as they arrived. Julia flew down from the carriage and smothered her in a hug just as she was curtseying, knocking her slightly off balance, much to the amusement of the farmer who received such a stern look from the housekeeper he immediately began to pull their luggage from the rack. Mary swiftly repacked Julia's trunk.

'Oh, it is wonderful, simply wonderful! Those parapets are just waiting for a forlorn damsel to drape herself over them to pine for her lover. The Signor would adore it.'

'I don't know about that Mrs... '

'Julia Margaret Cameron, call me Julia.' The housekeeper looked slowly down at Julia's dirty bare feet and then slowly back up, taking in her flowing robes and loose hair.

'She'll adore her in a few days,' whispered Mary to Rose. 'Everyone does.'

1860 Isle of Wight

Julia was enchanted with the quality of the light over the island and the perfect scenes of pastoral life. For the first few days she walked all over Freshwater with Mary, while Emily rested in the airy master bedroom with its high windows, eating the rich fruitcakes Mrs Ruttle insisted would do her good. As they walked, Julia spoke to every person they encountered; the men digging chalk at Alum Bay, and the women cutting grass on the lanes, their huge bundles resting on their hips as they talked. In the little church near Farringford she waited for Reverend Sheridan, asking so many questions about the paintings decorating the whitewashed walls that he began to think she was a test from above.

Military men in their high-necked red jackets were stopped and questioned about their station in the next bay along. They proved themselves so charming and knowledgeable Julia invited them all to dinner to discuss the Indian mutinies she had read about in the previous week's newspapers. When twelve smart soldiers arrived promptly at eight o'clock, Mrs Ruttle kept an inscrutable face and a tight rein on the drinks' cabinet. However, they proved to be excellent company and were so complimentary of her food that she raised no objection when they were invited back the following week.

With the sun still shining and the air sweet and clear, Julia's favourite place was the seashore, where she collected shells to complete the hanging decoration she planned to make for Emily's baby, and watched the women collecting samphire in huge round baskets they stuffed to the brim and then carried away on their heads. She was fascinated by the sight of two young men climbing carefully down the high white cliffs, swinging and bouncing precariously against the sides, clutching open leather satchels and short stout sticks. They were tied to thick ropes, which they pulled when they were ready to be helped up again.

Mary had seen such things before, explaining that cliffs harboured plenty of nature's bounty for working families to gather. 'At home it would be the weans, the men were too busy in the fields. But the women seem to farm here too. It would have been better, perhaps, if home was the same.'

'Surely children couldn't climb cliffs.' Julia was horrified, forgetting the reckless way she used to climb in India.

'They're not as steep as these ones but they did. No ropes neither. They used to hang off each other's arms and climb down in rows.'

'Goodness, I wouldn't want to see that.'

'Children did a lot worse than that ma'am.'

Julia glanced at Mary's clouded face and cursed herself for her thoughtlessness. Violetta had talked, before she went, about Ireland's violent poverty and the things it drove families towards. It would do Mary good to talk about them, but she had to give her time. She was so tough, such a self-contained girl. Sometimes it felt as though her trust was hard to come by.

'What are they doing then? Collecting herbs? I saw some plants growing out of holes in the cliff yesterday, they were fronded like fennel.'

'They're killing birds,' said Mary. 'Or taking their eggs. Cliffs are always full of sheltering birds; they nest in the grooves and dips. They beat them out and take their feathers for sale. They'd be tough to eat but their bodies are probably sold off for bait.' She indicated the lines of crab pots that hung from the low stone jetty, 'The fishermen need something to put in those.'

'Crabs will eat sea birds?'

'Crabs will eat absolutely anything ma'am. My pa used to say that if he ever killed a man he'd feed it to the crabs and there'd be nothing left the next day.'

Julia shivered. Here, despite the façade of idyllic countryside, was nature red in tooth and claw. It always took her by surprise. Even after India, where hungry tigers were regularly hunted and shot for choosing village children as breakfast. Nothing at all could shock Mary, who always thought the very worst of nature and men. But she seemed to like it here too. She'd grown comfortable in her skin in a way Julia could see now had been absent in their sociable London existence.

Island existence was so much more authentic. People led simple lives, whatever their social standing. Dinners were uncomplicated and conversation quickly serious without the constant need for competitive repartee. Among her new friends existed a great interest in science and discovery, much knowledge of fossil history and geology, but it was never used to score points or show off. They were truer to themselves than the London sets she had left behind. From a distance it was easy to see it all clearly.

A beautiful, idyllic island. All it needed was a community of artists and a genius or two and it would be perfect. Once she had found her true calling, whatever it may be. Here, of all places in the world, she was bound to find her creative self and understand how to share the Beauty she imagined. All she had to do was persuade Charles to another move.

My Dearest Herschel,

You have been unbearably cruel to deprive us of your company for so very long. I'll forgive you only if you promise to visit our new island at the moment I secure us a house. If you agree to build us one of your telescopes, I'll forget the matter. There is so much sky! You would smile to see it. At night this tiny island appears to be surrounded by the blackest of waters and the darkest of canopies. The stars are low, so low that one could almost reach out and touch them. Even in daylight it's the most beautiful sky in England.

Emily grows happier and stronger by the day, from the health-giving climate and from Mrs Ruttle's wonderful food. I do think that woman is quite the best bread maker I've encountered. Charles makes great progress with his work, I hope you'll write to enquire how he does—he's proud and won't tell you unless asked. Thoby and Sarah have added Mr Thackeray and Mr Trollope to their conquests, both of those great men are in good health and possessed of boundless energy.

Personally, I find that the lifestyle outside of the salon suits me better. Mary is also happier here at Freshwater than I've ever seen her. Her colour has returned, she no longer mourns her mother and is perfectly at home. It reminds her, I think, of Cork, and I can see her very settled here. She's a true and loyal companion and I often thank the gods for bringing her to me when they did. She understands as much of life as dear Alfred, but she doesn't let it upset her, or worry that she must try to change it, and that is the difference between them. Alfred is working, and working, and working, and I don't know when he will ever feel that he has finally made his mark. He drives himself hard and seems never to believe anyone who tells him how gargantuan are his achievements as they stand.

Emily is better off with us here, waiting for her time. We pass the days pleasantly enough, with our walks and crafts, conversations with the villagers. When she's better I'm thinking of setting up some entertainments and a school for the village children. But, for now, she needs me with her daily. Her thoughts are nervous, even without Alfred, and as her time nears her fears increase. I spend the evenings reading aloud to her, or talking to her of the constellations, as you once did with me.

I can't describe the Beauty of the fields and beaches. The island seems bathed in the light of happiness. I plan to spend the next few months looking for the right house and, when I do, I shall move here entirely. Charles will love it. And the three of us will sit and name the stars as we did under a warmer sky so many moons ago.
Always your affectionate,
Julia

'You must go, Julia, you've been cooped up with me for too long.' Emily sighed and turned away her graceful neck, burying her face in a pile of pillows.

Julia marched over and raised the curtain, indicating the torrents of water that cascaded the length of the windows. 'I know you consider me quite mad, but even I can't go walking in weather like this. Come now, what shall we do? You are a-weary, like Mariana in her moated grange.'

Emily pulled herself against the pillows with difficulty; her frame was slender and her stomach now so distended it hurt her to move even slightly. Instinctively, she put a hand to the swelling and felt the familiar kick that happened every time she changed position, the sharp little nub of a heel or elbow sticking out.

'I don't think you're mad at all. Quite the opposite, in fact. You're really the kindest person I know. The baby still moves, still breathes. I feel it. And I've only you to thank.'

'That's how us mad women operate,' laughed Julia. 'We get inside you so that you become one of us.'

'What is madness when everyone's mind is so different?'

'Quite!' Julia was about to suggest a game of draughts, but Emily was suddenly serious, leaning forward and rubbing at the small of her back. 'Here, let me do that.' Julia jumped up and sat behind her. 'Would you like me to ask Mrs Ruttle to bring you a hot pan?'

'No, stay.' Emily's hand gripped her own very hard, as though fearful she would disappear.

'What is it, Emily? The baby's fine, you know that, you can feel it. He... and it will be a he.' She smiled, knowing Emily did not believe that anyone could know what sex a child would be before it arrived. But she knew. Emily carried so high it could be nothing but a boy. 'He's a lively little thing! He'll be here so soon now. You must get all the rest you can before he arrives.'

'I know the baby lives, Julia, I can feel it and I'm grateful for everything you've done to help. But I'm terrified of what he, or she, will be. There's something in me that believes our baby will be a monster of some kind.'

'Oh Emily! Don't you think every new mother worries about that? We all have the worst of imaginations. It's what makes us good mothers. We worry for every possible iteration of what might go wrong for our children and subsequently we're there, one step ahead of them. Then we're constantly stopping them from tumbling, kissing them when they do, preventing them from falling for unsuitable actresses!' Emily tried to smile. It was what she had done for Henry and so like Julia to make fun of herself to make things better.

'That's not what I meant. I'm worried for the baby. If it will live…'

'It will live!'

'If it will live, I'm worried that it will be like him.'

'Like Alfred? It would be a travesty if it were not! He's a great man, a genius.' What mother would not want the same for her child? She would love to find great creativity in Henry or Ewen or Eugene, but all of them took after Charles, practical and scientific. Even Juliette set no store by her ability with paint.

'He's so melancholy, Julia, I don't think any of you realise how he is. Sometimes he'll sit for days on end looking at the plain wall of his study.'

It was true; she'd been called to bring him out of a slump like that many times, though Emily had never spoken of such things directly before. 'It's the muse, Emily.'

'It's his mind! I sometimes worry he'll succumb to the madness that haunts him. He speaks to Hallam every evening before he comes to bed. He sits and talks to him. While we're here he writes to me of what Hallam thinks. He barely tells me what he's doing, but he writes about what his dead friend is thinking. It's not right.'

'He doesn't do so with anyone else, Emily. He loves and trusts you. You should take comfort from that.' Perhaps a discrete conversation with a doctor who didn't already know them both would be a good idea.

'I do, I really do. And I love him dearly. I wish I could make him happy, but I can't, nobody can. And I worry that his child will be the same.'

Julia squeezed Emily's hands. 'This child will save him, you'll see. Once he has a child his life will need to happen outside of his head. Give him this child and you will all live.'

Hallam Tennyson won his fight for life, and his mother's eternal devotion to Julia. Even Mrs Ruttle was frightened by his timing, several weeks too early by any reckoning, but he was perfectly formed, with a mop of dark brown curls, and he was small, which was what Emily's slight frame required. His delivery was swift and determined, his hands bunched into fists that held onto his cord, pulling it away from where it caught around his neck. A baby so robust it appeared he had saved his own life, so vigorous he cried the moment he arrived and was feeding within ten minutes of being born. Yet Emily told anyone who would listen that Julia had worked her magic to keep him alive and safe and she would not have anyone other than Julia in the nursery until she was strong enough to leave her bed.

The young warrior's father departed London the moment he heard the news, arriving late at night and waking the household. Happier than anyone could remember seeing him, he held the child and then Emily as though he feared they may just disappear into dust. Hallam himself did not cry when awoken and was quiet for the rest of the night, staring up at his father's face with his dark blue eyes until he settled back to sleep. The following day, serious again, Tennyson vowed they would make their home at Freshwater from that moment; he would stay in London when necessary, but their home would be on the island, where the air was conducive to health and they

134

could hope to build on their family with siblings for Hallam.

It was the first time he had spoken with clarity about the future and it was the best news Julia could have heard. Still passionately in love with the island, she had already persuaded Charles to let her rent them a house and, with Alfred as a permanent genius, it seemed her Artistic Community would not take long to establish.

1860 Isle of Wight

'I've never seen so many windows in a single dwelling, there are barely bricks to hold the glass together.' Charles took a step back to admire the building's height. Three stories were topped with an eccentric row of gable ends and windows, the spaces in between covered with a beard of red-tinged ivy, the door mantel woven with a thick rope of wisteria that rippled in the breeze from the bay.

'It's an Artist's house, all light and air! Every one of these rooms could be a studio. Exactly how a house by the sea should look.' Julia's eyes shone with the possibilities the house would bring, its huge high-ceilinged rooms and generous gardens cried out to be filled with interesting people. It would inspire the muse in her. Moreover, it was convenient, a short walk to the beach and a ten-minute stroll through the fields to Farringford. 'And it's not a single dwelling, it's two. We've taken them both.'

'We?' Charles raised an eyebrow and took a further step back, losing his footing at the edge of the gravel drive so Julia had to put out her arm to steady him. She steered him to the right.

'See how the two are a matched pair? When we go inside, I'll show you, their layout is a perfect mirror image. They'll look wonderful joined and the gardens will truly come into their own when they're allowed to run around both. We can just remove this hedge and widen one of the doors.'

'Well, why stop there? Why not build a tower with a castellated roof right up the middle of the two and join them together that way?' said Charles, raising his eyes heavenwards.

'You're quite right, what a wonderful, clever idea.' She planted a kiss on his nose. 'You're the dearest man. I'll speak to the builders in Yarmouth tomorrow. It would be helpful, would it not, if that little piece of work was finished before the all of our things arrive?'

'My dear Julia, I was just…'

'Now then, don't be modest. It is settled. We'll honour your idea and we can live in one side of the house until it's completed. No, I won't hear another word about it. Let's go inside, I want to show you the long gallery, which will be rather marvellous as an actual gallery, we can showcase local artists and invite the reviewers to see their work in the same airy light in which it was painted. It really is such a dear house.'

'Houses… and I know when I'm beaten.'

'Soon to be house though. Thanks to my dear, clever husband. And you're not beaten; I know as well as you that you tire of Sarah's relentlessly fashionable London life. You'll find Freshwater a pleasant rural idyll.' Julia took her husband's arm, beaming at him. He was dressed in her favourite jacket of patchwork fabric, a straw hat covering his silver white hair. She steered him towards the wide front door of the house on the right, knowing he would approve of the stained glass around the wood and across the tops of the windows.

'There's a study just off the main hall, here, in which you would be very comfortable.' She threw open the heavy oak door, uncovering another empty room where their voices echoed. Or perhaps it would be too noisy for you? Come and see up here.' She darted back and ran up the stairs, her footsteps ringing on the bare treads.

'Why would it be noisy?'

'When all the others arrive. You wouldn't want to live here without guests. You'd be bored in a week.'

'I don't think I'd be bored at all. You promised a rural idyll.'

'So it is.'

'A noisy rural idyll full of your sister's fashionable entourage?' Charles raised his splendid silver eyebrows.

'Not all of them. Just the interesting ones. And new ones, of course; I've invited the Dawsons for dinner this evening, just with one or two others.'

'We have no furniture, Julia!'

'They're not the kind to mind. Besides, there are tables and chairs in the garden and Mrs Ruttle will bring up the food.'

Charles placed his hands on the oak railing, admiring the symmetry of the panelling and the colours of the glass. 'I have to admit you have a good eye. It will be a perfectly lovely home.'

'It needs a name,' said Julia. 'At the moment it's both Ranworth and Browe, but I can't think of a way to connect them that doesn't sound ugly, which doesn't suit the place at all.'

'Dimbola,' he said firmly, folding his arms. Julia knew how badly he missed the Indian climate. Hopefully the name, taken from their coffee estate, wouldn't make him want to go back to Ceylon at the first excuse. 'We'll call it Dimbola Lodge, and then it will quickly feel like home.'

Mrs Ruttle chose that moment to arrive with several boys from the village, all heavily laden with tableware and awaiting instruction. 'Welcome to Dimbola Lodge,' Julia called down.

Immediately their things arrived Julia set about collecting a menagerie of animals, aided and abetted by Mary and the two youngest boys who were home for the long holidays. Two fawn spaniels arrived from Bridge Farm and were soon joined by a pair of liver-and-white working pups. Altogether they wreaked such havoc, streaking through the ground-floor rooms in a perpetual game of chase, that Charles told visitors Dimbola was Senhalese for 'incurably mad pets.' An elderly black cat with matted fur and one white sock, who'd been left at Ranworth by its previous owners, made his home on the sofa in the garden room and hissed at the dogs every time they ran past. Julia named him Strauss and brought him three kittens for company before she was forced to admit that perhaps he did not wish for the company of other animals at all. The kittens, striped silver and black, reminded her of the gardens at Versailles.

A huge glazed chicken house was given as a present to the boys, who built warm boxes, packed with hay and straw, in which to hatch the eggs they begged from local farms. A dozen survived but, once they grew enough to roam free, proved so tempting for the dogs to chase that a cockerel and a small gaggle of geese were procured to protect them. It was Charles who ended it. Seeing Mary walking along the newly gravelled front drive, leading a small white goat on a long length of rope, was quite enough; he was growing fond of his kitchen garden and hoped to see it bear fruit the following spring. He walked with her all the way back to the farm at Ventnor, where Julia had swapped a china tea service for it, and insisted the owners keep both.

1860 Freshwater, Isle of Wight

Six women, dressed in similar shades of heather grey and oversized, wide-brimmed bonnets, stood evenly spaced along the low sea wall, each facing a slightly different viewpoint. Their easels were made from the same dark wood and each was heavily equipped with the accoutrements of fine art: tubes of colours, little water pots and different sizes of fancy brushes. Each artist painted in silence, with slow deliberate strokes and a look of fierce determination. Julia was immediately smitten. Here were Artists, all women, going about their work with such serious intent they must be preparing for exhibition. They were using brushes rather than knives, dipping the small tips into clean water between every stroke. How fascinating to watch them dabbing tiny dots of colour onto their miniature canvases. It looked terribly easy. Julia rushed down the slope to the bay, almost tripping over her skirts in her haste to reach them.

The nearest painter, the tallest of the group and obviously the eldest, held a pair of lorgnettes to her nose and peered over the top of them at Julia's wild hair and outlandish clothes. Julia had seen her before. When they had taken their own house and were no longer living as guests of the Tennysons, she'd been tireless in her house calls, visiting dozens of addresses gleaned from local sources. Julia caught this one peeping round floral curtains while her maid explained she wasn't at home. Well there was to be no hiding this time.

The woman put down her eyeglasses and carefully rinsed her delicate brush in the flask of water on her easel shelf. 'Mrs Cameron I believe? You left me a card. Forgive me; I've been remiss in my response. As you can see, we're all well occupied in advance of our annual exhibition.'

'Good morning Lady Eastnor.' Emily dipped her head, beckoning over Mary with the baby carriage. 'Allow me to introduce my dear friends, Mrs Julia Cameron and Miss Mary Ryan, and I don't believe you've met Hallam yet? He's the picture of health and I've dear Julia to thank for that. I do hope you'll make her welcome. She and her husband, Charles, have recently decided to make their home near us at Freshwater.'

So, this was the infamous Lady Caroline Eastnor, Chair of the Watercolour Society, a wealthy patron of serious artists, and with quite a reputation for drawing other artists to the island. Her personal reputation was less endearing, but out here, away from the mainland, she would be important to know. She should be easy enough to charm. Perhaps finally here was someone to teach Julia how to paint with skill, to translate the wonderful scenes in her head to something meaningful on paper; and watercolours did look so easy compared with all that scraping and fussing with oils.

'Quite charming.' Lady Eastnor barely moved her head to inspect the flounce of white lace inside the carriage.

'He's remarkable,' said Julia with enthusiasm. 'He practically saved his own life. When he was born he…'

'May I see your work?' interrupted Emily, throwing a glance stern enough to remind Julia that most people, particularly provincial spinsters, did not care for stories of childbirth. Julia, chastened, pretended to examine the painting carefully, though only the first few layers of wash and some detail of shingle were complete.

'You may find these of more interest.' Lady Eastnor drew from her portfolio a neat stack of four thick sheets of imperial, flattened and stretched over boards. Julia drew close. Although watercolours, especially these delicate landscapes, were her least favourite forms of art, she could see that they had been painted with skill and an eye for conventional composition. She had no doubt they would sell at exhibition, for they were suitable to be hung anywhere. They brought to mind the art of Paris railings.

'They're very pretty.' She cursed herself for the insipid comment, she would have been furious if someone had applied it to her own Art. Surprisingly it seemed to please Lady Eastnor. 'I've heard of your group. I'd like to join as soon as I can. I've often longed for the life of an Artist, but I've only painted in oils. I don't suppose that would do?' She was begging like a child, what was the matter with her? She should have simply told them she would bring her easel to the beach. There couldn't be that many women Artists in a community like this.

'No,' Lady Caroline agreed. 'No, that wouldn't do. But do try watercolours, I think you will find them more appropriate for ladies. And for the light of the island of course.'

'Appropriate?' said Julia. By whose decree? It made them rather less appealing.

Caroline fixed her with a cold stare.

'Do you always paint in your best dresses? You must be a good deal less messy than me. I like to wear smocks while I work. Or do you have a dress code?' Julia looked hopeful. If she could bring them round, she was sure they'd like some of her ideas. Smocks were a splendid invention, no need to be careful when throwing materials around and such handy big pockets for tools.

'Simply dressing as an artist isn't all it takes, Mrs Cameron.' She looked her up and down, taking in the red velvet cloak and green skirts, the Russian boots with bold embroidery along the leather and the long-stalked lily tucked behind her left ear. 'Mr Ruskin himself always paints in his morning suit.'

Along the bay the other artists were still pretending to paint, but straining to hear the conversation and Julia waved across the row, beckoning them. Caroline introduced them one at a time, but to Julia they looked so similar that she immediately forgot their names. 'I shall tell you apart by your ribbon colours.' She laughed, indicating the bright bands they wore on their bonnets, which were quite at odds with the rest of their clothes. None of them smiled.

'When is your exhibition?' enquired Emily. 'It must be quite soon now. Alfred has told me that we must get there early or there will be nothing left to buy.'

'It was very popular last year,' said the Bonnet with a pink ribbon. 'But we're not sure if we'll be able to hold it again. The roof of the church hall in Ventnor is so badly in need of repair Lady Eastnor fears it will cause damage to the paintings if the weather turns.'

'It would be a terrible shame,' added the blue ribbon, 'after a year's work.'

'Then what a marvellous coincidence that we should meet today. The works on the gallery space in my house will finish soon and it's crying out for a real exhibition.'

It was not enough to have met them; she wanted to be one of these women, so seriously applying their paint to paper out in the elements. She would never wear a ribboned bonnet, but they would grow to love her the way she was. Some of them might like more interesting clothes. And perhaps she'd be happy to dress in grey if it meant she could learn to paint with water. At last she might realise her potential, and it looked so much easier than oils. Though all their pictures looked very much the same, pale-washed and delicate, a little dreary. With brighter colours she could develop something Beautiful that would put their island on the cultural map.

'It's a kind invitation, but we can't accept,' said Lady Caroline in a voice that expected no argument. She began to pack her portfolio. 'It's a serious exhibition and will need a proper gallery space.'

'But I absolutely insist!' said Julia. She drew out her watch as if to signal the end of the discussion. 'You must all come for lunch on Saturday week, it will be ready to show you then.' Lady Caroline threw up her hands and was about to protest when Julia added, 'And my Artist friend will be here at the weekend, I would love to introduce you.'

'Would we know him?' asked the Bonnet with the trailing green ribbon that brought out the colour in her hazel eyes.

'You may have heard of George Frederick Watts? You must call him The Signor, we all do, he doesn't mind at all, it's from his travelling days. He's such tireless worker. I'm hoping he'll come for a rest, but I fear that if he hears of your exhibition he will want to help.'

Lady Caroline's eyes glittered, and her voice became polite. 'What time on Saturday will be convenient for you, Mrs Cameron?'

1862 Dimbola Lodge, Isle of Wight

Impatient to begin the next phase of her Artistic Journey, Julia travelled to the mainland the very next day. The only art supplies shop on the island, at Yarmouth, was too small to be trusted to carry everything she would need. If she was to join in with the exhibition—the first in her own gallery!—then there was no time to be lost. It was a purposeful visit, unusually devoid of social calls. Late that evening, she and Mary returned to Dimbola Lodge with a large packing chest, full of everything Julia considered necessary to make the kind of Art that would have Lady Caroline begging her to join the Society. Charles, who had waited up to see her home, sat on the conservatory sofa dressed in a richly embroidered dressing gown and Indian slippers, watching with amusement as she tore open boxes and lifted out brushes, pots and tubes, scattering them over the room.

'Do let the poor girl go to bed, Julia.' He smiled at Mary who was collecting the supplies and attempting to arrange them neatly on the table. 'I hope she's fed you properly today. There's no taming Julia when the thrill of a new hobby is upon her.'

Mary smoothed her dress and straightened, 'We've had a wonderful day, thank you, Mr Cameron, the crossing was as calm as anything and we took lunch at Parmenters, on one of the tables overlooking the sea. But I am quite tired and, if it pleases you both, I think I will retire now.'

'Thank you, Mary, for everything.' Julia seized her in a smothering hug. 'I really don't know what I would do without you.'

'You'd find someone else to terrorise,' said Charles. 'Do look in the kitchens on your way up, Mary, I asked Louisa to leave some supper, just in case. You've both had a long day.'

Julia watched Mary fondly as she disappeared. 'Sometimes I think you're a better mother than me.' Perhaps he always had been. She loved all her natural and adoptive children, far more than they would know, but the routines of childhood were so boring. It was Charles who remembered to feed them and make sure they went to bed. Charles who checked on their progress at school. A sudden image of the face of Juliette as a child came to mind, all soft curls and serious, reproachful eyes. Juliette and her husband had been conspicuously absent since they wed and moved to the Highlands, claiming the journey was long and difficult, that it was tiring. They had not yet visited them at Freshwater and her grandchildren must be running around by now, surely the little ones would love the bay. They should be paddling with her in the shallow waves, watching the boats at the harbour. With a deep sigh, she set up her station, putting together the new easel she had bought to match the ones used by the rest of the Society and laying out the pots and brushes on its little shelf.

'Surely, Julia, you're not planning to begin painting at this hour?' Charles took out his watch, 'It's close to midnight.'

'I just want to try it.' Julia inhaled a dusty smell from the pigment blocks and her fingers itched to seize the soft thin brushes. Watercolours would be so much easier than oils. They would be her saviour. If those Bonnets could hold an exhibition of their works, then so could she. With practise she would have the Society eating out of her hands. 'I will just cover a few sheets with wash, so it's dry and ready to paint over tomorrow.'

'Don't you need to plan your composition?'

Julia wished her husband would go to bed. In a moment he would be telling her to put down dust sheets and smother the mood entirely. 'I'm not sure I intend to paint landscapes, they seem rather dreary and washed out.'

'I believe that's the watercolour style.' Charles raised an eyebrow as he watched her fixing the easel's height.

'I don't see that it needs to be.' Julia swirled a new brush into her water pot and added a vivid blue. She felt a deep satisfaction in the drag of bristle across the rough surface, the way pigment pooled in the paper's deep pits. This was something. A renewed purpose; a reminder of her vows. She would be the very Artist to make watercolours relevant, 'A new style of Aquarelle, for a new Exhibition,' she announced.

By the time of the visit, Julia had used four full pads of her new thick paper, one almost entirely wasted by wash so liberally applied it curled the edges together when it dried, rendering the surface useless. Impatient with waiting for the fine washed layers to set before she could build on them, she tried the paints without dilution. The effect was brilliant! Strong, bright hues that streaked across the paper like Indian birds, flashing their plumage in the shadows. Charles said the colours reminded him of home. Mary thought they looked like stained-glass windows. They were wholly original paintings and The Society would love them. She could hardly wait to show them to The Signor!

When Watts arrived in the station carriage, the seamstress was still sewing the curtains for his room. Julia had decided there was nowhere near enough light in his allocated quarters, the blue bedroom at the back of the house overlooking the garden, and had impulsively called on local workmen to rip out the perfectly normal-sized window and replace it with a wide arch, which caused Charles to worry about the length of time the artist planned to stay, and which also meant that neither the curtains nor the existing drapes would cover the glass. Luckily, the villagers, more used to operating on island time, were beginning to understand Julia's restlessness and

147

seemed perfectly happy to drop whatever they were working on to help her, usually for an enhanced price.

Sending Charles out to greet him, Julia fussed over the final preparations in the rooms, throwing Indian shawls over the lights, smoothing the counterpane and adding a small glass vase of freesias to the dressing table. Her old oil painting easel had been casually erected by the edge of the new window, just in case he felt the urge, and Julia's painting of Strauss sat on the sill, edged in a plain silver frame. She tried to hurry the elderly seamstress over her last few stitches, to no avail, and left her steadfastly sewing the thick blue velvet while she whirled down to the gallery floor to check on the hanging of her paintings.

Lady Caroline, and her beribboned Bonnets, arrived at the exact hour appointed for lunch and were shown to the gallery, where Watts and Charles were contemplating a row of seventeen extraordinary watercolours, larger than average size and executed in wild streaks of vivid colour.

'I am charmed, Lady Eastnor.' Watts had brushed and oiled his beard and was wearing a new suit of navy cloth with a pea-green cravat, a thick gold watch chain hanging across his chest. As he took her hand, the chief of the island artists blushed a deep pink and threw a sideways glance at the Camerons, who stood together in their usual outlandish garb. Charles wore a pair of Indian trousers so bagged they could have harboured a small dog, and no one would have been at all surprised if they had. 'I've heard so very much about your art from dear Julia. I do hope you've brought some of your works to try on the walls?'

Lady Caroline inclined her head modestly and looked around. Julia held her breath. The long white room, flanked with deep windows dressed in muslin, could not have provided a more perfect space for their annual display. 'I haven't,' she admitted. 'I wanted to see for myself before we made any plans.'

'You'll learn,' he replied. 'You can always believe in Julia.'

Lady Caroline gave a thin-lipped smile. 'It's very nice. And it's a kind offer, Mrs Cameron, my Society will be happy to hold its little exhibition here. Mr Watts, I did not know you painted aquarelles?' She moved closer to the wall, recoiled and swiftly moved back again. 'But perhaps I have made a mistake?'

The brash strokes of one painting showed a black cat of strange proportions washing itself awkwardly on a bright yellow sofa; another two formless shapes walking hand-in-hand along a country lane flanked by bright green fields and wildflowers. Some of the paintings were of mermaids and other mythical beings draped across rocks or beaches, others entirely abstract, comprising swirls of thick pigment scattered across with the simple shapes of birds.

'Alas, I'm unschooled in the finer arts.' Watts affected a sorrowful face. 'This is Julia's handiwork. It's the first time I've ever seen watercolours that resemble oil.'

Julia, desperate to join the exhibition, had painted them all in a few furious days, stalking the house for subjects that differed from the pale landscapes favoured by the society. Her personal favourite was the slightly blurred portrait of Charles in his patchwork jacket, standing by the kitchen garden. She looked at Lady Caroline expectantly, feeling as though she might burst with pride. The Signor had said she may even change the face of watercolour painting forever, but what would Lady Caroline think?

'They are... very... different,' she managed.

'I did not use water,' Julia said triumphantly. The Bonnets looked stricken. 'I found it took too long for the paint to dry and it made the paper too bumpy. So, I painted directly with the paints. What do you think of them?'

'That would explain the unusual effect. There's a technique to achieving a wash that does not upset the paper, Mrs Cameron, I'll be quite happy to teach you.'

'I could try, of course, but I rather like these,' said Julia, waiting for a moment of understanding. 'Mostly I think it's the colours, they seem more real somehow.' She looked at Watts. Any moment now he would point out that hers were the first of their kind, works in a New Form, important for Art at this exact place and time. Lady Caroline must be overwhelmed, playing for time; she seemed transfixed by the paintings. Maybe they were all just trying to find the right words and needed her to prompt them.

'They're not typical, I agree, but then the watercolour style has always seemed to me like a picture of life seen through a wedding veil, blurred and cloudy.' Why could they not see the splendour of her works?

Lady Caroline's brow furrowed. 'It is an interesting thought, Mrs Cameron. Of course, they're not true aquarelles, and so they'll need to be removed before we begin to hang our exhibition.'

After all those hours, with such extraordinary results, how could she say such a thing? The woman was quite mad.

'Oh, that's a shame,' said Watts quickly, 'I was hoping you might allow me to add a painting of my own. I hear Julia has very kindly set up an easel in my room and the wonderful light on your island is already calling my hands.'

Did he think she could not see what he was doing? Far from backing her paintings, Watts had the temerity to offer himself as bait, as a bribe! As though her own Art was worthless.

'Naturally there are always exceptions,' said Lady Caroline with a graceful incline of her head.

'Naturally,' agreed Watts. 'And naturally that exception is always Julia!'

'I think I am beginning to realise,' Lady Caroline smirked at Watts. 'If you are certain these will not detract from the rest of the exhibition then we'll try to work around them. They can be placed at the far end, before the muslin drapes, provided Mrs Cameron doesn't think it too similar to the view through a wedding veil? I would so hate to seem conventional.'

Watts threw back his head and laughed like a traitor. Julia stood beside him, wearing a fixed smile. She'd been sure, so sure, this time. Beauty was there on the page, it was obvious to anyone with a mind to see it. But the ridicule was there in their voices. Although she was no longer beneath a table, for a moment she was twelve years old again, the stab of rejection felt as keenly as when she was a child. Tears clouded her eyes and she moved her pictures to the far end of the gallery, one at a time, while the rest of them went down to lunch.

Stories from the Glass House:
Mary Ryan

Julia liked to picture me as the Madonna. She never rightly said I was supposed to be the mother of Christ, but that was always how it looked in the end, all wistful and confused, cradling one or other of the poor village weans she had me fetch up to Dimbola. It was a fascination for her, the perfect mother figure, something she wanted to be. We all used to let on that she was a wonderful mother, not just to her own weans but to all of us; and no one's good at everything are they? She was always too busy for the routines most children need. But she had this ideal, this image of what motherhood should look like, and in her own mind she fell short.

Juliette didn't help all that. She was her ma's bar of gold and it made me awful fierce to see how little she cared. Always running off to the country with her fancy friends in the school holidays. Couldn't wait to get away. She never came to see or asked Julia up to Scotland, even once she had the wee ones. It was Mr Cameron who kept on at them to visit, after I found Julia on the beach. Still makes me shiver, thinking about that horrible time. We almost lost her then, and I know who I'd have blamed. All she ever wanted was for her friends to love her for who she was.

I don't know what it was that made me look for her that night, because she often walked out late. There was just something I didn't like about the way she got queer in front of that watercolour woman and I followed her out, quite a way behind. When I got to the bay she was nowhere to be seen. But her bits and pieces were all over the sand, and I raised the alarm just in time. She said she was just walking, got taken further than she'd expected. Thanked us for rescuing her and then that was that. None of us ever talked about it again. Not ever. She wouldn't let us. When you think, though…

People say she changed after that, especially after the camera and everything, but it didn't seem that way to me. She was the kindest person I ever met and I think that all she wanted was for people to notice her. Because such beauty surrounded her in her sisters, she thought no one ever noticed her, but they did. They just noticed her in different ways.

Juliette and her husband didn't come until nearly Christmas, even after something like that, after we almost lost her. By then she was almost back in her old skin. I remember they were cross she wasn't there to greet them, as though she'd just sit there and wait for them for years. They didn't know her at all. I knew very well where she'd be in the week before Christmas, she could never resist the drama of religion and sure enough that's where I found her. Sitting in the Church meeting room with the leaking roof, a bible on her lap and a box of biscuits in front of her, surrounded by children lying or sitting cross-legged on the tiled floor. Little Annie Philpott was shovelling biscuit crumbs into a white goose and a couple of the younger boys were piling up a tower of the tapestry kneelers. She loved having the children around her and she never told any of them off. She made me wait until she'd finished the last story and the tallest of the children had hung the Christmas star.

Julia almost ate my head off when I told her who was waiting at the house. I know she told Mr Cameron not to make them come, but he did anyway. She wanted them to want to come. I wasn't allowed to drive the trap back, she took the reins and hammered back along the lane at a fierce speed, scattering ducks and chickens, and spraying up frost all over the back wheels. And I understood it quite plainly. Juliette McKenzie was almost the only person in the world who refused to fall for her Ma's charms. And her Ma cut up

153

pretty thick about it. All she wanted was a daughter who was her very best friend; she had a deadly way of loving and she expected to be loved in return; she couldn't stand it when others refused to show the same emotions. When it was family the treachery was worse.

Part II
The Artist's Life

Shade of a shadow in the glass,
O set the crystal surface free!
Pass—as the fairer visions pass –
Nor ever more return, to be
The ghost of a distracted hour,
That heard me whisper, "I am she!"
                Mary Coleridge, The Other Side of a Mirror

1863 Dimbola Lodge, Isle of Wight

On the day Juliette and her husband arrived, England was gripped in a storm of biblical proportions and the crossing, delayed for two days, was treacherous. Arriving at Dimbola with their young son and daughter they found only Charles with Emily Tennyson. Mary was duly despatched to find her mistress while Charles gave them tea and made awkward conversation with the stranger who had married his child.

'Darling? I'm here. Was it an awful journey?' Julia burst into the sitting room, shaking frost all over the floor.

'Mother, your rugs!' Juliette winced watching her throw her wet cloak onto a chair just as the two spaniels chased in after her, knocking them into her youngest grandchild who fell flat to the floor. He cried and toddled towards the sofa, only to be confronted by Strauss whose contempt for people, especially small ones, had deepened with age and who set about growling in a low throaty voice. Staggering backwards the child bumped into Hallam, who had been playing nicely, but who nevertheless was beginning to fulfil his early promise as a fighter and took the opportunity to punch him hard on the arm. With the sense to act quickly Julia scooped up her grandchild in one arm, Hallam in the other and covered them both with her cloak. She peeped under the velvet at them, one at a time, until they stopped crying and then marched them outside. While the others watched through the window, Julia encouraged the boys to hit sticks across the double row of icicles that hung from the ledge.

'It's far too chilly outside for the children! It's too cold to leave the doors wide open as well,' said Juliette, pursing her lips. 'It will soon be bedtime and I'll never settle them after this. Really. I had hoped that her recent experience might have calmed mother down a bit. She is still quite incorrigible. Do you think she'll ever grow up?'

'I rather hope not,' said Charles. 'Shall I call for some more tea?'

Outside, Julia glowered at them both. Did they think she could not see them, thick as thieves? He'd made Juliette come, that much was obvious. If only she'd left her miserable husband on his estate, they might have been able to talk about her experience; she might have opened up properly. Now Charles was probably filling in all the detail they'd missed and they'd be tiptoeing round in mock concern just like everyone else.

It was hard for her to remember the events of that night, though she'd heard the story countless times and always in the same order. Dear Mary, worried by the quiet of her reaction in the gallery, had followed her from the house. Evidently Charles could not be roused—where had he been that evening? Why could she not just ask him outright? Mary had somehow managed to persuade Watts to join the chase. Neither were strong swimmers. What if something had happened to them? They must have been worried sick by the sight of her shoes on the beach if they called for the lifeboat. Old man Berry apparently appeared in his nightshirt, blowing a whistle that roused half the bay. Everyone came out to watch her pulled back in, unconscious, until she sat upright and threw up a bathtub of salt water. Old Berry said her petticoats had saved her; that she was floating on them like a raft on the still water, her head held up where they'd spread out behind her. Ophelia, though he was the last person to realise the dark beauty of the scene.

Why did they not stop repeating it? She was half sick from the tale and reliving the whole horrible exchange with Lady Caroline and The Signor. Half sick of shadows. Everyone pointing out how much the community cared, standing without their cloaks on a midnight beach, waiting for her to be brought back. Waiting to see if she lived. They repeated the story over and over, as though hoping to jog her memory, as though they could find out why, trying to make sure she didn't do it again. She might not remember the events, but she knew what it felt like to be in the sea. Especially after the anger of the gallery, the treachery of her friends. It felt easy and calm, the most natural thing; she just couldn't give them the promise they begged for. Impossible to say that she would always be able to fight the pull towards that dark cool nothingness, the overwhelming sense of peace. Without Art, it was a promise she could not make.

Christmas morning brought a sprinkling of snow, glittering the lane as they walked to church with the Tennysons, throwing an air of magic over the celebrations. A fragile fondness between mother and daughter blossomed, even when Julia embarrassed her son-in-law by wearing a crown to church and her disappointingly shy grandchildren spoiled the games by refusing to play charades. Louisa surpassed herself with a festive feast so vast Julia parcelled up portions to deliver to the village poor; nobody minded that she did this in the middle of the meal itself.

Presents were distributed after tea and cake, with the household gathered around the tree, which Jones had brought in from the garden on Christmas Eve and Mary had garlanded with bright red stars and twisted chains made from thin gold paper and paste. Charles received a splendid Turkish hat, with a tassel that fell rakishly over his left cheek. Mary was given a new dress and a penny whistle just like the one Julia had seen her borrowing from one of the village children; she played a tune that made her look as though she wanted to cry. When the last of the wrapped gifts had been presented, the givers thanked, Juliette led her mother to a large object by the window. It was as tall as her waist and as wide as it was long, covered in a length of deep blue velvet, which reached down to the floor on either side.

'Some kind of an easel? Perhaps a chair to sit in while I paint? I'm unsure those women in the Society would allow me to stay on their island if they knew about it, but it could double as a bathing chair?' Julia chattered to hide her embarrassment. Though generous with the gifts she gave others, she was bad at receiving them herself and could not shake the feeling that this gift, in particular, was a gesture to appease her daughter's guilt for her absence, or the embarrassment of what Julia had done. What could make up for years of daughterly disinterest and absence? Pointless to dwell on it, their relationship had to move on, or she would end up like Mama. If only the tears would stop threatening to come.

Conscious that she was being watched, her reaction tested, Julia felt along the length of the cloth. All the missed celebrations of childhood flooded to mind and she bit her lip hard. Pushing back a corner of cloth, she revealed a wooden box, large enough to house an infant and gleaming like a magician's chest. A vanishing cabinet? Perhaps, thirty-odd years too late. Had she been presented with one at the party in Grandmamma's garden she most likely would never have returned to the present.

'Do hurry mother.' Juliette's voice rose. 'There's no need for such a performance.'

Charles stepped round to the other side of the box, held up an edge of velvet and, raising an eye to Julia, indicated she should do the same. They pulled it away and the cloth pooled to the floor, uncovering a large camera, cased in highly polished mahogany and resting on a wide telescopic tripod with splayed wooden feet.

'We thought it may amuse you mother, to photograph during your solitude here at Freshwater. To keep you out of trouble.'

It was an expensive camera, clearly a gift that had taken thought. To Julia it was both a peace offering for all those years of disappointment and a message that her daughter did not intend many further visits. Keep her out of trouble indeed, what a terrible thing to say. Still, it was an extraordinary object. A shiny, magical instrument, alive with promise and hope.

'Solitude?' Charles laughed. 'Your mother would wait a long time here to be alone.' But Julia knew it was meant as a means of keeping her occupied; an assumption that, perhaps, this conventional mechanical tool might channel some of her bohemian creative urges. She was too delighted to find offence. Awestruck, she stroked the wooden casing lovingly.

'It's a splendid piece of machinery.' Charles ran a hand over the polished case. As he bent to take a closer look at the broad lens, his new hat fell over one eye and he made a face at Julia, hoping to make her laugh. But she only had eyes for her gift.

'It is beautiful!' burst Julia. 'And I can hardly wait to try it. I'm so very touched that you have given so much thought as to what would please me.' She seized Juliette in a violent embrace and did not mind when she felt her pulling away. Fascinated by the trays of glass plates and the small wooden boxes of chemicals, she barely halted her examination for the grandchildren's bedtimes, or Emily's recital.

When the others had retired to bed, she stayed up long into the night, reading the lengthy book of instructions and rifling through the papers on light writing Herschel had sent. Finally, the notes in his letters could begin to make sense. All the samples of talbotypes and daguerreotypes would help her understand what to do. Here was a chance and a destiny. For what was a camera but lenses and glass? What did this piece of machinery do but pull visions from the mind of the operator and translate them to magical paper? If she could master it, then her dreams would be at her fingertips. Hope flooded her veins. This time she would create something new and she would do it without anyone's approval.

1863 Freshwater Bay

Next morning, Julia rose late, finding the house empty. A note by the covered teapot on the breakfast table explained that the family had gone for a walk together, to enjoy the beautiful crisp, frosty day. Irritated by the lack of subjects for her camera and eager to begin work, she pulled out one of the wide glass plates and coated it liberally in what she hoped were the correct light-sensitive chemicals from one of the vials provided, before placing it carefully into the slot and replacing the wooden lid. The fumes were deeply toxic, filling her nose with a scent like rotten eggs. It was almost delicious to smell such a manifestation of alchemy. To think that such science could make Art!

First a sitter was needed. Julia hastily threw on a woollen shawl and Charles's new Turkish hat and strode down the lane. As luck would have it, she met Bolingbroke, a local farmer so named for his striking resemblance to that unhappy historical figure. Immediately, she longed to capture his image, to present him just as Bolingbroke would have looked, to make everyone viewing the image understand what it meant. But he was a farmer, taking a walk on a public holiday, and she chose her words carefully.

'Good morning Welles, and season's greetings to you. I hope you enjoyed a pleasant Christmas?' Albert Welles raised his cap and nodded, whistling to his border collie, Jim, to wait for him on the lane. Albert's beard and hair were freshly trimmed in neat lines of deep red-brown, like brushstrokes; his tweed trousers cinched tightly at the waist with a wide brown leather belt and strap. 'Are you on business?'

'No ma'am.'

'Do you have a few moments to help me with something up at the house?'

Albert eyed her warily, reaching down to pet Jim, who had circled back to his side.

'Aye.' The word seemed to surprise him, as though it came out before he really meant it.

Julia seized her chance and, instead of walking to the next farm for some seasonal spiced cider as planned, he found himself following her along the track to the front drive, Jim trotting beside him.

'Is it a birthing?' he enquired. 'I'm happy to help with sheep or goats, dogs even. But not cats, I can't abide cats. The farm's fairly overrun with them as it is.'

'No, no, nothing like that,' said Julia. Four dogs streaked through the door and out onto the front lawn when they reached the house, much to the disgust of Jim, who set out the business of rounding them up and restoring proper order.

'I'm afraid you're wasting your time with them, Jim.' Julia laughed.

'They just need some rightful training ma'am.' Welles looked as though he wanted to say more on the matter. Jim had managed to stop the chasing already and was lying in a half crouch, waiting for one of the other dogs to make a wrong move. 'Jim would stay like that all day.'

'Would he mind if we let him for a while? This won't take long.' She marched through the house, throwing her outdoor clothes onto the end of the stairs and waving at him to stop taking off his boots. 'No need for formalities. In here.' The farmer followed her through to the conservatory, where all the furniture had been pushed back to the walls except a single chair with an upright back, which had been half-turned to the light of the window. It faced a large wooden box with a round glass circle at the front and a frill of fabric at the back.

'I can't do anything to mend that thing I'm afraid.' Welles twisted his cap between his hands and made as if to go. 'I've only ever seen one of those once and I've no idea how it works.'

'Oh, I know how it works… I think… I hope so anyway. No, I want you to sit for me. I'll pay you, see.' Julia produced a half crown and handed it to him. 'You'll have one of these for every hour.'

He pocketed it with suspicion, sitting heavily on the fine-legged chair.

'Not like that.' Julia moved to arrange his arms, keeping up a steady stream of instruction. 'There, now turn your head slightly to me. That's not working; turn it the other way. Why can't I see that properly? You're very hard to focus, very hard indeed. Do sit still please. It won't work if you're shifting all over the chair. No, I said stop moving. There. Now, the camera works with light-sensitive chemicals, they make an imprint of your image, or whatever image the lens is pointing at, depending on how long the glass is exposed to light in the camera. I think it must take a little while; we'll try ten minutes. And it's very important you don't move for the entire time.'

Welles settled in the chair, was scolded for moving, then managed to sit still enough for the allocated time. But when Julia removed the plate nothing was imprinted; and she had barely an idea as to what had gone wrong. After all the excitement it felt as though her hopes were dashed. She had to hide it from him, make it look as though she was in control, or the news of his morning would be all over the island by tomorrow.

'I see. I'd like to try that again if I may,' she bluffed. 'Do check on Jim if you like while I coat another plate and I'll set the camera again.'

'Jim'll be fine.' Welles shifted his weight on the seat, which was small for his frame and looked as though it was already irritating his thighs. Julia rushed to her 'darkroom,' the smaller room of the scullery with a bucket wedged over the high small window to exclude all light, and mixed the chemicals for a second time, washing first one, then another, over the glass. Welles watched as she ran back with the dripping wet glass, lifting it carefully by the edges to slot into the placeholder.

'Looks heavy,' he added.

'It's not at all,' said Julia, brushing back her hair and leaving a dark slick across her cheek from her stained hands. She struggled to pull the heavy plate into place where it had dropped awkwardly. 'I'm sorry about the smell though. I can't open the garden door because of the dogs.'

'No worse than the farm,' he replied, gruffly.

By the time Julia removed a plate that contained a clear negative image to capture, Albert's back was aching, his thighs were chafed and he had earned one and a half crowns. Unfortunately, in her haste to show him it had worked, she touched the wrong side of the glass and smeared the colloidal film, leaving a wide smudge right across the image. But six plates worth of trial and error had shown her how the process worked and she was ecstatic with the joy of creation. This light writing was masterful, a medium to translate the images from her head directly onto paper! Not canvas but silvered paper. This, this, was her calling. It was surely the prediction from her childhood. What else so good, so Beautiful, could come from glass and mirrors? Possibility shone before her. How easy it would be to work, day and night, until her Photographic Art was perfect. She was filled with boundless energy for the first time in years.

But Welles had had enough. Even the saintly Jim could plainly be heard whining by the front door. His master, slightly mystified as to what had become of his morning, and more in need of spiced cider than ever, took his leave and mumbled a promise to return, though he could be heard mumbling to himself that he wouldn't hurry.

When the rest of the family returned, they found her alone with the dogs, sitting in a fug of odour that permeated most of the rooms on the ground floor, her hands stained a purplish black and her hair twisted up onto the back of her head, stuck through with an ivory letter opener to keep it in place.

'You look quite mad,' said Charles, with a cheerful smile. 'Have you worked it out yet?'

Juliette instinctively drew both children close to her skirts. 'I had thought you might take a photograph of the children before we leave, but these chemicals will do them no good at all. How many plates have you used? The fumes are already beginning to bring on one of my headaches.'

Julia gave a withering look. Sometimes she wondered if Juliette could really be her daughter. Perhaps Kali had swapped her baby with another, one of those tricks of fate the gods like to play on mortals. Here she was faced with the most exciting artistic development in history and it gave her headaches. She seemed to have forgotten about her earlier concerns for her mother's health and wellbeing. If she had really looked, she would have seen that nothing could make her happier.

'We saw Bolingbroke on the way, the poor man looked terrified. Did you tell him you were taking his soul?' asked Charles.

'He wouldn't have fallen for that. Though I do believe I made him sit for too long. Still there are plenty of other subjects. This island is full of handsome peasants; the men and the woman will make lovely subjects. Not to mention the children.' Julia held up her plate like a trophy. 'And yes, I've worked it out, thank you, it's different in practice to the hand lithographs I tried after Herschel sent his prints, but the principle is the same.'

'Herschel is always ahead of his time.' Charles took the spoiled glass plate from his wife's hands and held it up to the window, admiring the portrait with its clear outline of the handsome farmer's head.

'Indeed,' Julia agreed. 'He was wrong about one thing though. It's drawing or painting, not writing, with light. And if I can get it right, I'll have no more need of watercolours, oils or any other outdated medium. I can make these prints into the most wonderful paintings of light and shade.'

1864 Isle of Wight

The wonders of invention were wasted on the young, who all took them for granted. Julia was annoyed that Hardinge wasn't more impressed with her camera. But her son had seen a large lens used before and, with the easy technical skills of youth, showed her how to focus on her subjects. She was far too excited to be cross with him, especially as they saw so little of him in his time at Oxford. She couldn't wait to try out what she had learned. Again, she ran out to the lane and, finding no one around, knocked on the Tennyson's door, demanding they offer up children for Art. She secured two. Maude and Annie were daughters of the Philpotts, house guests of the Tennysons, and so bored with the company of adults and the relentless pinching of Hallam they skipped away with Julia before putting on their coats and had to be called back to dress properly against the bitingly cold air.

The afternoon was perfectly clear and frosty. It was important to make the most of the daylight. Julia arranged the sisters against the garden windows, framed with pale soft light, one leaning against the other's chair back. She kept up a running commentary of orders, desperate to ensure they did not move and spoil the plate. Unfortunately, it had quite the opposite effect. Her voice, rising in excitable octaves, proved to be irresistibly amusing and a splutter of laughter from Maude ruined the first plate completely.

'Help!' Julia yelled through the house for Mary, who took Maude's hand and walked her through the kitchen to see the dogs, knowing well that a single child would be easier than two to keep perfectly still. It worked. Julia pulled the lens closer to Annie so nothing else filled the frame. Really the child looked terrified. That wouldn't do at all. No one wanted a photograph of a terrified child. What did girls like? Dolls, of course, the old dolls were on a table in the music room, one either side of a tall potted parlour palm. She rushed to fetch them. Both looked slightly scary, but her Amina was probably worse with its dumpy body and flat face, the feathered stubs on its sunken shoulders all that remained of the magpie wings she had stitched to them. She ran back to Annie and thrust the doll towards her.

Whether it was the doll, the roughness of Julia messing the child's hair and puffing it out around her face, the exhortation to stop wasting her expensive chemicals, or simply Annie's desire to please, the child stayed immobile and the resulting image was exactly right. Julia rushed to her makeshift darkroom, fingers aching with carrying the plate so carefully as to avoid the wet side of the glass. She slowly developed and washed it, waited for it to dry again, then varnished it so that it could make as many prints as she wanted.

All the time spent in preparation was agonising. Had it worked? It seemed perfect. Such a clear light from the window, such a still child, with a wonderful expression. As she smoothed and rubbed the potions, she considered the process. It was magical. Conjuring faces from glass. No paint, no brushes or knives; no standing by an easel for hours on end dotting tiny little blobs of colour onto canvas. No judgement on whether she used things in a way prescribed by some silly Society. Art in its purest form.

The children had been made to wait until she had painstakingly transferred the image of Annie to paper. At first it was too faint, her impatience causing her to peel the paper from the glass before its time. She cursed herself. Even as she had begun to lift its edges, she had known it was too soon. Eventually the second attempt was ready. As she separated it from the plate, she could see it had succeeded. Annie's sweet face with its plump cheeks filled the print, with only the collar and top button of her coat visible below. Light streamed through the window and bounced off her hair, lending an angelic look to the wistful expression caused by asking a young child to sit still for any length of time. It looked exactly as she had planned. A portrait worthy of the name of Art. She ran from the closet, waving the print above her head and declared to Mary that this was her very First Success.

'It's beautiful, ma'am,' Mary agreed. 'I've never seen a photograph so absolutely real, and yet she looks like a painting.'

Julia, delighted, ran all over the house to search for gifts. When Mary walked the two children back to Farringford, they were laden with cakes, fresh eggs, a small book of sonnets and a bracelet of polished quartz. Julia printed, fixed, toned and framed the image that very afternoon, rushing down through the backfields to present it to the child's father with profuse thanks. At Mary's insistence she signed and dated the back of the frame with a breathless flourish.

Exhausted and happy, she stayed up late into the night, waving Charles away as he exhorted her to take some rest. She made dozens of prints, placing the negative directly onto the sensitised photographic paper she'd been given with her present. Each step offered so much room for error, required so much concentration. Though the glass plates were heavy they were still fragile, easily marked, scratched or dropped. It was such an exacting science. Such a wonderful thing to absorb and learn, improving with every print. The plates must be perfectly polished and clean before adding chemicals. Any specks of dusts would stick and magnify on the negative and could ruin the whole thing. She determined to find some new baths as quickly as possible. The old stone sinks in the scullery were not quite large enough to submerge the plates evenly; she would have liked more control than they gave her over the patches of light and shade.

Julia looked sadly at the empty bottles that littered the scullery. All those chemicals! How could she have used so many? They had to be prepared freshly each time, in correct combinations, and any errors were simply wasted. There was nowhere on the island to replace them. She would have to order an astonishing amount of materials from the mainland if the technique continually proved this difficult. Yet, despite all the challenge and uncertainty of creation, she was elated. She had imagined and created something undeniably Beautiful and she was the happiest she'd been since Juliette was born. The strange, compelling chemistry of this most modern Art felt more like her destiny than ever.

My Dear Herschel,

I write in haste to catch the last post boat, as I can't wait to share with you these prints, my very First Successes. You were the first to tell me about light writing and to spark my interest in its potential as an Art Form. There is so much I want to share with you. So much I want to create. Juliette made me the most wonderful present of a camera, with all the things necessary to make beautiful images. It has created in me an impulse towards my deeply seated love of the Beautiful, a chance to arrest all Beauty before me in a way that I've hitherto found unfulfilled. With my camera I have the wings to fly with my subjects and create beautiful Art. From the very first moment I handled the lens with a tender ardour, and it has become to me as a living thing, with voice and memory and creative vigour. Many weeks I've worked fruitlessly, but with hope and care, and I offer you these, my First Successes, to show how much you have inspired me.
With affection,
Julia

1864 Isle of Wight

Julia deliberately built her portfolio, planning and collecting scenes just as she had labelled slides for her microscope. Backdrops and props were acquired and stacked against the walls of the scullery until it was almost impossible to turn around in the room. They transformed the conservatory into fields and lanes, castles and seascapes. Every walk resulted in a new conquest, another face for the makeshift studio. There was no time to waste! Each print was a miracle. Breathless with excitement she would peel away the paper, finding new joy each time. How could she ever have thought those silly paintings were enough? No wonder they'd laughed. Such painting was the work of a child compared with these daring pictures of light and shade, their intensity of shadow, which brought Beauty to every person that sat in her chair.

Close up was so much more illuminating, it left the sitter nowhere to hide, though it did take rather a long time and they would wriggle so much. Children were the worst. And the chattier ones from the village. Alfred claimed they found it hard to sit so close to the photographer. 'You are terrifying to them, Julia, arranging them like that with no thought for their comfort, standing in front of their faces.' What did it matter? What was comfort when you were participating in the creation of the newest and most exciting Art? It was necessary, with a wide-open aperture, to stand closely by the lens. Who cared if her hair was a nest? Who cared if her dress and hands were stained with chemicals? They had to be mixed quickly; it was messy. It was Alchemy!

A new, larger, box was added to her growing collection of equipment. It held a negative of some fifteen by twelve inches, inspiring a series of close-up portrait heads to immense and unprecedented scale. They drew the very soul from their subjects. It was nothing short of miraculous and it was her duty to show them to the wider world.

'I fail to see how you think these might have anything at all to do with my Society?' Lady Caroline sat perfectly upright in her neat floral drawing room, leafing through a small album of photographic prints with a perplexed look and one hand constantly rising to hover above her heart, as though her physical peace might be threatened in some way.

'I'm merely offering you a joint Exhibition.' Julia spoke slowly and seriously, anxious that her suggestion be understood. 'I intend to show these to the people of the island first, before I take them to London, because these people are the subjects of many of my favourites and because this place, with its pure, clear light and handsome people, has inspired my Art. As I know it has inspired yours.' True, Caroline was an old-fashioned, straight-laced sort of woman, but she would come round. Their Art was so similar in some ways, the light of the island, the simplicity of the islanders and their pastoral life; yet so very different in others. These photographs were Art of the highest form and if Caroline couldn't see that, it must only be because she didn't want to.

'But this isn't art. It's photography. If it's art at all then it's the very darkest of arts, akin only to alchemy and trickery. These photographs bear no resemblance whatsoever to our watercolour landscapes. In fact, if I may say so, they bear very little resemblance to any photography I've ever seen.' Lady Caroline looked as though she wished she'd never opened the book. She continued to turn the pages slowly, holding the corner of the page gingerly between her thumb and forefinger.

Julia's intense close-up portraits showed all the imperfections that she felt revealed the inner being. All were softly focused, so the viewer must strain their eyes to right them; many wore mesmerising halos of light around their unbrushed hair. Why did this woman not see that they were adorable? People as nature intended, just as she loved them: flawed and raw and filled with emotion, their Beauty shining from their faces.

'Exactly! It is Alchemy, wonderful Alchemy. I intend for these portraits to shock the viewer with delight. My Photography will startle the world,' said Julia.

Lady Caroline, who had always been at pains to explain that the best art worked in an entirely opposite way, looked horrified at the idea.

'And I know that they will. You could not bring yourself to allow my paintings into your Society for the last exhibition. At the time I could not forgive it, and… we need not speak of it. But I understand you now. I understand what it is to make the kind of Art that people want to look at and admire. So, I thought it only fitting I invite you to join my exhibition.' Julia smiled, trying to forget that in her period of recovery she had fed Caroline's conciliatory chocolates to her pigs with a grim and childish satisfaction. She must accept, she had to, and not just to save face. It would be ridiculous in a small community like theirs if the only two real Artists could not find some common ground. It was not as though they led a London life with its warring social factions.

Caroline lowered her eyes to the portrait before her. A wild-haired man with a strong, handsome jaw, rendered in the deepest sepia, stared out from the page with half-closed eyes; his collarless shirt was unbuttoned, his waistcoat open, although only a tantalising glimpse of him could be seen below his face. Julia watched, delighted, as a deep pink flushed across Caroline's neck and ears.

'I'm flattered, of course, Mrs Cameron. But I think that if you wish to mount an exhibition you would be better served to show your own work in its entirety, without the dilution of art.'

'This is Art! It is the absolutely the most modern and meaningful Art.' Julia struggled to keep her voice polite. She was wasting her time. Ridiculous woman, how could anyone deny this was Art? It would serve her right if no one ever took a second look at her insipid paintings again. Julia turned the page to reveal a portrait of Mary Ryan, leaning against a trailing plant with a wistful, romantic expression. Surely this, of all the prints, was undeniable beauty? 'Maud by Moonlight' showed Mary resting against the spreading tendrils of a passionflower vine in full bloom, deep in thought and with all the vulnerability of blossoming youth. A lone vine tendril, impressed upon the negative glass itself, swept across the foreground as though the very garden was embracing the girl and drawing her in to its temptation. A perfect depiction of those lines, Maud about to enter the garden, seemingly through the veil of the vine itself. Her face betrayed the deepest emotions of the verse, her hesitance, the confusion of her burgeoning sensuality, the unrequited longing of her youth. Watercolours could never do justice to such an image, could never show the passion and longing, the utter tedium of the rest of life while a young maid waits for her lover.

'These titillating images won't sell here,' said Caroline firmly, closing the album and passing it back to Julia as though she wanted rid of it as quickly as possible. 'The rural folk of this island are not likely to enjoy your exhibition, nor buy these images of themselves in such wanton states of disarray.'

Julia considered this for a moment. Caroline was right, possibly, about the sales. But that was of no concern. She was planning to join the Royal Photographic Society and, once she was a member, would publish and sell as she pleased. What mattered, for now, was getting the people who sat for her to be able to see the way they looked in her images; the way she felt when she looked at the Signor's portrait. A better version of herself, the way she always was in her own head; the way she would be in a story. The exhibition Julia planned would get her subjects to understand that photography was a mirror of their souls. If they understood her properly, they would queue the length of the bay for the chance to sit in her chair.

Mary Ryan was an avid fan of the photographic method and made it her business to understand the process, spending hours helping Julia with the plates and chemicals and patiently holding papers up to dry. She was often persuaded in front of the lens herself; a handsome subject with her fresh complexion and rounded features. When Mary sat, acutely conscious of the need for stillness, her face naturally composed into a resigned and thoughtful expression that lent itself beautifully to Julia's experimental series of Renaissance-style Madonnas.

Many times, the housemaid was despatched into the village to find small children to complete the beatific scenes. The same three mothers, burdened with chores, would accept small coins for an easier afternoon and Mary later returned the children, bright-eyed from Louisa's pastry and their games with the animals of Dimbola. Usually they would be accompanied by a print of the negative, signed and dated with a flourish. Several dressers in Freshwater homes were crammed with such prints, all signed and numbered, part of carefully curated series, and viewed with some bemusement by the recipients.

'I believe these photographs are the most beautiful portraits I've ever seen. They've the light of halos, like the paintings in St Finn Barre's cathedral,' said Mary.

Julia peered over to see that the girl was examining her own portrait, taken as she knelt in a wide-sleeved dress, arms crossed over her chest. Such innocence and worldliness at the same the time, nothing but the camera could show it. The archness in the tilt of the head, the set jaw with its shadowed neck, the wideness of those eyes.

'That's the one Lady Caroline said was out of focus,' she observed.

'Then she's as cold as a fish! You've found, in my ordinary face, a light of beauty that shines like a light of heaven.'

Julia beamed. The girl had the most intuitive understanding. 'It's your own goodness and patience that shines from the page, Mary.'

'I wish with all my heart that Ma could see it.' Mary knew, because Julia was unable to keep secrets, that her mother had asked for her to be kept away from art. 'Surely this she would have understood.'

Julia's mind flashed with a painful image of Violetta kneeling in a little white church, her raw hands clasped in supplication, watched by the benign faces of the saints as she prayed for her remaining children. 'By no means is your face ordinary.' Julia peered over her shoulder with a feeling of satisfaction. 'And my lenses don't lie, they're a mirror. There's nothing coming from this image that isn't emanating from you.'

Mary's eyes shone with tears. If Julia had needed proof, she was now certain that she had the ability with her camera to draw out the inner self in a portrait.

'Your mother was proud of you Mary, as am I,' said Julia. 'How would you like to become my official Photographic Assistant? You can help me to mount the displays for my First Exhibition.'

1864 Dimbola Lodge, Isle of Wight

In the weeks before the exhibition, the housemaid was despatched to each hamlet of the island with a leather satchel of pamphlets announcing a new local talent and inviting the public free of charge. Still fearing a lack of crowds, Julia invited all the inhabitants of Little Holland House to stay from the day before the opening, and the group duly appeared on the first boat, complete with their attendant guests. Esteemed politician, Lord Alfred Gray, and family friend and novelist, William Thackeray, were seized and rushed to the conservatory where, to their consternation, Julia manhandled them into poses that were quickly developed and added to the displays already covering the long gallery walls. She was thrilled. Dressed in a magnificent plum velvet gown, girdled with a long silken belt, a crown of passionflowers on her hair, she was a vision not to be refused.

Thoby closeted in the drawing room for a long conversation with Charles; and Sarah took the opportunity to investigate the house, ending in the kitchen where she interrogated a startled Louisa about every guest the lodge had entertained. Virginia stayed away, frightened by Sarah's insistence that the provincial peasants of their sister's new home would be likely to attack her in their ignorance of beauty.

'As I suspected, you appear to have moved to a backwater.' Sarah sniffed on the day of the opening, watching the beribboned bonnets of the watercolour society gently pushing to be the first through the open front door. 'Good heavens, look at them.'

'Freshwater is beautiful, which even your eye must realise. And it is no more a backwater than London,' declared Julia loudly, attracting the attention of the locals who narrowed their gazes at Sarah. 'Allow me to introduce you to Mr William Holman-Hunt, his house is just behind Farringford, and this is Mr Edward Lear, who is staying with Alfred and Emily.'

She stepped back with a triumphant look as Sarah grappled with her manners, struggling between pleasantries and the overwhelming desire to capture the pair of them and invite them to her superior salon at Little Holland House. Of course, they were big names; in this provincial place she had almost forgotten. Freshwater contained a ready-made pot of fame, a salon for Sarah to envy. It also held a rich source of celebrity for a portrait artist.

'And these dear fashionable ladies are members of the Ventnor Watercolour Society.' She bore them no ill feelings; in fact, she had much for which to thank them. Had she joined the Society she would never have undergone her baptism, Juliette wouldn't have arrived with her present and the world of Photography would not have gained an Artist. 'I'm delighted to see you here to support my little show.' Julia, who struggled to remember any of their names, turned to introduce them to Sarah, just as Lady Caroline Eastnor sailed into the gallery. She wore an uncomfortably structured dress of deepest grey with a high neck of white lace and an imperious grey and white parasol, which swung from her right arm.

The Bonnets all gasped in unison. Julia covered her surprise by rushing over to greet her, regretting her decision to include a portrait of the youngest Bonnet, who would no doubt be ostracised from the painting circle. Lady Caroline's eyes glittered as she took in the gathered crowd, a number that already surpassed any of her annual watercolour events and clearly included a significant number of local and further flung dignitaries.

'Please, allow us to take your things.' Julia drew her towards the group she had just left.

'I'm afraid I may not stay long,' she replied loudly, gripping the parasol Julia was valiantly trying to remove.

'I'm expecting visitors from the mainland and they're not the kind to be kept waiting.'

'We thought you weren't able to come,' whispered the youngest Bonnet, 'Otherwise we would have come together, wouldn't we?' The other Bonnets nodded vigorously.

'My guests have been delayed, and so I found myself at some unexpected leisure. I thought it best used in supporting my dear fellow artist,' said Lady Caroline.

'Aha! I see you have changed your mind about the Dark Art! And if your time is limited then you must waste none of it!' Julia seized the unsuspecting Signor by the arm and reintroduced him. 'Dear Watts will accompany you. I find he does so understand my style and, being a Fellow Artist, will most ably guide you along the walls.' Lady Caroline had not a chance to protest and they began to stroll slowly along the length of the gallery, stopping to admire each print.

Watts lingered before an image of Anthony Trollope, splendid in a squat felt hat, his beard a vision of light and dark, his eyes observing the viewer in a fixed and penetrative stare. Light poured across his cheeks, which were slightly raised as though he smiled, although his heavy moustache obscured his mouth, giving the impression he kept an amusing joke entirely to himself.

'She's captured him perfectly,' Watts sighed. 'Do you know him?' Lady Caroline gave a prim shake of her head. 'He's just like this. Always. Really these portraits are quite divine. I wish only that I could paint such a picture.'

'It is hardly the same. Painting is a delicate art, each stroke a sensitive rendering of the artist's intent.'

'But the effect on the viewer is identical! I would, rather, suggest that these portraits are more compelling. And you have clearly never witnessed Julia at work. I've never seen an artist as sensitive as she when handling her lenses and plates. She washes chemicals in a veritable fervour of creative spirit.' Watts threw his arms around wildly.

'It's not ladylike to manhandle such huge machines, such poisonous chemicals.' Caroline's hands fluttered by her throat.

'My dear lady all paint is poisonous!' He raised his hands as though to strike something. 'All art is eventual death to the artist! But the technique is no matter. It's the resulting effect which we classify as art.' He stopped to admire a print of two girls, dressed in such a hazy swirl of white fabric they may well be ghosts, their white, anxious faces peering out from blackness.

'A dark art indeed,' muttered Caroline, momentarily forgetting her wish to charm the great painter. 'And, from what I read in the journals, there's a great deal of need to look at the technique. These images are a far cry from what I, or any right-thinking artist, would call successful photography.'

'You are a watercolour artist, a painter of landscapes, perhaps for you there is too much emotion, too much of real life here with its sweat and its passions…'

'Signor, you're not speaking with your London painters now,' Julia interrupted. Although she was enjoying the lecture, she was mindful that Watts's gathering intensity should not upset her neighbours. 'I think I heard you discussing technique?'

'Lady Eastnor believes that your technique may be flawed. Perhaps you should have asked her to contribute some of her own art to your display?'

'I don't photograph,' protested Caroline.

'Yes,' replied Watts, 'I know.'

'Ah, but in that Lady Eastnor is really quite correct, Signor. The First Successes in my portraits were indeed, as Hardinge says, a "fluke." That is, when focussing and coming to something which, to my eye, was very Beautiful,

182

I stopped there instead of screwing on the lens to the more definite focus which all other photographers insist upon.'

'Exactly as I explained.' Caroline nodded graciously. 'A slovenly approach to what is, in fact, an exacting scientific process. Something which, I believe, is best left to scientists.'

'But what you don't see,' said Watts, 'Is that Julia continued, knowing she would be criticised, and that these paint-like pictures were a most important contribution to the art form, and it is an art form, make no mistake. It is the most modern of all the arts and what we see now is only the beginning.'

Julia laughed, though secretly she was as delighted with Watts as she was furious with Caroline for her thinly veiled suggestion that photographers could only be scientists and, by implication, men.

'I merely played with the focus to make them more dreamlike. I wanted them to have that quality. As you know I'm a great admirer of the works of Millais as well as the Signor.'

'And you believe your photography to be pre-Raphaelite?' Caroline raised one eyebrow until it almost reached the brim of her bonnet.

'It's more than that,' declared Watts. 'It's like a Renaissance painting made modern in its execution.'

Julia felt she might burst with happiness. A true painter, one of the most talented of his generation, had declared her an Artist, and in front of Lady Eastnor! She could not have hoped for more.

They reached the end of the left wall and turned to face the opposite display, containing nine in a series of Madonna images, most of which featured Mary Ryan with some cameo appearances from the housemaid who, relieved of the tedium of dusting for the day, sat proudly a small distance apart, on one end of a mustard yellow love seat, graciously accepting the admiring comments of the villagers gathered around her.

'I would change the composition of some of these.' Watts narrowed his eyes, turning his head to get a better view. 'You'll never sell them as they are. There's too much complexity of emotion. Even as I view them, I'm wholly unable to explain whether the mother is cradling here a dead child or one merely sleeping. As an artist I enjoy the confusion of feeling that these seem designed to create, but I fear your buying public may not.'

'A dead child!' said Lady Caroline, 'Who could possibly want to buy something like that?'

'I don't wish to put them up for sale!' exclaimed Julia. 'I wish only for them to be admired.' What if no one bought them? She couldn't bear it; she would rather give them all away for free and tell herself everyone loved them.

Stories from the Glass House:
Edward (Charles) MacKenzie

Every damn person who'd been taken in by her amateur photographs spoke of her eccentricity as though it was an achievement in itself, or at least something to be admired. It was not. It was exhausting for her daughter, who wanted only for her mother to be conventional and elegant, like the mothers of her friends from school; and it was exhausting, in turn, for me. I much admired what Juliette tried to be, in the face of such a family. It took little to persuade her away from them.

Something had occurred that Christmas we were made to visit, something I barely understood, but Juliette was adamant she would take the children and I didn't want to leave her to make the journey herself. Parts of the visit were worse than I expected. When Julia left the house during the meal we were subjected to a good thirty minutes of Alfred and Charles quite seriously explaining the relationship between her eccentricity and the depth of her goodness; something Juliette professed to understand but I could see from the look on her face that didn't mean she had to like it. Being near her mother always made her tense, like a woodland creature listening out for some unseen predator.

The camera was blood money of sorts. But it brought the two closer, inexplicably. I was never sure she'd really learned what to do with it. I have always hated the family portrait she made us, myself and Juliette looking buttoned-up, benignly patient as the children rolled around our feet, half-dressed in nightclothes, tattered wings made from goose feathers hanging from their chubby backs. As soon as she received it, Juliette hid the picture away in a drawer as though she was ashamed of its petty drama.

I don't know what Juliette expected from the gift really, her mother was never going to take ordinary family portraits. The only other time I came down from the Highlands we were out walking, and we met a young couple in the bay, in some distress because the gentleman's hat had succumbed to a sharp gust of wind and been carried into the sea, too far for rescue by anyone but a chance fisherman. Naturally she dragged them back to Dimbola and invited them to take one that belonged to me as a replacement, as though she felt personally responsible for the whims of the weather on her island. Like all visitors they were treated to a tour of the Glass House and its darkroom, which the poor woman somehow mistook, and offered Julia money to snap them both on their holiday. I can still hear her response, but at least I wasn't forced to give away my hat.

1865 London and Isle of Wight

Despite Julia's protestations, and his own small reservations regarding her composition, Watts sent her album to his dealer in London. Buyers were found for the prints almost straight away, proving Julia's fears unfounded and sparking in her a desire to raise capital for purchasing more equipment. A series of images entitled 'Fruits of the Spirit', many of which were the strange Madonna-like prints of Mary Ryan, appealed to a buying public newly grappling with a difficult scientific discovery and keen to hold onto their faith. The prints, depicting love, joy, peace, patience, kindness and goodness, appealed to romantic sentiments and were purchased by visitors to the dealer's rooms within a week of him receiving them.

Buoyed by success, Julia experimented, including imperfections such as streaks and even fingerprints. These would surely help distinguish her superior Art from the conventional photographers. They would never create such deliberate exposure of the scientific method. Why not reveal the Alchemy by carving scratches into her negatives and creasing the prints? What would happen if she threw extra gun cotton into the alcohol with which she sensitised her albumen paper? These early wild exercises she posted to Watts, her champion and mentor, in great parcels of unfinished mounts, complete with the worst defects, to help him better understand her process and advise her on artistic technique. He adored them. The wilder her experiments, the more he praised her Art and she began to create images like dreams and nightmares—stark white faces against deep black backgrounds, deliberately devoid of collodion; faces swirling in chemical mists and ghost-like apparitions framed by the lines of a cracked negative.

'You are possessed, Julia. And you really must stop using the entire house as your laboratory. There are stains on every piece of furniture, and if you ruin another set of table linen then Louisa will probably leave the house entirely.' Charles sat on the conservatory sofa, absent-mindedly stroking Strauss, who had been stuffed and mounted following his demise the previous spring, and now resided in permanent rest on his favourite cushion. 'His fur is much improved on his living coat.'

'I rather miss him growling at guests,' said Julia.

'We must leave that to you now.' He smiled, as usual, at his own joke

'You're right. I'm working too much for the house. I need a studio, and a dedicated darkroom; otherwise I'll be simply unable to manage the work I find I must produce. And there's not enough light in here either, though I'm not sure anywhere could have enough daylight.'

'I am proud of you Julia.' Charles shook out his resplendent white beard. 'I know you think I don't take your work seriously, but your prints are remarkable. Though I wish you would sometimes sit still. I feel as though I've gained an artist and lost a wife.'

'You never did have a silly angel in the house.' Julia took up a piece of paper and sketched her ideal studio. 'You're a better wife and mother than I could be. I know that; everyone knows that. And you know very well that I can't stop. I'll never stop wanting to make things more Beautiful, to show people how Beautiful they really are.'

'Sometimes I think I prefer the way you make the roughest of faces appear, even more than I like the impressions you make with your most handsome subjects.' Charles began to stroke one of the dogs instead, surprised by the movement of its head.

'It is irresistible! The power to change things with a simple manipulation of light and shade. The arrangement of features to tell a story. The way the camera can make anyone look lovelier.' She was lucky to have him; Charles was always wise, always understood exactly what she felt, sometimes long before she realised it herself. And he was right about Dimbola; she resolved to please him by commissioning one of the local craftsmen to build her a studio the next day.

Ripping out the page of her journal she handed Charles the sketch she had finished, a rough working of a timber-framed structure that she intended to build as a studio, glazed all over, including the arch of the roof.

'You appear to have drawn the fowl house,' said Charles, amused.

The following day, Charles and Mary found themselves chasing around the house, trying to catch the dogs, which were, in turn, pursuing the homeless chickens. Jones, meanwhile, was hastily erecting a large pen of wire and stakes to keep them in, while shaking his head at the madness. Louisa, who had regained the scullery and a house free of chemical odour, was much happier. Having chosen the hen house as her studio, Julia moved her darkroom into the coal house next door and was delighted with both.

The coal house was a perfect windowless space and the huge fowl house, which Julia declared was wasted on hens, was renamed The Glass House. A glorious, light-filled studio that captured each last moment of the natural daylight on the island, enabling her to work with sitters for days at a time if needed. Deep-coloured velvet was draped across the glass to give her easy manipulation of the necessary depth of shade; theatrical props were rescued from all over the island and hauled inside. Julia even cleared a space on the wall to hang the certificate of membership she expected to get from the Royal Society on the next application. It was an area that remained empty, accusing her whenever she looked at it. Sometimes she cursed herself for her need for validation, the constant approval she sought in the absence of parental pride. Sometimes she cursed those officious men for their lack of understanding.

'They are charlatans!' Julia could see, without even opening the monogrammed envelope, that the Society had returned the prints she had sent them with a request for recognition. Which meant only one thing. She threw it across the breakfast table, knocking over Charles's eggcup and half-drunk cup of tea and causing Mary to jump back to avoid being splashed.

'Strange word, charlatan,' said Charles, calmly helping himself to another cup. 'From the French, who used it to label a particular kind of musical showman who also sold medicine, so not really a faker of skill, just a seller of something false…'

'For heaven's sake, no one's interested, Charles. It's a disaster!' Without the approval of the Societies there would be no high-profile exhibition, no professional status, no acknowledgement of the work she had put in and no ability to plan for the work she wanted to create. No future for the Artist she wanted to be.

'Why don't we have a look and see what it says?' Mary picked up the offending envelope and opened it carefully so as not to damage the contents. Five prints fell out. Not one bore any resemblance to a human face. Each was a wild swirled experiment, a picture of ghostly forms.

'Did you read their submission instructions?' asked Mary.

'I read them last time, and little good it did then, did it? I thought this time I would show them something new, something extraordinary.' Julia thought she heard a sigh, from whom she couldn't tell. 'Well since you have the letter you may as well tell us what they said.'

Mary took the stiff yellow paper and read its neat copperplate script. Julia tried to guess what it said but Mary's expression was serious, inscrutable. Why would she not read it aloud? Julia's fingers itched to take it back.

'For goodness sake! It's hardly a long letter, surely you're not falling for their waffle?' Unable to bear it any longer, she snatched the letter from Mary's hand and read aloud. 'Honoured that you have chosen to share with us your attempts—Attempts!—show no skill in technique... must recommend to you the excellent book by... and please try to stick to form, the Society is no place for photographs of fairies... Well!'

'There's more,' said Mary gently handing over the second page. 'They do encourage you to submit again, when you're ready.'

'I am ready!' said Julia, holding her head up and thrusting out her chin in a way that made her look like a queen, imperious, daring her authority to be questioned. 'It is they who are not.'

As Julia worked outside the house, with a clear view of the lanes through the full windows, it was easy to spot passers-by and drag them in, sometimes before they knew to what they had agreed. Mary was often more successful at securing subjects. Although she handled just as many chemicals and worked as hard as her mistress, somehow, she remained cleaner, less wild looking.

In the main, her sitters were less enamoured with Julia's Glass House than she was. It was cold or hot depending on the weather outside and contained just one chair amid a great bundle of drapes and backcloths. At the back was a rough wooden castle top, rendered as ramparts, which the gardeners had made for her old theatre. Village children, or Julia's own nieces and grandchildren, were tempted inside with the promise of biscuits and the chance to dress up and asked to climb on the scenery, sometimes with huge wings tied loosely around their shoulders. Julia would pull out their hair-combs and ruffle their hair to get rid of its nursery look until eventually the required anxious, wistful look of cherubim was achieved as the children longed to escape.

With no running water in the coal house, the chemical process became at once more arduous and dangerous. In the summer it was hard enough for Mary to draw one can of water from the well; and each negative required washing with at least nine full cans. In the winter months the water sometimes froze as it poured, leaving Julia furious at the wasted negative. The process took its toll. After a while, Julia noticed that her once soft hands were as raw and red as those of Violetta, but she cared little. Her only Beauty was her Art—and for that she would sacrifice anything.

Very few of her models agreed with such sacrifice, with the notable exception of the housemaid, who once consented to be locked inside the cellar for an entire day to achieve the desired expression for a photograph Julia intended to entitle 'Despair'. Friends and family viewed such unconventional methods with suspicion. Emily Tennyson, heavy with a third expected child, entrusted Hallam and his brother Lionel to Julia's care for a few hours one morning, becoming alarmed when they did not return by suppertime and despatching her maid to Dimbola to fetch them. After several hours of searching they were found, safe but cold and hungry, crouching in the straw of the lean-to where the elderly sheep overwintered. Julia herself, blissfully working in her darkroom, had forgotten all about them in the dream of a successful print.

Filled with remorse, Julia tore down the hill after dark that same day. She clutched prints of the whole day's photography in her hands, and was followed by a team of eight strong men carrying a peace offering of her own grand piano, which she exhorted Emily to play while she handed Alfred the portfolio of her work.

'I have no music in me today,' she protested. 'I am sure that my hands will reveal nothing but the strain of this afternoon's horrors.'

Julia began to apologise again but Alfred, frowning, held up a hand.

'The children are safe and sleeping. Nothing happened except that an artist lost track of time. It happens daily here does it not?' Emily scowled back at him. Julia beamed, delighted he had called her an Artist.

'These are lovely, Julia,' Tennyson continued, holding out an image of Lionel in which the boy had clearly wriggled on her studio's hard chair. His limbs were blurred, but the features of his face were clear and beautiful, framed with a halo of light. 'You have made him a cherubim, fallen from the heavens themselves. Extraordinary indeed when you consider what a little demon he can be.'

'Alfred! He's just a boy.' Emily stopped playing abruptly and flounced over to the pile of photographs. 'But you can hardly see them in this light, I'm straining my eyes to see but I confess I wouldn't recognise my own children.' She peered at the photograph of Lionel.

'That is the beauty of them. While most photographers aim for an exact likeness, what Julia has created is the opposite. Her backdrops are cracked and ruined but her people are softly painted, they all seem to be lit from within. These are portraits made in dreams.'

Julia wanted to dance; instead she lowered her head in feigned modesty. He had found in her Art what she intended. It was years since their first conversations on Beauty in his poems, on the transience of Beauty and the constant creative urge to pin it to the page. At that time, to imagine she could converse with him as an Artist of equal worth was unthinkable. Now it was reality.

Emily examined the rest of the prints with suspicion.

'Would you sit for me too?' Julia held her breath. If she could capture the poet in the way she wanted, it could spark a whole new beginning for her Glass House. She envisaged a parade of famous intellects, begging for her to show them in the light of their fame. If her lens transformed ordinary farmers, just think what fame might add!

'I will need a new portrait for my forthcoming collection. The publisher expects the poems by the end of the month. If you can find the time, then I'm happy to sit for you. It will make a welcome change from the cursed etching they have used in the last three works. That one makes me look like an ancient mariner.'

Julia walked home in a dream, stopping by the stile to admire the light of the full moon as it bathed the fields. Tennyson, the great Tennyson, had called her an Artist; he had praised her work and articulated what she herself had tried to show, that ordinary people could be elegantly transformed and made Beautiful. It was true. She had proved it with her lenses time and time again. But portraits of genius would surely be even better. They would all possess an indefinable light, and she would draw it forth with her lenses, allow their adoring public an insight into their characters.

When she finally reached Dimbola, she let herself in quietly, so as not to disturb the rest of the house, but her mind was alive with possibility. The hour was late, but she could not imagine being able to sleep. She tiptoed into the study and pulled down the arm of the writing desk, smoothed a fresh sheet of velum and filled her little silver pot with ink. By the morning she had written twenty-five lengthy and charming letters, inviting almost all the famous people she had met to sit before her lens.

1867 Kensington

'You have caused me the most extraordinary headache.' Sarah held her hand across her brow in a theatrical gesture of exhaustion and sat heavily in a bower seat covered in blooming tea roses. Guests of all kinds milled across her perfect lawns enjoying pre-dinner drinks and, despite her mock irritation, Julia saw a smile play across her lips at the sight.

Sarah should have been delighted at these people she had brought to her salon, it was hardly Julia's fault that intellectual celebrities were all men. Women were, it appeared, able only be famous for their looks. But it was an old argument and she didn't want to cause a fight by bringing it up. 'Why does anyone need to sit for dinner? It's a beautiful evening.' Julia plucked a tea rose, breathing its heady scent deeply before removing two thorns from the stem and tucking the flower gently behind her sister's ear. 'Have all the dishes piled up together, at the same time, like we did in India, and allow the guests to help themselves. Then they can wander and sit where they like.'

'That's actually a fine idea. A buffet meal. Do you remember the safari suppers in Calcutta?' Without waiting for an answer, Sarah jumped up to brief the staff, almost bumping into Virginia. She was walking purposefully towards the bower with Henry Taylor and Alfred who, despite his claims to hate parties, had refused to miss such a gathering of greats and left Emily at home with the children to indulge his need for deep conversation without feeling as though he needed to keep an eye on them all.

'Alfred has just shown me the portrait you took for his new edition. It is quite splendid.' Virginia leaned in for a kiss. Julia had not seen her in a while and, with surprise, she saw her barely aged at all. Now a mother of five, in her early forties, her porcelain skin was as smooth and plump as it had been in her youth, her hair free of grey. Julia self-consciously raised a hand to her own unwashed and white-streaked hair, piled on top of her head like a basket of washing and fixed with an arsenal of pencils and tortoiseshell combs.

'You look wonderful Virginia.' She could have kicked herself, knowing how much her sister hated such comments. 'I'm very pleased with that print. Alfred looks like an Isaiah or a Jeremiah, quite marvellous and biblical.'

'It makes me look like a dirty monk,' said Tennyson.

'Why Alfred that's exactly what you are! Your aura is most spiritual in that image, it simply shines from the page.' A dirty monk. If only she'd had the wit to call it as such.

'I didn't say that I didn't like it, it's by far my favourite of all the portraits I've suffered, and I've suffered many.'

'It's as fine as your finest lines of poetry,' said Henry admiringly and, between the praise of these two gods, Julia felt she might faint.

'It was almost worth the five years of my life spent in that confounded fowl house.'

'You very much enjoyed it and you are by far the most patient of my subjects.' The man never moved a muscle once she had set her plate; he was probably delighted to have some quiet thinking time.

'We're all helpless in that studio of yours,' said Alfred. 'Unfortunately, thanks to your photographs, people are beginning to recognise me. I may no longer walk the Strand without a dozen people clamouring for me to add my signature to a book or postcard or, yesterday, a railway ticket.'

'It's the price of fame,' said Virginia, looking wistful. The Viscount rushed over to her and she brushed him away with a cross gesture. To be stared at and adored by strangers every time one left the house would seem a heavy burden for one so delicate and Julia still struggled with the way it made her feel half envious and half protective.

'It's the price of portraits. And he's also to blame,' added Alfred, pointing across to Watts who, along with Sarah, was wandering around with a bowl of meat and potatoes and trying to persuade the other guests it was the perfect way to eat. He didn't look convincing. Since he held a large crystal glass filled with claret in his right hand, he had no easy way to get the food into his mouth.

'Come and sit here,' called Julia. 'We only ever eat picnics on the grass, or the sand, at Freshwater at this time of year.'

'Your island does seem to offer a more civilised pace of life. Are you there permanently, Mr Tennyson?' Watts arranged himself carefully on the seat, perching his glass on the arm.

'More or less. I only keep a house in town for business. And Emily almost never comes up. She's always struggled with London.'

'You must come and visit us again Signor,' said Julia. 'It's quite wonderful this time of year.' She was missing it already. There she felt like a queen, here she was back in Sarah's kingdom and for some reason it felt shallow and meaningless. It was not to her taste. The gathered guests spoke only in riddles; at Freshwater the conversation turned serious at the drop of a hat.

'If you promise to keep me from those dreadful watercolourists.' Watts pulled a face.

'They're not all bad, you'll see.' Julia's prediction that the youngest Bonnet would be ostracised from the group for her time in the Glass House had proven quite wrong. Lady Caroline still railed against the dark arts, but Julia's exhibition had slightly altered her. Like most social climbers she was won over by the whiff of celebrity and decided that an eccentric, well-known photographer was infinitely more tolerable than merely an eccentric one.

'Briarsfield, next door to Allingham's house, is up for lease at the moment,' said Tennyson thoughtfully. 'It has a very nice garden.'

'It's a perfect house!' said Julia, 'Though the neighbours leave a little to be desired.' Allingham, who was perfectly pleasant, had refused to sit for Julia on numerous occasions. He often had visitors of note, too, people not part of her own set; it was infuriating to have them only yards away and completely out of reach. 'You must come and see it the moment we get back.'

'Perhaps you're right,' agreed Watts. 'Perhaps it's time I joined the Freshwater Circle.'

Before she left London, Julia determined to take Virginia's portrait and risked the wrath of Sarah by setting up the camera in her siting room again, this time monopolising a guest bathroom for developing. To darken the room, she hung the only thing she could find big enough to cover it across the large window; the counterpane from the room she always stayed in at Little Holland House, a thin spread of Indian silk embroidered with star-shaped flowers, which made it necessary for Mary Ryan to distract Sarah in another part of the house until the deed was done. It had belonged to their mother and, aside from a few items of jewellery, was the closest thing they possessed to a family heirloom.

Taking an attractive image of Virginia was not an easy task, much to Julia's surprise. While she found it understandable that Alfred's friends, all those splendidly ungroomed men of letters, might need plenty of time in front of the lens before a suitably flattering image was shot, she had assumed that Virginia's classically sculpted profile might prove rather easier. When she eventually admitted defeat and put down her plates, her sister was exhausted.

'There, that's enough now. Your beauty clearly can't be improved upon. You're quite worthless to me as a subject.'

This, coming after a steady stream of grumbling complaint as she smeared and hefted her plates, was too much for poor Virginia. She burst into tears.

'I don't know why you weep Virginia; I should be weeping. This afternoon has cost me many times what I can afford in chemicals, plates and paper. It's money and time I could have spent on a subject of greatness.'

'I'm very sorry that you find your family such a waste of time,' sniffed Virginia.

Good god she was still beautiful even as she wept. Bright tears hung from the lengths of her eyelashes and dropped gently onto her cheeks. 'You know very well that's not what I meant, don't twist my words. It's our last day here. There are men of great achievement in the drawing room and now there's too little light for them.' Having finished the careful packing of her equipment Julia moved the furniture back into its customary place, spotting a large silver-nitrate stain on the armchair, which she hastily covered with a pair of cushions.

'And now I'm to be neither one of your famous people nor your fair women.'

'That's nonsense, Virginia, it's simply my style, I try to draw the light from within people to make them fair, but you are fair enough already. Painters adore you, do they not? Why even Burne-Jones remarked upon your beauty yesterday in the garden.'

'They all say that, that I'm beautiful, but they say nothing but that!' burst out Virginia in a torrent of emotion. Her marriage, though peaceable, had not been a huge success in terms of intellectual compatibility. While Julia and Charles discussed everything together, from the running of the household to evolutionary theory, the Viscount spoke to Virginia little regarding anything of matter. For most of their marriage he had avoided sharing important news, telling her she need not trouble her beautiful head about such things. 'I have the same loves and

199

thoughts and ideas as anyone, but apparently I've no substance. Why does everyone see your inner beauty and not mine?'

Calling on Mary to help her, Julia led her still weeping sister up the stairs and settled her to sleep on her own bed. She pulled their mother's counterpane up under her chin and dabbed lavender water onto her forehead. 'She's delicate Mary, as she has always been. See to it that she's not disturbed or exerted.'

Far from inviting Julia's sympathy, her younger sister's cry for help served only to increase her determination, both to make a name for herself as a Female Artist and further the cause of Photography as a valid and socially relevant form of Art. On returning to Dimbola, her first action was to reapply for membership of the Royal Photographic Society. Mary found her sitting on the floor of the long white gallery, surrounded by a jumble of prints and scribbled notes.

'You're going to miss supper,' she observed, knowing better than to question what was happening.

'Supper can hang!' Julia threw up her hands and a thin washed print of the dirty monk fluttered to the floor. Why was Mary even asking? She knew how important it was for these pictures to be seen by as many people as possible. Unless her prints hung in the national galleries she may as well stop working. Recognition was the holy grail of artistic endeavour and, after all these years, she deserved it. 'This is vital work that simply can't wait another day. I'm gathering pictures to support another application to the Society. Unless I'm awarded membership, I'm unable to submit my work to exhibitions. And I'm running out of time. The Summer show at the academy is in barely three months.'

'That's not going to be easy.' Mary sat on the floor beside her, smoothing her skirts tidily. She picked up and sorted the scattered prints.

'No, it isn't,' Julia agreed. 'It's yet another group of men who think women should not have ideas or talents of their own. And in this case, I'm afraid they know nothing about the Art of Photography.'

'Talking like that won't get you membership,' Mary cautioned. 'And unless you do you won't be able to sell your prints in any quantity. You'd do better to play along with them and let them think you agree.'

'I care very little for sales,' said Julia. 'I simply wish for more people to see my work.'

'You forget who it is that orders your materials. You burn through it all. And the results are wonderful.' Mary held up her hands to calm the inevitable protest. 'But you can't pretend that this is just a hobby. It must surely pay for itself.'

Julia thought of the crates of chemical vials, the specially coated paper, the single-use glass plates. Mary was right; they were expensive. She knew their entire household existed on the profits of the Ceylon estates, an income that fluctuated wildly year on year and made no provision for savings. But it wasn't something she cared about. Money was always found, somehow. It struck her that Mary may know more about the family's finances than she did. The girl was sharp, had lived through years of surviving on nothing and must be acutely aware of money.

'If I might offer a suggestion, ma'am,' Mary said, 'I think the Society will want to see examples of your work that better suit the conventions.' She pulled a portrait of Watts from the pile Julia had set to one side. If the viewer did not know the painter well, he would surely not recognise him from this. Facial features were indistinguishable in the deep gloom and he seemed about to sink inside his oversized greatcoat and disappear.

'It's a perfect image,' protested Julia, 'A masterpiece of definition within blackness. It's very difficult to get an image at all in such a thick wash. Besides, this is an exact representation of the Signor's mood.' She remembered the day well. It followed an afternoon at Little Holland House Watts had spent entirely with Virginia and her husband, a man he descried later, knee-deep in claret, as a coward and a simpleton. Afterwards he had hung his head and cried for letting her go while Julia stroked his hair. Cruel, really, to have got him before the lens at all, but the temptation had been too great.

'To you, yes. And me. And to anyone who knows the afternoon in question. But the Society is traditional. It says in their literature they base their membership acceptance "purely on technical skill." You're only allowed to submit five prints of your own. Why not make those five more conventional?'

Mary took the print and placed it on the pile of rejects, avoiding Julia's gimlet stare. She drew from the other pile one of Julia's choreographed haymaking scenes at Freshwater, portraits of strong honest peasants steadfast in their gaze at the lens. The image, though taken in the conservatory rather than the studio, was filled with a sense of the island's clear light. Julia sighed. In her mind she had moved the Art Form years beyond these original amateur works.

'Well this one stays.' She pulled out Tennyson's dirty monk and Mary nodded, picking her battles. 'And this one?' Henry Taylor sat in a brooding pose, his heavy-lidded eyes turned down to his hands, bunched into fists. So keen was the contrast of light and dark that each strand of hair on his head and beard were distinguishable and so full he looked like a sad and elderly lion. Julia's customary softness of focus could only be seen around his eyes.

'Absolutely,' agreed Mary. 'They can't criticise anything in its technical execution. Why does Mr Taylor always look so sad in his photographs? I've ever really seen him anything but happy.'

'He believes he must be serious to be considered seriously,' said Julia, rummaging through the pile and discarding another part of the collection. 'Unfortunately, people consider his work too serious already, especially his plays. How many do we have now? Four? What about this one?' she passed Mary a print of William Holman-Hunt, dressed in a badly wrapped cloth turban and striped Turkish tunic, his thin, youthful beard spread and his face set in a reproachful stare.

'Good,' agreed Mary. 'You know you only have to conform until you are a member. That will allow you to sell your prints widely. Then, of course, you can do as you please,' she hastily collected the permissible prints before Julia changed her mind, 'Shall I wrap these in paper?'

Membership was duly, if grudgingly, accorded the following month. Julia's certificate arrived with a curt note, congratulating her for achieving the status of first female member of the Photographic Society of London, but exhorting her to use the medium for realistic purposes.

'The selecting committee,' she read aloud to Mary, 'do "not wish to see subjects in any pose other than the standard portrait, and especially not as elves and fairies." Fiddlesticks! "We wish Mrs Cameron the best of success with her camera and hope that she will continue with her practice, producing conventional portraits, landscapes and still lives that she may proudly call technically perfect." I'm proud of all my Photographs thank you very much.'

'Well done,' said Mary.

'Well done to you,' replied Julia. 'Given this absolute nonsense of a letter I believe you were quite right, I don't think I would have been awarded this for the first prints I chose. Heavens above it gets worse! Look at this.' She thrust the letter across the table and Mary began to read.

'They do seem rather full of their own importance.'

'They are insufferable! A hobby photographer, that's what they called me, a hobby photographer.' It was an insult to her Art. People like Tennyson and Watts had been calling her an Artist for years. If they recognised her talent, why could the Societies not see it? Why were they so pompous and old-fashioned? And why did she feel such a craving for their official recognition? It shouldn't matter to her. But it did.

1867 Freshwater

Membership of the hallowed society was granted the day Herschel made his first visit to Freshwater. Julia, filled with excitement at the thought of welcoming her oldest friend to her home, had spent the previous week decorating the ceiling of his room with deep blue paint and silver paper stars; individually cutting them and mapping their constellations accurately before pinning them, one by one, into the plaster.

Herschel, now living in London as Astronomer Royal, was already a great age. Yet he remained as playful as he had been when they met at the Cape and his conversation was equally stimulating. Mary adored him and wanted him to teach her how to use the telescope in the tower that joined the houses of Dimbola. Charles clamoured to take him off for a long walk to explore the island and rekindle old interests. Julia would permit neither. Desperate for her dear friend to see her talent and skill, and still incensed by the inference of the committee that her work was merely insignificant dabbling in technique, she dragged Herschel off to the Glass House before he had even seen his room.

'Something's not right,' she muttered, staring at the reversed image on the third plate she tried. 'Something… something…' Herschel, for whom the experience was a delightful game, peered into the corners of the studio, which were stuffed with props and clothes.

'Perhaps I should put on a cloak?' he enquired politely 'Or a turban? I've barely had a chance to freshen up after travelling. It might be useful to cover my hair.'

'Your hair, that's it!' Julia dragged him back to the house and up to the bathroom, where she insisted that he let her wash his fine white hair. She did so with vigour, drying it so roughly that it stood up around his head like electrical currents. Bemused, weary from his journey and now forbidden to speak, the astronomer sat patiently through his plate, moving only when released. The resulting portrait was declared A Masterpiece.

'It is extraordinary it should be the camera, the other side of the mirror, the instrument with which I captured your interest those years ago, that has given you your voice.' Herschel studied his image intently. 'You create a poetry and mystery far removed from the work of the ordinary photographer. It is deeply me.'

Herschel's soft white hair stood out like a halo, focussing attention on his face and giving it an intensity of expression that was almost divine. It was exactly as she had intended. He appeared as a saint.

'I will never allow another photographer near me,' he promised, much to Julia's delight. She signed and numbered a copy of the print, and showed him the letter from the Photography Society's selection committee.

'I am officially a Photographer now. You may, if you wish, use this as your official portrait as royal astronomer. Really it is only thanks to Mary, who persuaded me to send my most conventional portraits, otherwise I do believe she's right, they would have said no.'

'They are fools.' He shrugged. 'You would do better to create your own society. Why not start one here on your island?'

'Because it would be a society of one,' laughed Julia. 'I want people to see my prints. But I'll prove them wrong about your light writing, you'll see. Using light to reveal the sitter's inner life is a trick that painters have used for years. It's a technique I believe other photographers will emulate. And my prints are so successful, even now, they'll find them hard to ignore.'

'You will be ignored at their peril!' said Herschel. 'Must you join them?'

'I fear I must. They control all the exhibitions in London, and without membership I would not be able to participate. But I won't submit the tedious works they wish to see. My aspirations are to ennoble Photography and secure for it the character and uses of High Art, sacrificing nothing of Truth by all possible devotion to Poetry and Beauty.' Julia swept up the print and raised it heavenwards. 'And the very first one I shall exhibit will be this!'

Briarsfield proved as perfect as his friends had claimed and Watts moved in at the end of the summer, bringing with him all the things from the studio Sarah had made for him in her breakfast room. Unable to let anyone else touch his things, she helped him pack, wrapping brushes and paints into scraps of oilcloth. Julia listened amused to her sister's dramatic outpouring. What a reversal of fortune, indeed.

'It's worse than losing a child! Dear Signor. I did not anticipate feeling so alone. You've lived with us for so many years I can hardly remember a time before we met.' She struggled to keep an even tone and Julia willed her to cry, to show something other than her customary cool collectedness. Mama had been the same; though she was prone to bursts of anger that showed the stress she felt from keeping her emotions to herself. Sarah never cracked and it was irritating.

'Please don't be sad, it's a new beginning!' said Watts, cheerfully patting the back of her hand. 'Briarsfield is perfectly large enough for you and Thoby to stay. Why not come and join the Freshwater Circle in the summer?'

'Is that what it's become? A Circle? Run by my sister and the Tennysons I suppose, with all the visitors that great poet attracts.' Sarah gripped the back of the kitchen chair until her fingers whitened.

'I've never heard anyone call it anything else,' said Watts, oblivious.

'Then I will invite the Freshwater Circle here to stay as soon as they can attend.'

How like Sarah to try to poach everyone. Clearly, she didn't understand the difference between a salon and a circle. She would soon enough. Watts would tempt them to the island eventually and she looked forward to the day she'd be in charge. For now, though, Julia had little need to visit London. With a steady stream of famous guests, her Glass House was occupied most of the time. Alfred, thoroughly disheartened with sitting in her uncomfortable studio, threw her his many guests like sacrificial lambs. Browning, who had already enjoyed considerable commercial recognition for his dramatic monologues, Julia considered to be less a poet because of his smart coat, society manners and neat whiskers. He seemed like someone Sarah would enjoy having at Little Holland House. She left him sitting two hours on the hard studio chair as she went off to fetch more equipment and got side tracked. His ignorance about the technicalities of photography enabled her to persuade him the exposure had actually taken that long and he was surprised to receive rather an ordinary print the next day, along with a curt comment that Julia disliked his hat.

Tennyson threw them all into Julia's hands, warning his guests they would have to do whatever she told them, or it would be the worse for them and the ordeal would be prolonged. He was not wrong. One actress was made to clutch at the ankle of a poet for hours at a stretch so Julia could find the right arrangement for a study of Hippolyta. A politician suffered the indignity of a composition interview without his trousers, when Julia burst into his bedroom to talk it through. One esteemed American poet was practically thrown into the Glass House and Tennyson was seen half running away, calling over his shoulder a promise to come back later to see what was left of him. It wasn't much. Darkness enveloped the final print, Longfellow's coat barely distinguishable from the curtain behind him, a furious helpless look on his face. He faced away from the lens, his right arm across his body, his hand clutching the fabric of his coat as though warding off demons. Julia declared it An Enormous Success.

Stories from the Glass House:
Lady Caroline Eastnor

Mrs Cameron tried to drag me into her hen house on countless occasions and I refused her every time except one. Whenever I look at that image, I wish I had acquiesced, that I might know what else she could have done with me. But I was proud. I had a reputation to maintain. And our views on Art were wildly different. Entering the Glass House felt like capitulation, but when I saw my portrait I realised what she had tried to tell me from the outset, that women should always be sisters, first and foremost, whatever they think of one another.

I knew that she was unconventional, but the first time I saw her album of prints I don't mind admitting I was shocked. Iago—I believe it is now in the hands of the Royal Academy though I can barely believe they would show it—was the worst. A portrait of a man, shirt unbuttoned, hair ruffled, not quite handsome but so intensely male he might appear so. By the look on his face he was transported in a moment of madness, or lust, or possibly both. It was quite impossible for any genteel person to look at. Worse, I knew the man, a local blacksmith. I would hardly be able to look at him the same way. And I have no doubt that, had Mrs Cameron understood what I was thinking, she would have been delighted.

She had no reason to like me. I had been unkind to her, as I said. I'm afraid I viewed her as some sort of gypsy, not quite fit for my circle. But she always ignored my dislike, as though one day she knew she would bring me to my senses. When she heard about my eyes, the degeneration that prevented me from doing any close work by candlelight, she initially invited me to live at Dimbola, just like that, extraordinary really. She was so terribly impulsive, free of respect for social convention. But it was only after dark I struggled and so each night for two months Julia, or Mary, came to my house to read to me for an hour, a gesture so unbelievably touching I could barely speak to thank them. They organised others too, so a different reader comes every evening and I'm able to choose my own books.

Her portrait of me was strong, and beautiful in its strength. The way the light played across the cheekbones and squared the jaw. The simplicity of the pose; the determination in the angle of my neck. She asked me to wear what made me feel like an artist and I chose a striped dress that I thought was daring. If I knew she could make me look like that I may not have been so proud. What she managed to find in me was extraordinary. It is her and me. It is all strong women.

1868 Kensington

Each morning, before she prepared her plates and draped her studio, Julia would sit at the desk by the bay window at the front of the house and write to a new potential conquest. Poets and painters, scientists and politicians, all the great names were added to a growing register she kept on a scroll, pinned to the wall in the study and annotated every evening before she shut down the lamp. She drew inspiration from the great taxonomists of the day, many of whom were, themselves, pinned by the wings to her carefully curated albums. Hopeful names were drawn from magazines and newspapers. Charles was frequently exasperated to find an article partially obscured where Julia's sweeping pen had circled another name.

Mary expressed her concern that such ambition would not make her happy. But Julia listened to neither. She wrote to her potential conquests care of their publishers, of the newspapers, via any network of her own society that may be able to achieve an introduction, sometimes going back to connections in Calcutta to ask for details on an individual that may help her cause. Often the latter approach was the most successful. A creative environment to equal Sarah's was already in full bloom on the Isle of Wight, with Watts having joined the community permanently, and Tennyson the bright star of the constellation around which others gathered. Still her letters did bring many more names to the Glass House, not least because she made no secret of the fact that they would meet these revered persons once they arrived.

Only one conquest was tempting enough to persuade Julia to bring her studio to London again, a massive undertaking involving chartering several modes of transport and the constant accompaniment of two strong men to lift it in and out. Porters without knowledge of the delicacy of the instrument could not be trusted anywhere near it and, even with such security, she still insisted on travelling in the hold, so that she could fold one arm around the lens and thereby cradle it against the indignities of the journey. She revelled in the amount of kit she needed. Who was to tell her now that Photography was not for faint-hearted women? She was the foremost Dark Artist in the country and her Studio was by far the most Scientific!

Glass plates were packed in straw and oilcloth and labelled as dangerous livestock, to prevent the chance that they may be handled with anything other than the utmost reverence. Vials of chemicals were despatched separately, one after the other, as any upset of their volatile contents may lead to violent explosions. On this last export of her studio she was in such haste to meet the specified agreed time that in the resulting commotion she forgot to write to the Prinseps and warn them of her arrival, upsetting Sarah's personal quest to capture Robert Browning and causing a family rift that lasted the best part of a year.

It was all worth it. All the upheaval and sulking. There could hardly be a better opportunity. Thomas Carlyle, the Scottish essayist, historian and social commentator, was visiting London to present a series of lectures to the Royal Society on the subject of 'heroes'. Here was surely someone who could help her to understand the whole charade of fame, as well as make an excellent conquest for her own portfolio. His was a household name and yet no one knew what he looked like. If she could capture him in the spirit of her now well-known Dirty Monk photograph then the name alone could secure her an exhibition, perhaps at the newly opened Kensington Museum.

'All history revolves around great men. When you really consider it, no progress would be possible without such key figures.' Carlyle leaned back on Sarah's dining chair and Julia wondered whether he might actually snap its legs. Such a huge, solid, presence of a man; rugged, tough and entirely out of place in the drawing rooms of London. 'All history revolves around great men and without them there is no progress.'

Tempting to believe him. But the pantomime of public adoration was troubling and what he described was not far from the awful experiences of poor Virginia. 'Don't you worry that you are creating a cult of hero worship? There'll be many people who don't read someone's books, but who would like an autograph, something signed as a memento of meeting their hero. Does that not concern you?'

Carlyle grimaced, 'Hero worship is both fitting and necessary if the great thinkers of any age are to be allowed to fulfil their potential and genuinely contribute to a society. In no age is this more important than our own, an age where industrialisation and the commercialisation of life has blinkered the public to true greatness.'

Julia was taken by his looks and manner. A hard-faced, unsmiling man whose appearance gave his words the veneer of absolute authority, Carlyle was exactly the kind of sitter to test her theory of fame. Now she was more determined than ever to bring these men to the world through the extraordinary medium of her close-up lens. And he had all the answers she needed in her search for the meaning of fame and the achievement of greatness, even if he wasn't likeable.

Thoby, delighted with the prospect of interrogating Carlyle over dinner, was a willing ally in the covert operation to set up another makeshift studio at Little Holland House. Initially removing Sarah to their daughter's house in Barnes, he was forced to call her back again when he realised that Carlyle's wife, Jane, had accompanied him on the visit and would be bereft of female company. It was an unhappy arrangement. Jane, who had no children, and Sarah, who talked incessantly of her brood of seven, did not warm to each other and found the conversation so awkward Charles was brought in to rescue the proceedings. Julia worked away in blissful ignorance in the back kitchen, where Thoby had firmly wheeled her equipment to prevent a repeat of the previous damage to the best guest bathrooms.

The sitting was long. Although his wife was well known as a domestic tyrant Carlyle was not used to being ordered to keep silent and the experience did not suit him. Julia trapped him in the kitchen on the hardest of chairs, surrounded by a makeshift curtain fashioned from Thoby's travelling cloaks hung across broom handles. Carlyle, far from the promised hero worship of his invitation, felt as though he endured a bizarre afternoon of amateur dramatics, pushed and pulled by the most unsympathetic of stagehands. The more he spoke, the less Julia warmed to him and the harsher her treatment became.

By dinner the deed was done and four portrait prints, facing various directions, were presented to the gathered table. They were masterful. Carlyle appeared to be chiselled in the startling contrast of shades, his craggy face rough-hewn from rock. His broad brow was furrowed from the anguish of the chair, his dark eyes deeply brooding and his shock of white hair and white cuffs framed the whole so perfectly all attention rested on his expression. Julia knew they were her finest yet, though they bore no resemblance to any other photographic portrait. Pride swelled as she watched the guests' faces. Surprise from Sarah, no doubt shocked her big sister had finally grown into the Artist she'd yearned to be. Approval from Watts, always gratifying, though something she'd come to expect. Mild horror from Jane, which probably caused the look of amusement on Charles; he was incorrigible, how could he not take this seriously? Carlyle himself was harder to work out. She willed him to approve.

'He is a Michelangelo!' said Watts joyfully. He had valiantly accompanied Julia as her mentor, risking the patronage of the Prinseps in the process, and when he saw the print confided in Julia that he was delighted the expedition was not the disaster it had earlier promised to be. 'I knew you proved to be fierce competition for painters, but this is the first photographic print I've seen that so closely resembles a sculpture. Bravo. It is one of your finest portraits.'

'There is something in the character of this man that resembles the strength of rock,' replied Julia, ignoring the disgusted look that his wife was directing to her end of the table. 'I have never had anyone quite like him before my lens. The Art of Photography is not, as you know, an exact Art but a process of drawing out from the subject whatever masterful elements of character should emerge.'

'Anyone who manages a successful print for you would need the strength of rock,' said Carlyle. 'But you have made me a hero. And, though I never wish to sit for you again, for that I'm grateful.'

My Dear Herschel

A great change has come about in my Art since you last sat before my lens. You've opened my eyes to a new form of Portrait, one that flatters the mind of the subject and draws his intellect from the very page. I've enclosed for you an album of these prints, entitled Great Men, for you to view at your leisure. Many of these men will be known to you: Tennyson, Holman-Hunt, Browning and Trollope. But it was Thomas Carlyle who taught me to see them as they really are, not just distinguished or famous men, but Great Men.

When I've had such men before my camera, my whole Soul has endeavoured to do its duty towards them in recording faithfully the greatness of the inner as well as the features of the outer man. The Photograph thus taken has been almost the embodiment of a prayer. Every print I make is become an act of homage; necessary to highlight the contribution of these great thinkers and men of letters to the society they helped to create. Yours was the first of these that made me realise this and put to words the process of this creation. So, I hope that you enjoy your gift, for you, above all others, deserve my thanks. You were my first teacher, and to you I owe all my first experience and insights.

Ever in Your Debt,

Julia

1868 Isle of Wight

Julia's appearance grew increasingly eccentric. Free with her use of chemical dyes, she sported long streaks of violet on her arms and throughout her greying hair; rough cracked skin developed on her face and hands from the length of time she spent working outside. The lure of the Glass House was stronger than anything, or anyone, in her life. When not actively working, she was furiously penning hopeful letters, inviting celebrities to be immortalised in the new Photographic Art. Mary, keen to support her guardian's burgeoning career and knowing only too well how hard she would need to work to make any kind of commercial success, took it on herself to run the household.

After the London Photographic Society rejected eighteen of the twenty prints she had sent for an exhibition, Julia threw herself into a fit of despair. Not least because she had sent two of the men from the village to deliver them by hand, ready mounted on large boards, which had cost her a small fortune. The prints had been returned by standard post, the week before the exhibition start date and most were irreparably damaged by careless carriage. Perhaps it was her own fault; she should never have allowed herself to be proud of her work. This time she had assumed that they would bend to her will. Was that foolish? No, they were foolish; they were ignorant too. Why should she chastise herself when it was their mistake not to accept her prints?

'Along with the temerity to ruin my priceless Art they have sent me this!' Julia waved the offending letter in the faces of Mary and Charles, who were valiantly attempting to finish a light breakfast of Louisa's wildly spiced kedgeree. 'This! They claim my Photographs are possessed of a complete absence of definition, as though they were amateur line sketches in charcoal! Sketchy they've called them... sketchy!'

'It's not the first time the critics have proved themselves unwilling,' said Charles, clearly trying to be helpful. Julia gave him a look intended to show him that he was not and he retreated.

'Out of focus!' Julia fumed. 'Only the focus I use can create what I can with my Art. The roundness of form and feature, the modelling of flesh and limb as though painted, or even sculpted, as the Signor so kindly remarked. They call it out of focus. I call it the only work of focus they will ever have seen!' She threw herself into the chair next to Charles, pulling down his newspaper and thrusting the letter onto his plate. Adjusting his spectacles along his elegant nose he picked up the letter carefully, removing the flakes of rice and fish, and began to read.

'You needed their introduction to submit to other exhibitions, and to the museums,' said Mary calmly, handing Julia a plate of buttered toast and a pot of thick-cut marmalade. Julia nodded, spreading one of the slices, enjoying the sharp tang of burnt orange skin. Louisa always made the very best marmalade.

'Must you really have their approval?' continued Mary.

'What do you mean?' Julia felt wary. Approval, from everyone, was all she craved. These pompous critics must be educated in the way of her Art until they saw it for what it was. Why else was she working like this unless it was to be recognised? She had finally found a way to capture Beauty and it simply must be shared.

'Do you need them to approve of every single one of your prints, or are you happy to exhibit them elsewhere? You have their letters now. They won't be able to strip you of your membership.'

'That's true.' Julia began to feel calmer.

'Would you not try to get your prints included in the other exhibitions? There's one in Scotland in the Autumn, the annual showing of the Edinburgh Photographic Society, I've been asking. I wrote to Mr Colnaghi. You know there are loads of shows in Germany, where photography fares even better than here. They're far more advanced, Herschel was describing that to us the last time he visited and with his connections there he could help. They might be more advanced, but I bet they're not doing what you're doing with your portraits.'

It was a long speech for Mary, and she sat, with her hands folded on her lap, a slight tinge of pink on her cheeks the only sign that she felt herself brave. Julia could not have loved her more.

They set to work without delay. Within three months of their conversation, a series of prints was exhibited in Edinburgh, and a second in Dublin, both to broad critical acclaim. Julia won a bronze medal at her first exhibition in Berlin, followed by gold in the same exhibition in the subsequent year. Medals! Huge and shining and testament to the opinions of others. Her Photography was most certainly not just a hobby. She had precious metal discs to prove it. Even the Signor did not have medals. Such accolades were a New Reward for a New Art Form. If they weren't so heavy she would have worn them around her neck. Instead she had them mounted and framed and hung in the entrance hall of Dimbola Lodge. They would be the first things that visitors saw.

Mary herself presented Fruits of the Spirit to the British Museum and was thrilled to convey the news that the South Kensington Museum intended to purchase a further twenty. With some encouragement they were persuaded to give Julia an exhibition room of her own in May, and she set to work on the plans, finding time to invite the Signor as the first guest of honour.

1868 Dimbola Lodge

Charles's illness was a shock to Julia, a stark reminder of their difference in age and the first time she had really been conscious of it. The fever drew his cheeks, flushed his skin and took his appetite until the flesh hung in folds from his bones. She saw he was old. As she sat by his bed for hour after hour, watching his burning cold shivers, she told herself that if he didn't recover it would be her fault. Hadn't she neglected many of her duties as a wife, as well as failed her daughter? Just as their children were grown, a time when they should have been drawing towards each other, rediscovering their friendship and interests, she had run off to chase her creative dream, leaving him to fend for himself. The pair of them had never really talked about it. Why had she always just assumed that he would understand?

Looking down on him as he slept, Julia realised she had always made a lot of assumptions. She would have given anything for the chance to show her gratitude to him for the wonderful life they had led, for the freedom she enjoyed. There must be few husbands in the world who would have been so tolerant and understanding. Against all odds she had enjoyed a marriage full of happiness and had never shown him how grateful she was. She had taken it for granted, and now it may be too late. It mustn't be too late. What was the use in finding Art if she was to lose Charles?

Contrite, and wracked with guilt, Julia stopped working for the first time since she was given a camera. Tenderly she nursed her husband for a fortnight, asking Mary to cancel visitors to the Glass House and shooing everyone away from the sick room. On Louisa's advice she laid rosemary stalks in bowls of boiling water on the floor, wrapped his head with cotton and his feet with mustard plasters. Remembering Calcutta, she arranged their carved wooden pantheon along the dresser to watch over him, and peeled onions and garlic to place in the folds of his sheets, by his chest.

Doctor Walpole, a trim, impeccably dressed man with a profound knowledge of modern science and a deep mistrust of eccentricity, found Julia's methods exasperating. 'The man needs warmth and rest, not talismans,' he chided, returning every couple of days to supervise the movement of his patient during the changing of the sweat-soaked sheets. On the tenth day his face became grave; he took Julia to one side. 'Is there anyone that should be here with you?'

'I prefer to nurse him myself.' Julia refused to allow others to help or sit in vigil, fearful that the moment she turned away something terrible would happen.

'Another family member, perhaps, someone to assist with the burden of care. You're in danger of becoming ill yourself if you do not rest.'

Why was he so concerned? Surely if she became ill his bill would just increase. No, she would stay; it was her duty. 'I am quite well, thank you.'

'I have to tell you, Mrs Cameron, I'm not entirely sure your husband will recover. He grows very weak and is not able to take on enough fluids. You must prepare yourself, at best, for a long illness and a longer recovery. It will not be possible to nurse him alone.'

The look on Doctor Walpole's face was troubling.

'Thank you so much for your concern, but he's strong, the strongest of men. I'll call for you if we see any further deterioration.' Julia stood to close the discussion. What ridiculous words. Charles would never succumb to a fever. He'd faced worse in India. Though he was old now, older than she cared to admit, and if she didn't write then Juliette would never forgive her if anything happened, she had always loved him more.

Swallowing her pride, she wrote straight away, asking Juliette to visit without the children, in case they succumbed to the fever as well, but really because she hated to see the way they were fussed over. If Juliette didn't allow them to get a little messy and muddy, they would never grow up at all. At least she had always given her own children freedom. Though in Juliette's case no amount of freedom from the family had seemed enough.

'I can barely believe the speed of your arrival. I hope Edward will forgive my insistence.' Julia didn't notice her daughter's haunted guilt, any more than she'd noticed her own dry skin and tired red eyes. She was dressed in a plain grey smock, a shawl of red openwork across her shoulders, her usually wild hair brushed and pinned into a neat loaf shape, a shocking semblance of normality.

'When did you last sleep?'

Julia shrugged. She couldn't remember. What did it matter? She wasn't the one who was ill.

Juliette called Louisa to bring a tray of hot food, then fetched her a large pillow and a woollen blanket, arranging it around her in the chair when she'd eaten.

'I thought you might tell me to go to bed,' she said sleepily, stretching into the blanket like a cat.

'What would be the point? I know how you are. Mary says you've been here for the best part of two weeks. She seems terribly worried about you. It would seem foolish to finish yourself off at father's... bedside.'

Julia knew she had almost said 'deathbed'. It was frightening how old he looked, with his long white hair spread on the pillow, his beard full of moonlight, stretching silvery white across the counterpane. 'Thank you, but we will manage.' She stifled a yawn, soothed by the blanket. It was good to begin to let go, to have someone else care for her.

'You wrote to me, though, to come. Did you think that…'

'It was a purely selfish request,' interrupted Julia, afraid to articulate her thoughts. 'I've been much in my own thoughts in this room and I just wanted to see you. To talk.' She had Mary for that and Juliette knew it. Mary had always been easier for her to get along with, but closeness and conversation were all she had ever wanted from Juliette. From a young age her daughter had been closed, perfectly self-contained in a way Julia found difficult to penetrate; she had always taken it personally. A note of sadness hung in the silence between them and for a moment Julia thought they might embrace.

'Your Scottish exhibition was a great success,' Juliette observed.

'Thank you. It was a relief to me. I had wondered whether anyone else could really see my Art in the same way as myself and my small Circle.' Juliette had never seemed to approve before, despite being the one to start it all off. Why this sudden interest in her work? Was it possible she had changed her mind? It was too much to hope that Juliette would be proud of her achievements after all. Perhaps she would like to see the medals? A stab of guilt drew her mind back to the bedside. For now, they were here for Charles. 'I've wondered in the last days if it's really what I should have craved. There's a great deal more to happiness than chasing recognition. I suppose you saw the Edinburgh Review?'

'I visited the exhibition. With Edward. And don't try to tell me that you feel guilty for your success. Father would be furious with you for such thinking, and you know very well I tell the truth. He's always been your absolute champion, even when you had no calling that was recognised. He is happy for your success, you should know that. Whatever happens.' Juliette looked directly into her mother's eyes, cool and collected. 'As am I.'

It appeared that, since the effusive praise in the Edinburgh Review, Juliette had begun to look at her mother's work with fresh eyes. Julia had sent her dozens of prints over the years, all signed and meticulously numbered. Many featured her nieces and nephews, and many more the village children or the offspring of visitors photographed only once or twice. Yet only since the review had she looked at them properly. It proved everything Julia had assumed about value and recognition.

'Your portraits show a tenderness and compassion that people are only just beginning to understand, myself included.'

'I didn't ever think to hear you say it.' Julia gave a sleepy smile. 'Can I change these clothes now?'

'Not for one moment do I believe you are dressed so sensibly to please me.' Juliette looked across at her father. His bedclothes moved in time with his ragged breath. 'I believe you're making pacts with God. They don't work you know.'

'That's just where you are wrong, Juliette. I made a pact with the gods a long time ago. And they brought me you.'

1869 Isle of Wight

In a moment of guilt over moving his studio to Freshwater, Watts built a brand-new home, The Briary, in the grounds of Briarsfield and offered it to the Prinseps as unspoken recompense for the devastation of their salon. Now he and the Taylors were living on the island for most of the year, Julia had gathered most of the Holland House set to her island and it was virtually impossible for Sarah and Thoby to continue. Designed to his exacting specifications, The Briary was a labour of love: a cottage of artistic proportions, with an intricately woven pattern of thatch and an Arts and Crafts interior. With their children grown and their beautiful gardens attracting mainly political thinkers, there was little enough cultural life left to keep them in London and they moved as soon as the roof was secured, unable to unpack for several weeks while the decorators finished the plasterwork. Setbacks caused them to move in with Watts, initially temporarily but, after a time, the idea of moving out again was forgotten. Sarah was particularly reluctant to downsize to cottage life and The Briary remained empty, an expensive folly in the grounds of their more imposing communal home.

All of the Freshwater Circle were delighted to welcome them back, not least because Julia's calling now took so much of her time that, while the company at Dimbola was always wonderful, the catering and entertainments left much to be desired; even distinguished guests were left to fend for themselves. Sarah's tireless organisation restored comfort to the proceedings and, for Alfred and Charles at least, Thoby provided a reliable intellect and a wealth of information on any subject. 'Less like conversation and more like leafing through the pages of an encyclopaedia,' declared Charles, who credited much of his return to good health to the long hours he spent with Thoby during the weeks of his recuperation.

Juliette, delighted with her father's recovery but painfully aware of his advancing age, persuaded her family to take a house in Lymington in the New Forest to be within travelling distance. It was not an easy decision. Edward, never entirely comfortable with his eccentric in-laws, would have preferred to remain in the Highlands and, even after their move, spent much of his time there tending the estates and managing the shoots. For Juliette, newly reconciled with her mother, it was more than a matter of taking sides. As she reached middle age, with years to recover, she spent more and more time across the water until she and her children were almost permanent houseguests at Dimbola. A happy arrangement for Julia who fretted whenever they visited Lymington because the harbour reminded Charles of Calcutta, with its tall white ships, and made him threaten to move back again. Since his illness he had talked even more frequently of the pleasant climate and benefits for their health.

With her favourite people around her, in the midst of a cultural storm, and on the beautiful island she loved, Julia found happiness. Encouraged by her growing closeness with Juliette, she also began to feel like a mother, to let go of her own family ties. It brought a welcome emotional freedom. At Dimbola the doors were open to friends, family and strangers and, when her dear friend Reverend Sheridan died of tuberculosis, she offered a home and an education to his three young children, without a thought for the expense. Far from meeting Charles's careful financial calculations, which accounted for their own children growing and moving away, they were faced with supporting a large and busy household with a constant stream of guests.

'Must we offer five kinds of cake every time the kettle is heated?' Charles tried to keep his voice light, though he meant his complaint. 'I counted three separate afternoon teas yesterday, one for every new visitor! What is more, we now seem to have two cooks. I assume this is all for their benefit? To give them something to do?'

'I won't listen to any more of this Charles,' said Julia. 'It's penny pinching of the worst kind. The new cook was hired to prepare special meals you needed for your recovery. And we have four young people in the house who have suffered the worst of tragedies, am I to tell those unhappy souls they may not be permitted anything nice to eat?' On such days Julia showed more of the soul of James Pattle than she would care to admit, waving away all mention of the tawdry details of finance and looking only to those comforts that could be assumed to make people happy.

'If we carry on like this, they won't be able to eat anything at all! And I'm fully recovered now, or will be if you allow me any peace, so why is she still here? And have Juliette and the children also moved in?'

'She's the Meredith's daughter! I can hardly turn her out after everything they have suffered. No, she is better off here. And Louisa is happier with the company. So, it's settled.' Julia gritted her teeth, prepared to stand her ground. How dare he complain that their daughter was staying? After all the years she'd been absent from their lives, surely he could find it in him to accommodate her and the children?

Charles sighed. 'I know you always operate with the very best of intentions, Julia, but you work in rather mysterious ways.' In the last week of his illness she had hired twelve men to turn the vegetable gardens into lawn, believing it would aid his recovery to wander green slopes rather than worry over carrot fly. 'The gardening bill is still unpaid; and now the grocer's bill is doubled. If you don't at least try to rein in the expenses you will slice up the estates in Ceylon. Perhaps,' he asked tentatively, 'Perhaps you could ask Mary to help you review the way you work in the Glass House?' He looked around for a sign of support but Mary, sensing trouble, had disappeared at the outset of their conversation.

Julia drew herself up to her full height, which was considerably lower than Charles's, and folded her arms. 'Please tell me how you propose to change the way I make my Art?' Her voice became dangerously soft. No one, not even Charles, was permitted commentary on the artistic merit of her work. Hers was an Artist's intuition and it was vital her methods continued as they were. She had medals for goodness sake. Her review exhibition in Germany had attracted the attention of a raft of younger artists and she now received regular praise by post.

'I simply meant that you could sell more. And, perhaps, stop using fifteen plates for every print?' He gave her a nervous glance. 'Your technique is so well mastered now, of course.'

'Would you like me to set up a tedious little shop, charging by the minute to take boring family photographs? I would rather sell my camera than my soul. Anyway, since the Societies still insist on calling me an amateur because a woman can't be a professional, I'm unable to charge for sittings of that nature. So, I can't.' Julia stared at him defiantly, arms still folded.

'We may not go on indefinitely wasting money and adopting orphans.'

'Wasting? What is wasted? Our home is filled with young people who would otherwise be in dire straits, and my Art is growing successful. I had hoped you would be happy for me. I suppose you think I should be charging dear Juliette for bed and board?' The look on his face! Goodness he was almost agreeing. She had been virtually estranged from them for years and now he grudged her children a mouthful of bread. He'd better not mention it to Juliette herself; the girl was so headstrong she'd pack her bags in an instant. And as for Art, clearly it must be allowed to continue in the same way. After a lifetime of longing she would not give up on it now. Just when she was getting somewhere. 'Well? What's it to be? Shall we evict our daughter or am I to be prevented from working?'

'You are always so dramatic, Julia.' Charles gave a weary sigh. 'I can't produce money for these things when it isn't there. So, I must go back to the valleys in Ceylon, to improve production. And Ewen will come with me.'

'It sounds as though your mind is set. How long will you both be gone?' Now that Juliette was with her, in her heart she knew she would survive. There was always such a houseful, and so much to do to keep the galleries fed with her work that they would probably be back before she had a chance to miss them.

'It's hard to say. Eugene has written to say he needs help. It's a difficult place, less developed than India, and everything he tries to do takes twice the time it should. He needs help and Ewen needs work.'

'Do you mean to say that Ewen will stay out there!'

'He's old enough Julia; don't look at me in that way. It will be for the best.'

Julia flew into a perfect rage of activity. The threat of Charles leaving for months on end and, worse, taking another of her children out to manage the estates, worried her immensely. Income from their plantations was all that they had, but she had always managed to ignore the fact, finding thoughts of money not only distasteful but an impediment to the way she chose to live. Her parents had died notorious socialites, but virtually penniless; the sale of Charles's family home in Barbados, a country little more than a landing spot for trade, had fetched little. If she wanted to carry on the work that she relied on for her happiness, that she knew was important for Art, then she must try to find a way to make it pay. People wanted her prints now, though the amount she felt impelled to give away for free had only increased with her popularity.

Letter after letter was written to societies and exhibitions and many of them accepted her work, though never paid for anything and the huge cost of protective post and packaging simply added to the escalating Glass House bills. Mary worked hard to get prints bought by museums and many of the key collections in London and Europe now held at least one original Julia Margaret Cameron. Some simply accepted the first one sent, which she found irritating, but Mary considered a form of advertising, and a few went on to order a full series of works. Those featuring the Great Men were to prove the most popular and soon surpassed the sales of Fruits of the Spirit at Colnaghi's dealing rooms.

It was Juliette who suggested they start sending prints direct to the publishers of the works of these great men. 'After all,' she said, 'they need to take a likeness from somewhere. May as well be a photograph as a line drawing.' She was not entirely reconciled with her mother's wild working appearance, or the dark art itself, but she spoke of it well enough for Julia to find a certain peace in her company.

'Juliette's right,' said Mary. 'We should be doing that. Mr Tennyson adores his photograph.'

'Yes, he does,' said Juliette, 'It's not a favourite of mine, I'm afraid he looks as though he could do with a visit to the barber.' Alfred himself was not a favourite of her daughter, either; he was too brooding and low-spirited, too simply male for her tastes. 'But there are plenty of others. Your island is brimming with the men you call the great and the good. Have you captured Mr Allingham yet? He has, I believe, Mr Rossetti staying with him again. It wouldn't surprise me if he were to be the latest artist to move here.'

'I've tried many times,' replied Julia, pulling a gloomy expression that suggested unaccustomed defeat. 'Allingham has set against me for some reason and as for Rossetti, I believe he considers me to be competition for the affections of his mistress.'

'Such a shame,' added Mary, in soft voice. 'He's a very beautiful man.'

'He is a very loose man I might say, Mary,' chastised Juliette. 'Not at all the type that mother would wish to have making his home here. And you'd do well to avoid him lest he try to get you into his studio.'

Julia smiled. She would love to see the young artist move to her Circle; he would be just the thing to shake up some of the stuffier elements of its edges. How like Juliette to assume the mantle of propriety.

Mary coloured prettily and busied herself making notes on Juliette's suggestions. 'Mr Taylor then, and, of course, Mr Watts. We could try with an island series. Would we set up something on the front at Freshwater?'

'Lady Eastnor says that tourists will only buy from a shop, or, if they do buy directly, won't pay what it is really worth.' Juliette stopped to think. 'She does very well with her aquarelles at the little hotel in Ryde, there's a shop at the front selling local things. It's definitely worth a try.'

Mary scribbled it all down. Julia badly wanted to comment on Caroline's boring seascapes, but Juliette seemed taken in by the title and the respectability. Anyway, if unsuspecting tourists were willing to purchase such bland paintings it really was worth a try. Juliette had almost managed to tame the old bat, though they had little in common except their paints. She'd joined the Ventor Watercolour Society, of course, was accepted first time. When the Edinburgh Review came out, they'd tried to make an exception for her too, but she'd refused. Hadn't she left them behind? Not one of them knew how to use a camera. If Juliette started wearing a bonnet, then she would have to say something.

'In fact,' Juliette continued, 'If you could get the prints signed, they would sell even better.'

'I always sign them.' Julia looked puzzled.

'No, no. Get your 'great men' to sign their own. You said yourself that Mr Tennyson adored his photograph, why not ask him to help?'

Had Alfred known who had made this suggestion to Julia, he would have visited her armed with the musket he kept to clear Farringford of squirrels. The first stack he accepted with good grace, taking time after dinner to embellish them with his signature. When she returned to collect them, she left a bigger pile for signing, which was less well received. Juliette's prediction had been accurate and the island's tourists clamoured to buy the autographed pictures. Why had Julia been surprised? She could have kicked herself for not spotting it sooner. Celebrity obsessed people wanted proximity to their idols, to touch them, pretend to be them. It made sense they would want something signed by them. Even when Hardinge was at university he had joined the trend of carrying an autograph book around. The money was marvellous. Charles would be delighted when he returned.

On her next visit to the Tennysons, Julia brought so many mounted copies it was necessary to bring a carriage. Had he possessed commercial sense himself, Alfred would have asked his own publisher to send more of his poems for signing and sale by the same medium. But he was no more a natural salesman than Julia and, in the end, the constant requests to sign her Art became too much. One evening, watching her drive along the path to the front of the house, a full pile beside her, he locked the front door and forbid Mrs Ruttle to answer it. A locked door was the last thing to stop Julia. She simply climbed in through the open front window and handed the prints to a startled Emily for safekeeping. Happily for Alfred, Charles returned from Ceylon with a windfall from the sale of part of their estates and Julia lost interest in autographs, being more concerned with the taking of new images than the commercial side of art; their turbulent friendship was quickly restored.

1869 Isle of Wight

'Must we sit in the same places for the entire evening?' Julia felt she was being slowly strangled. Why should it matter if people wanted to walk around between courses? The Campbells would prove to be rather dull neighbours if this evening was anything to go by.

'I can't remember an evening like it,' said Watts, who'd already professed his envy of the great limestone hall. 'It's rather thrilling. It reminds me of dinners a hundred years ago.'

Julia considered the room's pale silk walls and ancestral paintings. 'I suppose it's tasteful, if not exactly Beautiful. And it was kind of them to invite so many of us. I keep losing count halfway round the table. It must seat sixty at least.'

'People of honour. I expect they felt duty bound after their wild arrival.'

'You would have had the best view of that,' Julia smiled. For a bohemian Artist, Watts was a terrible scandalmonger and had been the first to share news of the arrival of this new family from London. They'd brought with them a whole team of expensive and highly-strung horses, apparently in need of training, acquired to suit their new country life. They hadn't really caused much disturbance. It was his retelling of the story that prompted the poor mainlanders to host an apology. Kind of them, but she was finding the atmosphere mildly strained. It was by far the most formal dinner they had endured for a long time. Probably since Lady Macbeth's tortuous evenings in Calcutta.

'Charles seems to be enjoying himself,' observed Watts, gesturing to where he sat with John Campbell. Julia rolled her eyes, though she understood. Their host, rotund and cheerful, was a lawyer of repute, and Charles enjoyed a little legal rambling. She knew he missed the company of other businessmen in her cultural circle. The wife was a different matter. Arabella Campbell was neither learned nor cultural and fussed a great deal over everything, including the servants. How could they be friends? She had an alarming elaborate hairstyle and a deliberate straight-backed posture, both of which lent her the air of a tall wooden doll.

'They seem to be rather ordinary girls,' said Julia in a stage whisper to her son, straightening his waistcoat. 'I do hope you'll find this evening worth your while.' Henry Herschel, still home after finishing at Oxford, had heard there would be young ladies and agreed to accompany his parents for the evening.

'Mother!' He looked quickly across the table but Hatty Campbell showed no sign of having heard. She carried on listening intently to the Signor excitedly explain his ideas for painting new frescoes around their dining room walls.

'Well you wouldn't have come for the food, would you?' Julia hated the bland British fare they were eating, thin cold soup and poached white fish. Why must they be subjected to it after so many years of colonials bringing back interesting flavours? She would get Louisa to take some spices to the Campbell's cook the next time one of Rohit's parcels arrived.

'The food is perfectly edible,' hissed Henry, 'And you might have dressed appropriately.'

Julia swished the trumpet sleeves of her velvet medieval gown and followed the line of his gaze.

'Hmm, you may have something. Something about the mouth perhaps.' She began to stare unwaveringly at Hatty, until the poor girl felt the pressure of the gaze and turned her head helplessly.

'You're being sized up,' laughed Watts. 'I've seen that look many times before. Don't worry, she won't eat you, she just wants to take your photograph.'

'Oh.' Hatty looked relieved. 'Mother said you were… I hardly know the word. It isn't photographer is it? Because I've seen your prints. You paint with photography rather.'

Julia beamed. What a clever girl. Henry could do much worse. 'I'll expect you at eleven tomorrow. Dimbola, it's the double house with the tower, can't miss it. Come straight to the back where my studio is.'

'You are not obliged to go,' interjected Henry. 'She assumes nobody has anything better to do than sit around in a draughty hen house while she paints poisons onto glass.' Hatty gave him the pretty smile that had caught Julia's attention.

'Of course she doesn't have anything to do, they've only just moved here. And don't get any ideas about hanging around, Henry,' Julia wagged a purple-striped finger at her son, 'I don't like people in my Glass House while I'm working. You could do with some gainful employment yourself.'

Watts, who was quite used to the way the Cameron family spoke to one another, carried on eating his fish. Hatty looked shocked.

'Don't mind mother, she's perfectly lovely… provided you do exactly as she asks,' Henry grinned and made a throat-slitting gesture, 'I'll check on you at noon to make sure you're still alive.'

The arrangement made, the evening passed in pleasant conversation and would not have been in the slightest bit memorable had it not been for the after-dinner entertainment. The Campbells had occupied a high standing in City business circles, largely bereft of guests gifted in the musical or creative fields. They were used to formal dinners followed by popular music and the latest craze of tableau vivant, where the evening's hosts dressed up in elaborate theatrical costumes and adopted dramatic poses under artful lighting.

When Mrs Campbell and her three daughters appeared dressed in costume, as various characters from A Midsummer Night's Dream, the gathered islanders did not know what to think. It was Julia who led the applause, who shouted her appreciation and silently determined that these were the next kind of photographs she would take. It would be a stroke of genius. Already she used splendid, unusual clothes for her portraits, but to dress up her sitters as characters from Shakespeare, or heroes and heroines from the mythologies, would be something. No other light-drawing Artist could compete. Costumes, properly planned, theatrical costumes, would give her prints authority; they would tell stories without words. It was the most exciting revelation. At the end of the evening it was as much as Charles could do to prevent her from running to their storehouse and rummaging through the costumes.

Arriving at the Glass House obediently on time, Hatty was faced with a barrage of questions: where were the best costumiers? What sets did the Campbells own? Might Julia borrow them? Might she borrow all the sisters at once? Then she asked her to sit, her mouth upturned just so for seven minutes at a time until she achieved the plate she wanted. When Henry was finally permitted to rescue her, the young girl was close to tears.

'Whatever is the matter?' he asked, concerned.

Hatty steadied herself against the doorframe, as though the experience had been wholly physical, 'I feel as though I shall never smile again!'

'You'll never have to,' replied Julia. 'For your smile will be immortalised, like the mouth of the Mona Lisa.'

In the grounds of Dimbola Julia built a stage with a sweet thatched roof. Trunks of theatrical clothing accumulated in the summerhouse, the scullery, Julia's bedroom. Every visitor was marshalled into some kind of play, every villager newly assessed for heroic potential. The idea that ordinary men and women could appropriate the persona of a legendary figure from history or fiction provided Julia's Art with unlimited potential and she used tableaux to create narrative; Charles found it virtually impossible to keep a straight face.

'This is the very last chance you have, Charles. Merlin would never, ever have laughed.' Julia was attempting to create a scene featuring Merlin and Viviana, the enchantress, which required the utmost seriousness. Charles was naturally cast as Merlin, no other islander wore such a perfectly silver-white mane of hair and beard. But he laughed on so many occasions, his shoulders shaking and causing the plate to spoil, she had been forced to use an entire series of Vivianas. 'If so much as a trace of a smile remains on your face the entire effect will be ruined. Stop it. You know very well I mean it. Annie Fortune is coming in less than thirty minutes and you're not even dressed.' It was hard to find the heart to be cross with Charles; if she had to live with someone who took things seriously, they would drive each other mad within a couple of days.

He cast down his eyes with a sheepish expression. 'I've something to tell you that will, perhaps, cast a sombre mood over today entirely.' Julia took a soft piece of cloth and rubbed the glass of her lens.

'You've asked the Campbells to dinner?'

'No, Julia, and don't be unkind. I don't know why you speak so ill of that poor family; they've given you much for which to be grateful.'

'You don't have the monopoly on humour.' He was about to say something she wouldn't like; she could feel it coming.

Charles took a deep breath. 'There's no easy way to say this… I must go back to the Valleys. The boys have written to ask. Crops have failed for a second year,' he held up a hand to stay her concern, 'Not ours, thankfully, but they don't know why, and any disease on the neighbouring plots will be hard to contain.'

'But what can you do about that?'

'My dear, the crops are our only hope. We managed this year with the income we received from the sale, but we can't keep slicing up the land. The reality is that we must work to improve the estates in order to earn what they're worth.'

'We have a nice enough life.' Why was he suggesting they couldn't manage? Things were perfectly fine, weren't they?

'We won't manage our debt if crops fail for even one year! All your parties, the materials for your work, the building of theatres... at some point it must be paid for Julia. Do you see?'

Julia shook her head. Did he have to look so long-suffering? She was nowhere near as profligate as he suggested.

'The natives are, understandably, finding it hard. There's a lack of food, there's poverty and there may be fighting. I can't leave Eugene and Ewen to manage things alone. Would you want them in that danger?'

'If they're in danger then they must come home!' Julia thought with horror of the Indian mutiny that had claimed so many lives. It made her sick to think her sons should have to make their livelihood in the midst of such danger. Around their hill-station the jungle was unforgiving, but if anyone wanted to attack it then it wouldn't be difficult.

'And leave our lands for others to plunder? We must go to them Julia, myself and Henry. The boy wishes to work, and his brothers want him there. There's no harm to anyone.'

No harm to anyone but me, thought Julia, though she was sensible enough to see when she had lost. All that talk of money, they were hardly reduced to taking in washing; it was so vulgar to contemplate. Papa had never discussed money, and he would certainly never have done so in front of Mama. But then, there were many things he didn't tell his family. Things he left them to find out themselves. She should be grateful, really, that Charles was truthful. If only the lot of them weren't so keen to run to the other side of the world. He was to blame for infecting them with his love of the climate. Soon only Hardinge would be left of the boys.

Annie arrived at a silent house, dressed silently in the coalhouse next door and was taken to a silent studio where Merlin awaited, dressed in a long velvet robe, resting on a thick knobbed cane, his silver hair spread out over his shoulders. She was instructed to lift her arm in an act of enchantment, an uncomfortable angle, but she was used to modelling for Julia and affected a slight rise of the arm with the elbow held to her side, which allowed her to hold the pose. Merlin was struck dumb and perfectly still, in the grip of an enchantment. When the image was printed, two tiny droplets, like tears, were left on Merlin's robes. As usual Julia refused to clean the negative, 'It's a perfect print,' she declared. 'And as to spots they must, like all of the blights on our lives, remain.'

Stories from the Glass House:
Sir Joseph Hooker

Darwin's theory may well be better understood than the changes that take place in all of us throughout our lifetimes. Personal evolution is a gradual process and it can be very hard to recognise. I only knew Julia after her transformation, but I'm assured by all who knew her that she certainly didn't realise until she stopped.

In the Glass House I found her delightful. That's possibly why I look so much more cheerful in my portrait than her better-known subjects. None wore smiles, even Herschel, and I never once saw him in the flesh without one. In every photograph she took of me I look as though I'm about to cause mischief, and I rather like that she saw that in me. She was right, too, though most people wouldn't have noticed, would not have looked at the man beyond his title or the collection of letters after his name.

Julia worked with a kind of invigorating energy, the way a scientist is driven once he develops a theory he must prove—with a single-minded determination and to the virtual exclusion of all else in his life. For a scientist with an exciting theory, the business of everyday life doesn't matter. He'll dress in whatever is to hand, forget social convention and eat nothing but cold cuts for months. Julia lived like that with her camera. The Glass House was her laboratory and there is no doubt, to me, she was proving something. Whether that something was scientific or artistic, or simply personal, depends entirely on the way you see the world yourself.

1870 Isle of Wight

Nothing mattered to Julia but getting onto paper images she pictured in her mind. If she asked a sitter to roll down the neck of their dress, to give the impression they were partially clothed, she would undress herself to make them more relaxed, despite the full windows in the studio. After one such sitting, Juliette found her in the coalhouse, shocked to see her still in petticoats, and Julia simply showed her the resulting print, an image of May Prinsep as Beatrice, a wrap of cloth around her head, her long hair tumbling over her bare shoulders. 'She is Beatrice! Abused and abandoned by her father, pushed into murder! She is perfect. How can you talk about petticoats when this young girl's story needs to be heard?' May's face was soft lit, beatific, her eyes downcast but without shame. Later Mary sold the print to a private collector and it fetched more than either of them thought possible.

Even fully clothed sitters sometimes confided to Mary that they found Julia's intensity terrifying in the hours they spent in a cold outbuilding, watching silently as she experimented with depth and focus in a room strewn with costumes and offering a choice of hard chair or dirty floor for poses. Her adopted children soon learned that she was only stern in the studio and managed to be absent whenever the need for a set of cherubim came over her. Even children from the village needed ever more coaxing.

Julia spoke of the Glass House as though it was a fairytale castle. Her sitters agreed it must be enchanted, because time changed inside, either dragging with the aching of limbs in uncompromising poses, or rushing past in a blur of Julia's energy until they were sent away, disorientated in the daylight, still wearing remnants of the person they had been asked to become.

'What do you know of Hamlet? Of King Arthur? For heaven's sake why don't you leave such subjects alone and go back to taking photographs of peasant girls? There's a beauty in those simple portraits of simple people that it seems to the viewer you entirely understand. But when I look at these, these silly renderings of high drama, I'm left cold.'

Julia clasped her hands tightly, as though she feared her arms may just fly out to strike him of their own accord. Her nails dug hard into her skin. Ruskin was a good friend of the Signor's and she had been made to promise not to upset him, though that was before she realised what a pompous, self-important man he was. With cold and piercing pale-grey eyes he leafed through her portfolios, his elegant nose wrinkled, his too-large mouth curled in an unpleasant disdain. To think she'd looked forward to this visit! All her life she'd read his words, wanting to question him about Beauty. Over twenty volumes of essays on the subject he'd become the foremost living expert and she could not resist the opportunity to meet him in the flesh. Yet now she had the chance to show him her most modern creation of Beauty it seemed he was determined to reject it. He was a fool!

'I believe I'm as well placed to create allegorical Art as any Photographic Artist,' she said through tight lips, knowing she mustn't displease him. As the country's foremost art critic his approval was paramount, and essential to achieve the status she desired for her prints. It wasn't enough to be popular, though that was nice; she must also have the endorsement of the art world. Not just painters, like Watts, but the critics, the essayists; the ones that told the public how they should think. The ones that created Artists. Provided their words were sensible, of course.

'That's a ridiculous statement.' The eminent, opinionated man of letters sucked in his cheeks, which Julia thought made him look quite a lot like a tortoise. 'As a woman you are simply unable to feel the way an artist would feel. A man's power is active, progressive, defensive. He is eminently the doer, the creator, the discoverer. How many great explorers were female, Mrs Cameron?'

'How many explorers' fathers would have given money for ships rather than dowries to allow their daughters to sail, when their daughters were prevented from owning property or keeping money of their own? Your argument simply shows that men are favoured, it has nothing to do with the nature of men and women.' Julia struggled to remain in control of her voice. In a moment he would tell her she shouldn't be dealing with chemicals; an argument she'd heard many times, but had somehow not expected from him.

'It has everything to do with that. A man, by his inherent nature, has an intellect built for speculation and invention, his energy is for war, where war is just, and conquest, whenever conquest is necessary.'

'When exactly is war and conquest necessary?' asked Julia. The Signor threw her a warning look and shook his head quickly. Ruskin was temperamental, important and, lately, emotionally scarred. His marriage, to a young and beautiful family friend, had recently been annulled in a scandalous divorce and Watts had invited him to stay to give him some peace and reflection, both largely impossible once Julia had discovered his arrival. He hadn't asked to see her prints; she had assumed he would want to.

'My point exactly. There's little point in me explaining to you, because you wouldn't understand. A woman's interest is neither for invention nor creation, but for sweet ordering and arrangement. A woman's place is not for battle and war but for making a comfortable home in which a man can return from his work.'

No wonder poor Effie had enough of you, thought Julia. She'd heard that their marriage was never consummated and had broken down as a result of Ruskin accusing her of unnatural behaviours. Whatever they might be. Having emotions perhaps? Watts himself had confided that the great critic was terrified of women in the flesh and she would have loved to throw that at him now. But she protected Watts, who needed this awful man's approval too, and held her tongue.

'I have many other portraits to show you that may well change your mind. But I fear, seeing the direction in which this discussion is headed, I would merely waste my time and yours. You are a painter, Mr Ruskin, perhaps you don't try to understand Photography?'

The critic gave a short, humourless laugh and turned to the Signor. 'Perhaps you would care to correct your friend, Mr Watts? I've been a photographer for many years, dear lady. Truly I would like to show you my own dageurrotypes, which are taken as the medium intended, as real and honest works of art, representing truth and beauty in close work.'

'And you see no Truth and Beauty in the images of these faces? These stories made flesh?'

'They are amateur theatricals. An old man with a wizard's staff, a child wrapped in a curtain! How can such spectacles speak of either beauty or truth? With my dageurrotypes it is as though the building could be taken home and viewed through the lens of truth, as accurate as seeing it brick by brick. Every chip of stone and stain is there in the image.'

'That is not Art, Mr Ruskin. It is simply a copy. How can it make you feel anything?'

'The truth of mere transcript, in photography, has nothing to do with Art properly so called. It doesn't matter how much you people try to popularise the medium, it will never supersede Art.'

Watts remained stricken at the edge of the room. Julia visibly bristled. You people! How dare he speak to her in that way?

'Perhaps,' ventured Watts bravely from his corner. 'It may be possible to walk around the truth. Viewing it sometimes from a distance as well as examining it with a magnifying glass, lest your eye and taste become microscopic and fail to take in the length and breadth.'

Julia shot him a withering look and he retreated once more.

Ruskin continued to leaf through the portfolio, growing more and more impatient with the images. 'All artists should strive to create beauty; there is little enough of it in the world. I can see from these ugly portraits that you know nothing of that calling Mrs Cameron.'

Julia seethed. His remark was as far from the truth as it was possible to be. All she had ever wanted was to draw the Beautiful from the everyday, and she had succeeded, she knew she had. Who was this ridiculous man, with his sneer and wealth, his impossible attitude to women? Who was he to tell her how to think?

Ruskin came to her favourite photograph, the print of Herschel with his newly washed halo of hair. The beautiful clear light of intelligence shone from his aged face. Surely this one, of all my pictures, will be enough to change his mind?

'And as for this one!' Ruskin spluttered, 'the poor man looks deranged. It's as though a battery of fireworks was let loose behind his head!' He slammed the book shut, whereupon Julia leapt forward and thumped him violently on the back, exclaiming angrily, 'John Ruskin, you are not worthy of my Photographs!'

It was to be a week of unsettling visits. Although Julia and Ruskin eventually regained civil terms, the remainder of his visit to Freshwater felt strained and none of the Circle would dare to engage him in discussion of the subjects in which he declared expertise: Art, Beauty and the nature of life. Which, since he was spoiled and fussy and not at all an easy man with whom to live, rendered his once highly anticipated visit a disappointment. Even Charles restricted his conversation to small talk, which left him quite exhausted. Since his return from Ceylon he had, in any case, been restless, questioning the sense of the life they led in Freshwater when they could be back in the glorious sunshine, in wonderful landscapes, enjoying the simple life of plantation farmers and reunited with their eldest boys.

Barely four days after Ruskin left, he was replaced by another visitor to Briarsfield, Sir Henry Cotton, who enjoyed an old acquaintance with Thoby Prinsep, from their days in India, and who had written with an urgent insistence that he should visit as soon as he could. Sir Henry had recently acquired his title for an outstanding contribution to the Indian Civil Service and it was assumed he was coming to offer an important job to Thoby.

'I must prepare!' cried Sarah.

'It's not a State visit,' said Julia. 'And I thought you'd no wish to return to India?'

'I don't, but I'm not averse to Thoby achieving political status at home.'

Watts, still raw from the Ruskin experience, had no desire to entertain in his own home a man he didn't know, and decamped to Dimbola for a few days.

Much to Sarah's disappointment, Sir Henry was no sooner settled in the East bedroom, which she had decorated for his visit, than he was requesting an introductory visit to Julia, whose photographs he had seen for the first time on his recent visit to London. He had barely noticed the lotus blossom theme she'd used for the dining room, hastily replacing at the last moment the original peacock feather theme, which she had chosen especially and had caused her to fight with Thoby. Having been stationed in Madras, he claimed they were unlucky to keep in the house and insisted Sir Henry would no doubt think the same. She had flung at him that Sir Henry would not have reached his considerable social standing had he been so superstitious as to believe that, and the pair were still smarting when their honoured guest arrived.

Sarah sent message to Julia to expect them all that afternoon; an imperious missive, which was received as such, and which made Julia determine to be as unwelcoming as she could. Who was this man to request her? He was as pompous as Ruskin. What on earth did these men think gave them the right to self-declare as experts and then spend the rest of their lives ordering lesser mortals around, taking their self-esteem, deciding who was to be fashionable? When the deposition arrived at the appointed hour, she was still in the Glass House, where she remained a good forty minutes before stomping into the house, dressed in her slate grey working smock and covered in chemical dyes. It was a beautiful afternoon, with a valiant sun peeping through scudding clouds, though too chilly to sit entirely out of doors, and Charles had served tea in the conservatory instead.

With the long windows thrown open, their collection of exotic houseplants shivered in the light breeze. A richly embroidered arch of fabric, tasselled with silken loops, hung from the far wall and the guests sat on mounds of silk cushions. It reminded Sir Henry so much of Madras, and he found he liked Charles so much, he had immediately felt at home, meaning Julia's minor protest passed quite unnoticed and she was mildly irritated to find them all in excellent spirits when she arrived.

'I am to understand that you are interested in my Art, Sir Henry.' Julia sat cross-legged on the floor cushions, revealing shockingly dirty bare feet, smeared with dust from the floor of the coalhouse where she finished her plates. She was annoyed at his lack of reaction. 'Please do excuse my dress. I find it easier to work like this than to suffer soaking wet boots and stockings for an entire afternoon.

My process of development requires a veritable waterfall of cold water to wash the plates cleanly.'

Sir Henry himself was dressed in the most immaculate and expensive clothes the Circle had seen since Browning's visit, with a long-tailed coat of smooth new wool and spotless white linen. Next to him Charles wore the air of a man of the road in his bagged and faded trousers and Moroccan hat.

'Please don't worry on my behalf,' he said. 'I'm newly returned from a country that has meant very little would shock me now.'

'How is India?' asked Julia. 'Charles misses it badly, it wouldn't at all surprise me if he decided we were moving back, and yet we hear such dreadful stories! Mutinies and murders! Is it really so very changed?' Sir Henry gave a delicate, meaningful glance towards May and Adeline Prinsep, who rested on cushions nearby.

'Perhaps that's a conversation for later in the evening. But I confess I've much sympathy for the agitators, they wish to have their country returned, it's simply a question of how best we manage to return it for them,' said Sir Henry with his customary political sensitivity.

'You're right, a conversation for a later time. But I'd very much like your insight, when we can speak freely,' said Charles. 'I've only spent time in Ceylon in recent years and the mood there is not so much political as desperate in light of the recent famine. We're to hope that's a temporary thing.'

'Do tell us about your work, and the opportunities it brings,' said Sarah, who listened intently as the peer described his recent office, clearly waiting for the chance to mention Thoby's experience.

While Sir Henry spoke, Julia watched him. He was elegant, not quite handsome but with a noble bearing, slim build and fine high features marked by intense dark eyes. He wore a thick, perfectly oiled and curled, moustache and his hair was brushed smooth and neatly parted. As he spoke, he gestured frequently with his graceful hands, seeming to draw the company in to lean towards him; and he gave, in Julia's opinion, a deeply moral and honest account of his liberal views.

When he'd finished and his audience had drawn back, Julia asked, 'So, you wish for me to take your image? I'd be happy to, Sir Henry; you've a face that my camera will love. And from what you've already told us, I feel I know your soul well enough to draw it out.'

If he was surprised, he didn't show it and he took the chance to accept, agreeing to return for his sitting the following morning.

1871 Isle of Wight

Julia did like Sir Henry. When he sat in her Glass House he'd known, without instruction, how she wanted him to behave and his portrait was drawn forth in two plates, both as neat and unmarked as his own appearance. Sir Henry was earnest, intelligent, imposing and, above all, kind. He cut a dashing figure in their little community. Over his first and second visits they had listened much to his liberal politics and agreed that, although he spoke sensibly and held a great deal of expertise, he was in no way opinionated, a trait which had become the lowest of attributes since Ruskin's unfortunate holiday. Julia liked his manners, his approach to politics and, in particular, she liked the way he spoke about India. Even Mary, who was generally indisposed to the company of politicians, hung on his every word. But her family was unsettled when he left after a third visit and she could not help but lay the blame at his door.

Perhaps the mood was caused by nothing more troubling than the absence of a new friend? After all, he'd done much to ingratiate himself to her circle, in a flurry of visits, and then left the country again, with no hope of returning quickly. But something had changed. After Sir Henry left, Charles, who always wanted to escape to Ceylon, talked of almost nothing but India until Julia felt her head may split in two. Mary took long walks alone, or in the sole company of the youngest Bonnet. After these walks, she would sit directly on the stone sea wall around the bay and watch the waves crash against the rocks, staring into the ocean. Mary's temper was slightly brittle, as though something preyed on her mind, and she made mistakes with the chemicals in the coalhouse, mixing incorrect proportions so that the painted image cracked on the plate and made lines on the prints. Julia watched her carefully, worried she may be pining for a home and family she no longer had.

'Nonsense Mother, the girl's in love!' Juliette laughed delightedly as her mother described her concerns. 'You never did see what was in front of your face, did you? You look too far for truth that's close to home. It's obvious that she's in love. She's behaving like one of Tennyson's damsels.'

Julia blinked, astonished. Was it that obvious to everyone else? Although she'd been quick to encourage her children to grow up, she'd never thought of Mary as anything other than a child. Could she love Sir Henry? It would be an extraordinary marriage for a girl like her to achieve. Julia remembered the day she'd met her begging on the heath, dressed in rags but still strikingly beautiful and strong, with all the quiet and resolute determination she bore as an adult. No wonder he'd fallen for her; she would make him a wonderful wife.

'Do you think it's Sir Henry?' she asked.

'I think it's all rather coincidental if it's not. I haven't seen many other striking and eligible bachelors for a while. It would be a good match for her,' she said, suddenly serious. 'I know you love her, but don't try to stop her if it's what she wants. Talk to her. You're her mother now.'

'I promised I would keep her safe,' said Julia, pleased to hear her daughter use such words. There was no jealousy between the girls, as Charles had predicted and feared. In fact, Juliette had once admitted she was grateful to Mary for keeping her mother at arm's length from herself.

'Well if it does turn out to be Sir Henry then you probably have kept her safe. At the very least you have you'll have fulfilled your promise to keep her from artists.'

It took only one question for Mary to confess all, weeping on her adoptive father's shoulder as she talked. She fetched all Sir Henry's letters and spread them over the table, as

253

though she wanted to prove she had no secrets from them anymore. Julia gently folded them again, unread, and retied them with their silk ribbons. So, it was not her own work, after all, but her sitter that had held fascination for Sir Henry. He'd seen her repeatedly in the series of works she had prepared and listed for sale at Colnaghi's shop, which he'd visited with the aim of purchasing a gift for his sister. At once he'd bought the whole print run, found out from the dealer what he could about the sitter, and determined to go to the Isle of Wight to find her. In one of his letters to her he claimed from the outset he could 'see through' her beauty to 'a steadfast, morally upright woman with a streak of determination' that gave her 'the air of a mythical goddess; a modern-day Diana'. Such insight was pleasing. Nothing bad could come from marrying such a man.

'You must marry him if you wish, of course you must. But only if you love him.' Mary lifted her head and nodded tearfully at Julia. 'Then what's there to stop you? You mustn't worry about us, we'll manage.'

'Indeed,' said Charles mischievously, 'Julia will simply keep adopting more children the moment she begins to feel lonely.'

'You're not helping,' scolded Julia.

'He seems so sure, but I find it overwhelms me. I'm not sure how his words make me feel. I know Ma would've warned me not to believe him,' said Mary. 'And I've never imagined a life without you both. I owe you everything.'

'What about how much we owe to you? It's not luck that shapes our lives but fate, and our own inherent goodness. You deserve everything you've gained,' said Julia.

'How will you manage the Glass House alone? You'd never show any pictures, you'd just forget to send them off anywhere!'

Julia was about to take offence when she realised it was true. All the societies, the museums and galleries, it was all Mary. The girl had pushed her hard at a time when she almost gave up her fight for recognition, and saved her life more than once. But she had to stop living for other people. It was time for her to choose the life she wanted, with the man she wanted. 'I know you love us, and you're loved in your turn, believe me. You've done so much for me, Mary, I've no wish to lose you.'

'You mustn't worry, Mary,' Juliette spoke up. 'If you teach me, I can try to help. I want to.'

Julia's heart sang to hear it. To be close to her daughter, to hear acknowledgement that her creative work was important, was all she had wanted. No one could match Mary's skill and judgement, but in time Juliette would be a help and the time they spent together while she tried would be precious. 'You love this man, and I can see why. What else is stopping you from going with him? What are you worried for?'

'I don't know what India is like,' confessed Mary. 'I've tried to picture it, from your words, from the paintings I've seen, the way Sarah and Thoby talk of Calcutta. But I can't. And I'm scared I won't like it. The heat and the jungle and the danger.'

'India is those things.' Charles stroked his beard along its silvery length, closing his eyes as he conjured the heat and the smell of his favourite place. 'It's hot—unbearably hot sometimes—but it's also the cool of a fat raindrop running down huge leaves, and the whirr of a fan in the sleepy afternoon. It's the orange flash of a tiger through trees, and the steam on the flanks of a chestnut horse in the maidan.'

'It's monkeys,' added Julia, joining in and smiling across at her husband. 'Chattering through the neem trees as they go from house to house for their supper. And it's cows. So many pretty pale gold cows! They wander wherever they will, because they're sacred there, as you know. They may never be hurried. Outside of the city, life in India may never be hurried.' Julia looked at Juliette, who had been listening intently, and noticed that her eyes were shining with unshed tears. Was she, too, sad for the journey they'd never managed together? Might things have been different if they had? They could go and see Mary together, once she was settled.

'We could go to visit them, Juliette, make our trip after all,' said Julia. 'I'll take you to the house where you were born.' She remembered the soapstone turtle and was filled with a longing to see temples again, to see the way people worshipped the smallest of things, making each day extraordinary. There was such Beauty in it all.

'Sir Henry's house is in the country, he has more sense than to cram into one of those streets in Madras,' said Charles. 'The lands around the city are beautiful there. After the monsoon the sky is simply filled with butterflies, as big as your hands, in all the colours of the rainbow.'

'I would like to see that,' breathed Mary, her eyes, dry now, opening wide.

'Everything is beautiful in India,' said Julia. 'You know that there you won't be so special.'

'I would like that, very much,' she replied.

'Then tell him,' said Julia softly. 'Tell him you will go.'

My Dear Herschel,

I hope your recent illness has passed and that you are restored to full health. As to my news, I hardly know where to begin. Mary is to be married to Sir Henry Cotton and she is brave and afraid at the same time, which is wearing to a mother's nerves! Ewen and Henry have both joined their elder brother in Ceylon and I'm left with Juliette and Hardinge for company. My family seems to dwindle, though you'd never know it from the constant company.

You're a man who has lived a great deal in the public eye, and been known to fight with public opinion, and so I feel you will understand these last few weeks on the island. We're at once a community of culture and sophistication of ideas and a 'backwater', as my sister continually reminds us. The ideas of Mr

256

Darwin, describing what you yourself have called that 'mystery of mysteries' caused some of our number, not to mention himself, significant distress.

Sir Joseph Hooker, I believe, enjoyed every moment. Like yourself, he was a delight in the studio, a man of science, unselfconscious and simple, with no need for reassurance, just an unwavering faith in his science. Mr Darwin was not the same. Still he is a deeply charming man and his family is delightful. We hope he'll choose to visit us again next summer. I'll let you know if he does as you're sure to like him very much.

Charles was much taken with Sir Joseph and has already been to visit him at Kew, to discuss the rust fungus on leaves of his precious coffee plants. I'm glad he has someone to help with his research, but he continually talks of return and I'm not ready to leave. There is much to be done with Photography, if we're to achieve its elevation to Art, as we discussed, and I've barely even started.

With much love,
Julia

Mary married Sir Henry Cotton in the little church at Freshwater. The Bonnets took charge of decorations and smothered everything with so many wreaths and garlanded flowers it was difficult for some guests to find a seat. Julia, whose eyes watered throughout the service, blamed the overpowering lavender, a fragrance that could be relied on to draw tears. Seizing the happy couple, she escorted them to her studio on the way to the wedding breakfast, which the Campbells kindly hosted on their rolling lawns. In her photograph they looked happy and handsome together, and fresh with the promise of their lives made new in each other.

Julia thought of the way she felt on her wedding day, the triumph over Grandmamma and her coven, the safe knowledge that something she had done had finally pleased Mama, the gnawing fear that her purpose in life would disappear. She and Charles had been full of hope, and where had that gone? Was it replaced with her own selfish ambition? In India they had wanted to work together, but she had stopped that. Or had he? It was hard to remember the last time they had sat and listened to each other. Mary smiled below her veil with a new-found approval of the world, a face that Julia loved and missed, and the print found pride of place as the only photograph hung in the Glass House itself, housed in a silver frame.

1872 Lymington

Julia threw herself into work, though no one else had Mary's expert touch with the plates, or patience with the photographer, and she found herself without useful help, working long into the night to create the prints alone. After the celebrations, Alfred sunk into one of his slumps and preferred to spend his days in solitude, leaving Emily to manage unaccompanied, occupied with her growing family. Watts, newly interested in Ruskin's Venice, had travelled to Italy with the Prinseps, who were treating him to the trip by way of thanks for the permanent use of his home. Charles was occupied in his research on coffee, encouraged by Sir Joseph's advice, and spent long hours in the library writing letters to the botanist and his sons in Ceylon, or travelling to London's botanical gardens to discuss the plants with the experts there.

Thank goodness for Juliette. After the years of absence, the relationship Julia had always wanted was blooming. With all the others so occupied it was hard to know what she would do without her daughter. At least once a week Julia abandoned the studio to travel to visit Lymington, often staying the night to spend time with her five grandchildren, who still needed a little 'unbuttoning.' She'd looked forward to working with Juliette, had allowed herself flights of fancy about developing the same relationship she had with Mary. If Juliette saw the way she worked she would surely love her more, or at least find increased respect for her. But Juliette was with child again and couldn't bear the chemical smells in the close confines of the Glass House any more than she could the movement of the boat on the journey to Freshwater.

The sickness was nothing unusual; she had sickened throughout all of her other pregnancies. Julia had been travelling to see her instead, enjoying the peace of the crossing and the change of scene in the bustling market town. She was planning a further visit when the news arrived from the dawn ferry that Juliette was in a difficult labour, early, and had asked for her mother. But Julia had finally persuaded her reticent neighbour, Allingham, to sit for his portrait and didn't dare to postpone him lest he changed his mind. It wasn't even him but his regular houseguest, Rossetti, she wished to capture, partly for Mary's sake and partly because she knew it would complete her collection.

Allingham was not what Julia would call 'easy to draw' and she was frustrated in her attempts to uncover his soul for her lens. It took seven plates before she declared one a success and released him. Once they were developed and a further promise to bring Rossetti was extracted, Julia had missed all but the late evening ferry. She paced the harbour, looking for a boat to charter, to no avail. It was a calm day and every working boat had been despatched to fish or take tourists around the headland.

Sitting on the bench overlooking the ferry stage, Julia stared out at the still, dark water with an increasing foreboding. Remembering the water on her skin, the way it wrapped around her and took her cares, made her tired and fretful. In the year she was saved from the sea she had told herself to be careful, to remember what mattered, to be thankful for all she had. That was the year she'd been given her camera, discovered her talent, found her daughter. She should not have spent all day ignoring her message. As she watched the pale sun sink and the moon rise to take its place over the water, Julia felt the rising shame of success. She'd achieved her heart's desire, only to become absorbed by her work. A selfish fame-hunter, worse than Sarah, whose shallow life and opinions she had disparaged.

When the ferry left for the mainland, only four other passengers joined her. One was Bolingbroke, on his way to a horse fair, who eyed her warily and asked if she had her camera, only relaxing when she reassured him that she did not. The others were family from a farm in Ventnor, on their way to Lyndhurst for a funeral. Their mood was not sombre, though they all wore weeds and Julia disliked herself for judging them.

Three seabirds circled the spray for most of the journey. Three for a girl. Juliette had promised to call the baby Violetta if it was, a touching gesture showing she understood her mother more than she let on. It should be a girl. Someone to whom she could make amends, be a better grandmother than the job she had made of motherhood. Leaning over the ferry rail she made promises to the baby that this time she felt able to keep. When she'd laid down her heart for Juliette it had been more about her than her daughter, she saw it clearly, it had been her declaration of what she would do, how her child would be. At the time she'd been full of a desperate, unfulfilled longing. She had not listened to Juliette, or even tried to understand what she wanted from life. Thank goodness they had time now.

While she waited for the ferry, Julia had not thought to secure a carriage and cursed herself when they docked and no one waited. But her valise was light, the road well-lit and she walked the three miles with an anxious swift tread, willing herself to stop thinking the worst.

By the time she arrived at the house in Lymington, Juliette was dead, unable to survive the troublesome delivery and subsequent loss of blood. There were no goodbyes, no embraces, no recriminations. The housekeeper took her bag silently and the butler poured her a glass of brandy. The doctor had gone. Edward did not appear. Julia showed herself into the parlour where her daughter lay and stared at her unnatural form. Even in death her plainness carried an elegance Julia knew she'd never possessed herself. Why had she never told her that? Why had she never told her how she felt? After all the years of hurt, Julia finally found herself ready to forgive, apologise, understand, and what she found at the house was nothing. No second chances, no conversations.

Later the butler would describe the look on her face as 'a wife by the gallows, stricken with grief and too proud to show tears.' The child, robustly healthy and with the deep-throated cry of a survivor, was already with the wet-nurse, the other children in bed. Edward had named her Henrietta, a name Julia despised, and he appeared in the morning as a wraith, dry-eyed and stiff-limbed. He prevented Julia from turning the mirrors, or draping the lamps, and rejected her attempts to bring the children to Freshwater, pledging instead to take them back to Scotland where, he made it plain, the Camerons were unlikely to be welcome.

Julia was heartbroken. Her photography, already ethereal, developed an increasingly dream-like quality and her interests focused on haunting female characters from mythology. Pictures full of ghosts. Repeatedly she staged Tennyson's 'Lady of Shallot', lonely in her enchanted tower and forced to stay for an eternity, weaving a representation of the world she saw only in her mirror. None of the models was right. Alfred, long familiar with the harrowing stress of depression and bereavement, thought privately what she sought for her Lady was Juliette herself; and, since he knew she would never find her, he took it on himself to suggest that she work on a series of photographs to illustrate his final, complete publication of The Idylls of the King, a lengthy poetical homage to the legends of King Arthur. Tennyson was enjoying a heyday of popularity and the book was hotly anticipated.

It was her first significant series commission. It was also a creative risk, carrying the danger of widespread critique along with the potential to bring her the best of the fame she craved. Immediately, she began to reread the cycle of narrative poems.

'I don't fully understand why Guinevere must be blamed for the fall of the entire kingdom.' Julia pulled at the cloth with which she had wrapped the hair of Lancelot, valiantly played by local tenant farmer, Albert Read. He had sat for her often enough to remain silent, unwilling to be dragged into another discussion for which he had no time or care. He'd already received payment for his trouble and would be unlikely to receive more, even if he remained in the Glass House for hours.

'It's an allegory,' said Tennyson, who was being made to attend every sitting, much against his will. Home comforts were important to the poet and Julia knew he was thinking of the fire that would be raging in his drawing room, the claret warming on its hearth. 'It's not the woman but the act of betrayal itself.'

'She has sent her lover away,' Julia quoted. It all sounded complicated. Far better a happy life with a man you knew than chasing lust. But then perhaps Guinevere had not the luxury of choice? Mallory seemed to think that. Had her own life been happy because she was plain? It seemed beautiful women were always in trouble. Or causing trouble.

'But not before she has loved him.'

'You've asked us already, how can she help who she loves?'

'And that's the tragedy of the human condition. That we may not choose. Our hearts and emotions, weak as they are, may simply not be guided by our heads and intellects, no matter how much we try to force them. Besides, I believe that Lancelot is worse.'

Albert furrowed his brow and tried to look hard as though he was not listening. Julia felt mildly guilty at the methods she had used to bring him to the studio, waxing lyrical about the shine of the armour and Lancelot's gallantry. Poor Albert would undoubtedly feel let down. 'Lancelot is the weakest of all. He loves Arthur, more than any of the knights, more than Guinevere herself if we're honest. And yet, at first sight, allows himself to fall for Arthur's queen. And he stays. And then he confesses his love to Elaine when she tries to court him, effectively killing all of them.'

Hatty Campbell, playing Guinevere for the fourth time and thoroughly in character, drew away from Lancelot and folded her arms. Julia smiled encouragingly; Hatty was just a young girl, a few years older than she'd been at the Cape when Keats had so impressed her. No doubt all of the Idylls had made her cry on first reading.

'There! Now it's ruined. You must stop talking Alfred, I can't work when you're like this.' Julia pulled off Albert's right chainmail gauntlet and thrust it into Hatty's hand. 'Now come back together, you must hold his bare hand in yours, his glove, the symbol of his loyalty for Arthur, should be clasped in your other hand, as though you crush it. You seem to dislike him now, your face... but that's good, good. It is a difficult story.'

Julia moved Albert's left arm behind them so the hilt of his sword was visible, leaving a threat of violence and battle in the background. She carried on talking to the pair through the exposure of the plate, which she left for ten full minutes. When she finally allowed them to move, Albert's neck was cricked from the strange angle and the draught of the studio. Hatty looked as though she might cry. They waited until Julia had developed a print she liked, talking together in low whispers while she worked in the coalhouse next door.

'Which of the poems is your favourite Mr Tennyson?' asked Hatty, shy without Julia.

He considered a few moments before replying. 'If you'd asked me a few weeks ago I would have said 'The Passing of Arthur'. Now I find I must wait to see what Mrs Cameron makes of them.'

Stories from the Glass House:
May Prinsep (Elaine)

We sat often for Aunt Julia and so nothing in the Glass House surprised me much. People who weren't used to her found it difficult sometimes, sitting in that weird smell for so long, in all the clutter and mess. But all her nieces and nephews were used to it. We were pulled in there on every visit and quickly learned that, if we did exactly as she asked, we'd be allowed out sooner. I was, in any case, quite a passive child and happy to be told what to do, which is probably why she kept asking me back once I'd grown. Mummy didn't like it at all, because Aunt Julia never asked her to sit. I don't think she ever took one photograph of her. They were always quarrelling, always trying to get one over on each other. But they were quite inseparable really; they couldn't leave each other alone.

By the time I sat as Elaine, I already had children of my own and Mummy had moved again—to be nearer to Aunt Julia and her whole circle, I think, though she had her list of other reasons. It was among some of the last pictures she took, a series based on stories of King Arthur. I was to be Elaine because I was a new mother, and Aunt Julia said I was learning patience, though I'm not sure that was true. Elaine, she explained, was the soul of patience, alone in a tower, weaving the image of Camelot in a mirror because she was banned from looking down on the city.

Aunt Julia was very excited about the tapestry she had found for me to pretend to be weaving; it was huge and round and heavy, propped on an uneven music stand draped around in a velvet throw. I worried it might fall on me and tried to hold it up with the hand that was supposed to be weaving, which made her constantly fuss over the placing of my arm. We came to a compromise in the end and I held it up with the other arm, but it was agony; you can see it in my face.

What I found difficult to believe about Elaine was that in the story she did not even know if it was true, if she really would be cursed if she looked at Camelot. She had only heard, or thought she heard, someone say it. And it seemed strange to me that someone would live their whole life like that, in thrall to some chance overheard conversation.

1873 Camelot & Freshwater Bay

Over fifty different costumes were gathered, made and altered to fit more than thirty sitters before Julia was satisfied that the resulting twelve images were the best they could be. The chainmail was borrowed from the theatre in Southampton, the armour from the metal suits that lined the Campbell's draughty hall. Dresses were easier. Most of Julia's wardrobe consisted of medieval velvets and she was happy for them to be cut and re-stitched in the name of Art. Swords were borrowed from the long hall of the manor in Shanklin, and a group of local craftsmen were employed to make the ship for Arthur Lying Wounded in the Barge.

'You were dreadful in that sitting, even Alfred wanted you removed.' Julia and Charles together looked through the first edition of the Idylls; a beautiful, cloth-bound book inset with twelve thick vellum pages printed with Julia's images. It had been rushed to them by Mrs Ruttles's son, along with a bottle of champagne, a sincere letter of thanks and a promise they would be joined for celebrations that very evening.

'I still can't believe you made me stand with my back to the lens.' Three figures turned away from the scene, each dressed in long black coats and with heads covered in wide strips of cloth. They appeared as ghosts behind the image of Arthur, played again by the fine lithe figure of Albert Read, his face obscured by a full helmet as he lay against the side of the barge, his arms drooping across his chest.

'It's how you should always be photographed,' admonished Julia. 'I don't know why I didn't think of it before. You'd never know here that your shoulders were shaking.'

'I can never help it; it's the costumes and the seriousness of it all. You know how serious things make me laugh.'

'I thought I did. Yet you didn't laugh in either of these.' She indicated the pages depicting the death of Elaine, first in the barge and again surrounded by people of the court. In both Charles appeared as Merlin, dressed in long grey robes and carrying a wide staff, his white beard pointed sleek, his face a perfect mask.

'There were too many people who wanted to go home.' He pointed to the gathered crowd at the deathbed. 'Some of them made that very plain.'

Julia remembered Jeremiah Bevan, who ran the island's abattoir, glowering over the many wasted plates. Large in stature and wealthy for a villager, he had volunteered himself for the Glass House when he heard about the project and, though he seemed to enjoy the costumes, was not the kind of man to be kept hanging around. The high pointed helmet he wore was heavy, requiring a thick pad of fabric underneath to protect the skull, and he sweltered under the cloth and armour.

'I think, of all of the prints, this one is my favourite.' Charles pointed to the picture of the Little Novice and the Queen. 'It's an extraordinary photograph. The girl is wrapped in cloth up to her eyes, but her cloth won't protect her, see how the queen sits, her eyes proud, she won't repent. They seem set on opposing sides.'

Julia began to explain how she had deliberately developed the print unevenly, leaving the left-hand side as pale as the nun herself and the queen enveloped in darkness, then stopped. Her pictures should speak for themselves and these ones did. She was right to be proud; she would never be able to make better prints. They were the pinnacle of what she hoped to achieve.

'You've interpreted these words as perfectly as if Alfred himself could have wielded your lens.' Charles smiled.

'I wonder if that will be enough.' Julia closed the book, suddenly weary. 'I know Alfred likes them, but will it all be enough?'

'Enough for who Julia? For what? Everything you've done has been enough for others, for those who enjoy looking at your work. It's beautiful, enchanting. If you're asking whether this is enough, the only person who can answer is yourself.'

Julia leaned back against her husband, felt the hard leanness of his body through his thin dressing gown. She closed her eyes. Was it enough for her? It was what she'd envisaged and it was wonderful to see it finished, but the series had taken immense creative energy and a formidable effort. When she thought of the Glass House now, in place of fresh creativity all she felt was a nagging doubt that there was little left for its stage. Her great work was complete, her great men mainly captured. The idea of beginning a new phase filled her with something close to dread.

She placed the book on the trunk they'd brought back from Calcutta, its dark wood smeared with a green-blue paint and pinned with scuffed metal studs. A delicious waft of sandalwood rose and scented the air, bringing visions of India. 'And your work Charles? We have barely spoken of anything but these confounded plates since you returned from the valleys.' India always reminded her of him, of them as a pair. Here they had drifted—no, her work had pushed them apart.

He eyed his wife warily. 'I've been unable to visit the Library much since Ceylon, and what with the visits to Kew and...'

'Actually, I meant your work on the estates. I've been meaning to ask you but these,' she waved a hand across the album of prints, 'I'm afraid they've occupied my soul.' If they could only talk about it, perhaps he would forgive her. Perhaps he felt there was nothing to forgive.

'The boys are doing well with managing the lands, as we knew they would.'

Julia tried to picture their faces and was alarmed to find she could not easily call to mind a clear image of Eugene. Had it been so long?

'They have good staff, a lot of staff I might add as people seem to choose where they want to work and simply show up every day, smiling, until you realise you need them and give in. But they need more help with the plants. Hooker's been immensely helpful, he's even offered to come out to see them, but I fear we may need to replant the estates with tea. It's a native plant and copes better with the weight of the monsoon.'

'Is it so bad?' Julia imagined warm rain running down her face in fat drops, the feel of wind in her hair.

'Heavier rains than India, and they sweep across in two directions, so it's not always possible to be entirely prepared.'

'Is it ever possible to be entirely prepared?' said Julia, half to herself. A sudden longing for real rain had caught her off guard. The smell of water-soaked earth, staccato drops on broad leaves. 'Do you miss it?' she said abruptly.

'Julia, you know I do. If you weren't here, I would never have returned the last time. This house is fuller than ever and yet it seems there's nothing left of our family now. The boys are in Ceylon, Hardinge wishes only to join them, and Juliette…'

She took his hand, understanding his inability to speak of their grandchildren. They had not seen them since they returned to the Highlands after Juliette's death, when Edward had made it plain they were not welcome.

'I find I'm weary and I feel that heat and peace is what I need,' said Charles. 'But you know I'll stay with you if you must be here.'

With her free hand Julia stroked her husband's long silver-white hair. She would be happy to see him happy. Moving would mean the end of Photography, but what more did she have to prove? She had been called an Artist, not once but countless times, by other Artists, Great Men, people whose opinions mattered deeply. What's more, she'd found the means to take back the world's Beauty and understand her destiny. It was enough.

'I'm weary too,' she said at last. 'And it feels as though there's little left for me to do in my selfish life but make my husband happy. So, if you say that we need to fix our estates ourselves, then that is what we must do.'

1873 Isle of Wight

In the fortnight before they left Freshwater, the Camerons threw open the doors of Dimbola Lodge and invited their neighbours to take what they wished. 'We've no use for any of it where we're going,' said Julia, and Watts began to worry for them even more.

'Dear Signor,' said Julia gently. 'We need nothing to live our simple life in Ceylon and this will be our last move. I'm 63 years of age; Charles is over 80. I'm sure you've heard my sister's horror that we plan to take our coffins with us?'

Watts had not and he was shocked. Charles, for all his white hair, walked perfectly straight-backed, his long limbs supple with the morning yoga he had practised for most of his life. Julia seemed no older than when she had first arrived on their island like a storm, and worked as tirelessly in the studio as she had ten years before.

'We wish only for a monastic existence in our hillside villa, spared from all this clutter.'

'If only that were true,' said Charles ruefully. 'I believe she merely wishes to begin the collection all over again.'

'But your work, everything you have achieved!' Watts swept an arm across the wall that held a dozen of her favourite prints and Julia smiled.

'It's all more than I ever thought possible. Besides, I'm not sure what more I can do here. Nothing's left. Nothing of my family is left. I'll take my camera and perhaps something else will come.'

'We both know it will not.'

'Perhaps you're right. But if it doesn't, I still believe I'll be happy. In these ten years I have contributed much to the Art of Photography—and I find it means more to me than fame. It hasn't brought me quite what I'd expected. I am weary of pushing and fighting. And Charles has talked for so long of where there is peace, warmth, few people, wonderful animals, that I find myself dreaming of the same things.'

Thoby, the only member of the family other than Mary with any kind of a head for business, urged Sarah to set up a discreet box for donations. Villagers dropped in pennies and carried off pots, pans and umbrella stands; the Cameron's circle gave generous gifts for sentimental mementoes and Alfred kept most of the props used in the Idylls series, even those that belonged to the local theatres. The photogenic housemaid, who was due to marry Watts's gardener that year, shyly asked Sarah to keep for her the baby things stored in the attic.

All Julia really wished to carry with her was the Glass House, an impossible desire, though she had it dismantled and moved to The Briary where it was lovingly reassembled and restored. She rehung the back curtains and sat inside it alone, remembering all the scenes and stories, triumphs and disasters of her years behind the lens. Bolingbroke with his set jaw, her First Successes, the men of science and the characters of legend, they were all there, remembered as they were.

Thoughts of Juliette brought tears. She should have set less store by her artistic pride and taken the family portraits her daughter so desired. At least she'd have the faces of the grandchildren. It was too hard not knowing how they'd grown, forgetting even how they were as children. They didn't play enough, she remembered that much. Was that her fault too? Was Juliette's childhood so marred by her own loose parenting that she had swung the other way with her own and been too hard on them? Too late now for blame, at least they had found a peace with each other and, who knew, maybe one of the boys would marry soon, give them some grandchildren they could help raise. Charles was sure Eugene would have found a bride by now; perhaps he was waiting for their arrival to tell them.

As the low evening light drew down on the windows, memories flooded to mind; Mary's patient hands on the plates, her nieces and nephews cross-faced from her fussing with their hair, the electric shock of Herschel's halo. She picked up the last remains of the clothes and costumes, the props and crowns, folding the fabric slowly, wanting to pull it all into herself. Then she closed its door for the last time, knowing what the Signor had told her was true—the Glass House was her and she would carry it with her always.

'I should never be helping you at all,' Watts complained, removing from the wall a print of Emily Tennyson with a young Hallam and wrinkling his nose at the depth of dust on the frame. 'When was this room last properly cleaned?'

'Why should I be expected to know?' asked Julia, surprised. 'I have maids.'

'I believe they spent more time on the chair in the Glass House than in here.'

'You say that as though it's a bad thing. I'd rather possess a hoard of fine prints than a sparkling drawing room. Besides, you taught me everything I know about abandoning Life for Art.'

'I certainly did not, you were quite incorrigible before we met.' Watts made a show of cleaning another heavy frame. 'And you don't seem to possess such a hoard as I had expected to find. What have you done with them all?'

'I've sold them, on your advice I might add.'

'You've taken many, many more than you've sold.'

'There are some at the societies and galleries of course.'

'Not enough to account for the rest. I've seen you giving them away Julia, to all and sundry, you really should have kept more. I don't wish to see you give another print away for no reason other than the pleasure of hearing someone say it's good.'

'That's not why,' Julia sulked. 'I wish only to share Beauty. Not everyone can afford painters. There are some people who may never have something Beautiful hanging on their walls if it weren't for my Photographs.'

'Well it has to stop,' said Watts. 'Where are your plates? Surely you've not been disposing of those too?'

'Mary took care of those,' she replied. 'Come and see.' She led him into the crockery store at the end of the dining room, now empty of everything except her archive of photographic plates. Carefully stacked piles of negative glasses, all wrapped, numbered and labelled in Mary's neat, clear script. To Julia the sight of those careful letters was somehow heart wrenching.

'There's a company that will reproduce these. I'd strongly advise that you allow me to work with them for you. Colnaghi asks always for more prints, we could make numbered editions of many of your series. While there's such an appetite for your prints it'll keep your name alive.'

Julia shrugged. After all the years of desperate longing to make a name, now she had done so it seemed enough. 'Perhaps,' she said. 'But how do you know they would print them correctly?'

'They're experts. They'll charge for the service, around thirty per cent of sales I believe.'

Julia whirled around from the pile she was inspecting, incensed at the temerity of such practice. 'But that's daylight robbery!'

'You've been giving them away! That's seventy per cent of sales you would not otherwise have made!'

Common sense had little impact on Julia, but something must be done with the plates; she could not take them to Ceylon, where the humidity would destroy them within weeks.

'Very well,' she said at last. 'You may do as you wish with these thieves. But my photographs should only be sold to collectors now, ask Colnaghi to see it is done.'

Watts inclined his head. 'So beauty is for everyone, but only if it is free? With such a temperament, Julia, you could never have been anything other than an artist.' He paused at the plate of himself, pretending to play on Julia's battered violin, two of her small nieces nestled close to his head. 'What did you call this one again?'

Julia glanced over. 'The Whisper of the Muse,' she replied. 'It is very you.'

'It is,' he agreed. 'Though, before I saw it, I could never have imagined it. May I keep this one?'

'You may keep them all, if you wish.'

He shook his head. 'I believe it's a good thing you're disappearing from civilised society. You may very well have caused the death of portrait painting with your photographs.'

'What a nonsense! There will always be the need for reflections and distortions, in any form.' She did not add that it was his ability to render beautiful her portrait that started it. Perhaps he knew, she hoped, but she never discussed her appearance with anyone. There was no place for platitudes or flattery. If he didn't understand now, he never would.

The sea was still on the day they left their island for another. A huge gathered crowd waved them off at the dockside: their friends, staff and all the many subjects of the Glass House, the farmers and girls, the grown-up children, along with several tourists caught up in the throng.

Charles moved as calmly as the water, dressed in a long, smart frock coat and holding nothing but a pink rose, given to him by Emily Tennyson. Alfred refused to say goodbye at the harbour and was notably absent in the crowd. Julia herself rushed from pillar to post, marshalling parcels and packages and, when she ran out of small coins for the dozens of porters, trying to persuade them to accept one of her prints as payment. Watts, watching from the harbour wall, shook his fists at her. But she was occupied with her cargo, doing her best to persuade along the gangplank a nervous cow, a present from Virginia to ensure they would have fresh milk at sea. Before the cow, eight porters struggled under the weight of two rosewood coffins, fitted with brass and filled with their glass and china, a sign to their friends that they did not plan to return. Charles walked to the ship, serene amidst the chaos, with an overwhelming relief that they were heading for a quieter life. It was as much as Julia could do not to cry.

1874 Dimbula Valley, Ceylon

Transported back to the East by the smell of sandalwood and the call of family, the Camerons arrived in Ceylon. Their sons were surprised to see such meagre luggage, the cow not surviving the full journey and the coffins accompanied by just two trunks of what Julia called 'the essentials', which contained mostly photographic equipment. Neither she nor Charles had brought clothes, intending to adopt the traditional dress more suited to the warm, damp climate and the work they knew awaited them on the plantations.

Julia liked that Ceylon was an island, with a wildness of water in rivers and waterfalls coursing through its interior lands. Though she missed the high, clear light of Freshwater, she liked their dark, spreading colonial villa, built from orange-streaked teak and covered in a sloping roof of twisted palm fronds that absorbed the sound of the rain and swiftly dried in the heat, whispering and rustling with the breeze. It merged seamlessly with the dense forests, a cave in the shadows of the canopy. The bedrooms were on the same floor, but, since they spent most days and evenings out of doors, the lack of space and privacy with their four grown sons didn't really matter.

Equally, she liked the sharp peaks of the mountains that framed their view and the way the tea and coffee plants ran down the hill in neat, thick lines, to meet with the untamed jungle. It was fertile country, with abundant wildlife and a humid climate that encouraged the indiscriminate growth of vines and weeds, as well as crops, and all the Camerons grew used to slashing and taming the vegetation with long curved knives. Plants sprouted easily from the rich red soil Charles liked to rub between his fingers as he squatted on the ground. Coffee rust was no longer a problem, but the lack of local expertise and the reluctance of the local workforce to manage anything but tea plants, meant most of the estate was now turned over to growing tea. A few lines of coffee remained, and the family, who sold a small crop locally to other colonials, mostly tended these.

Animals roamed the grounds and Julia did her best to tame them, but the shrieking monkeys and slinking civets evaded her attempts to draw them in. The lands were less populated than India, less changed by human hand, and the animals had no need to inhabit any other worlds than their own wild kingdoms. Julia adored elephants, finding them gentle and intelligent company. Two large females were kept for some of the heavier work, hauling trees and baskets of leaves up the steep sides of the hills. But she also began to collect retired log-haulers and babies orphaned by hunters, which exasperated Charles because they took up so much space and cost so much to keep. Each animal needed a handler, to train and work them, to bond with them and keep them constantly entertained; if they became bored, they could take out a coffee plant, carefully cultivated over a number of years, in one easy trunkful.

Charles's planned monastic existence was not to last long. Julia acquired possessions almost as soon as they arrived, finding it impossible to resist the travelling sellers with their carts of carved wooden ornaments. Soon the villa was crammed with low tables, footstools and carvings of a hundred different deities, the once-plain walls hung with masks and colourful paintings on long scrolls of bark. Space under the stilts of the house was surrounded with planks and lined with dark fabric to make a cool darkroom and a place to store her small stock of chemicals, some of which she poured on the ground in a bid to deter snakes. As soon as the urge to create returned, she would be ready.

'You've finally learned to close your aperture,' said Ewen, admiring the print of the elderly herbalist. 'I can see every line on his skin.'

Julia had been in Ceylon for over a year before using her camera and it was necessary to break it down to its components to wipe the damp from the glasses before it would properly work. She had fixed and set the lenses differently to the settings she had favoured in the Glass House and found she liked the new challenge. Here it seemed pointless to create dreamy medieval scenes. It was impossible to imagine battlements or castles. All that was needed was a clear, clean close-up of these fascinating faces.

'I couldn't get him to do anything other than smile.' Julia narrowed her eyes at the image, remembering his excitement at seeing the equipment. Llanku was the first local she'd persuaded to sit for her and he'd waved away the protests of the others that the camera would steal a part of him, laughing at their superstitions.

'I'm not surprised, he has a fine set of teeth. Look at these, he has most of his bottom set left and only two missing on the top row, I wonder what his secret is?' Most of the local men sported bare pink gums, their teeth ruined by the twin habits of chewing paan and sugar cane.

'Funnily enough I did ask him,' said Julia. 'He gave me a packet of leaves in a little thin cloth and said he drank it every day. Then he stretched his leg up behind his ear and said it would help me to do that when I was old. I told him that I was already old and had never felt the urge to contort myself in such a fashion.'

'Did you tell him he could move into the elephant barn?'

Julia shook her head, but she wasn't surprised he had and did not mind. The Singhalese people had a special way of getting what they wanted by simply not listening and going about their plans with the most impeccable manners. Llanku did move in, but he spoke excellent English and

280

proved an unwavering source of help and support, advising Charles on his planting and willingly recruiting other subjects for Julia from the local villages, even suggesting people to her once he realised the style of photographs she liked. For his original sitting, she'd paid him with a long string of beads made from pale orange stone and he wore it wrapped twice around his scrawny neck, always looking for the chance to acquire more jewellery. Whatever the weather, he wore the traditional Singhalese dress of a long white cloth, wound round the body in a feminine style, something Charles liked to copy when relaxing after a day's work. With his darkened skin Charles might have looked native but for his imposing height and the length of his hair and beard, which Llanku disliked and was always trying to cut. Eugene and Ewen had quickly adopted white trousers and tunics, cool and comfortable in the heat and rain. Often Julia wore the same, which worried some of the women who sat for her.

Knowing she could not easily get any more glass or equipment shipped to their station, Julia learned to become sparing with her plates and her photographs became stronger, more exacting. Experiments with focus were no longer affordable and from the very first trials it was obvious her style had changed; the faces that stared out from the prints were clear, natural and in focus, the images swept of their ethereal quality. Allowed to pose as they wished, the sitters mostly stared at the lens defiantly. Although Watts's careful disposal of her vast image library in England ensured she was still well known there, her new prints attracted a different kind of collector. They were popular with colonial tourists, especially those touring the region before returning home to Europe.

'You should really charge more,' chided Charles, as they watched the visitors depart. 'If only for the trouble of having to listen to their stories. I dread to think how many of your lovely photographs will be used to illustrate dreary memoirs.'

'They're not my best Art. Besides, they'll carry them home, where more people will see them.'

'People see them here.' He indicated the wall above the long rattan sofa where she carefully hung a copy of each new print as she made it. 'It's like a museum. You should have brought your others.'

'I'm not sure they'd understand them.'

Neither of them had much time for the tourists who came for a break from their posts in India and flocked through the nearby hill town on their way to Kandy. The local temple was said to hold the tooth of Buddha, smuggled from India in the hair of a princess, which was paraded through the town once a year in a riot of colour, reed pipes and drums. Once the temple guard had shown it to them, a huge pointed lump that could not possibly have lived in a human mouth.

'No, you're probably right,' agreed Charles.

'They asked me for whole family groups,' said Julia, indicating the local family that had now reached the end of their plantation, their elephants picking their huge feet delicately through the lines, managing not to damage a single leaf. 'They were quite insistent. I didn't like the way they talked about it.'

'They will have heard about the husbands of course.' In the surrounding hill country, once a separate kingdom, the women were permitted to have more than one husband, often two, sometimes more. There were several such families working in the Dimbula Valley, the children calling all the men in the household 'father'.

'It's nothing but protection of property and land. Either way the women lose out, they're not allowed their own land. In that respect it's not so different from home.' Julia had never lost sight of the fact that her husband had allowed her to behave as she wished, to make a name for herself in a man's world, and she was grateful. There couldn't be many like him. It was right that she'd done as he wished for the last years of his life. He was so happy here and there was nothing left for her to do at home. Had she started out a younger Artist, found her medium sooner, then she might have been able to grow, to change, but it was hard work and without Mary, without Juliette... She reached out to take his hand and squeezed it gently for a moment. 'It isn't for us to do anything about these matters now. Besides, I find I don't like to take group photographs any more. I'm done with storytelling. I prefer to take portraits again.'

'They're lovely,' said Charles, reaching to lift from the wall a portrait of a young woman, wearing a clean white sari and gold arm bracelets, a bride ring through her nose. Her right arm was on her hip, showing dominance, and her chin jutted fiercely, yet her left hand swung her skirts playfully. 'I feel as though I know everything about this woman.'

'You do,' said Julia, 'It's Seema, she helps with our laundry.'

'You know exactly what I mean. She's sharp, really sharp, her features are all in focus and her character truly visible to me. I've always admired your art, the dreamy quality you gave your images, but these seem to me truer to the people here. They suit the style.' He replaced the print next to an image of a young girl, wearing a blouse with long cotton trousers, her legs curled beneath her like a child, her elegant neck held proud, like a woman.

'I've no need to dress people up anymore.' Julia shrugged. And finally, perhaps, learned what it means to be a mirror, a real mirror. Such close detail is a way of showing the sitter that someone sees them as they are. In some ways that awful Ruskin had been right.

'Well they're really very beautiful in their way. I'm not surprised they're in demand,' he considered for a moment.

'You might do better to post the plates themselves to the Signor and have him make more for you.'

'The only person I would ever have trusted with my plates is Mary, who's busy, or dear Herschel and he's sadly no longer with us.'

Most evenings, as they sat on the porch and listened to the calls of the night creatures, the spreading canopy of stars around them, Julia thought of her old friend, looked for his face in his beloved celestial bodies. Together with her husband and daughter, and Mary, he had shaped her life; they had all shown her the glass and mirrors that made her whole. Although her god sometimes escaped her, still her fervent wish was to be reunited with them all beyond the stars.

1874 Ceylon

Sir Henry Cotton had been posted to Galle, ostensibly to head the burgeoning civil service there. In reality his opinion on independence for India was becoming unpopular within government circles and he had been politely requested to move. Julia left that conversation to her husband, delighted that she had the opportunity to spend time with Mary again. The town was a half-day from their hill station, by elephant and two of the local public carts, which were so uncomfortable most of the locals preferred to walk everywhere. They walked miles on the dusty roads in bare feet, toes splayed out the pads of mountain animals. Julia would have liked to do the same, but was no longer young and it hurt her to even try.

Galle itself was a bustling small town, a long-established trading centre crammed with dozens of nationalities and religions. Its narrow, dusty streets were filled to bursting with fakirs and fortune-tellers, magicians and snake charmers. Street vendors jostled for position with trays of hard and bitter fruits, or polished stones, strips of cloth dyed yellow and painted with symbols to ward away evil eyes. Julia adored it, though it felt as though Mama was always closer than comfort. She willed herself to ignore the calls of the scribes.

Mary and Henry had three young children, all girls, all pretty like their mother but slightly wild in a way that she had never been. 'They will kill me,' said Mary wearily. 'I have half a mind to sell them at the West Street market.'

'I know for a fact it would take more than a few children to finish you off, Mary Cotton. What would your mother say?' They smiled to remember. 'I complained I had no shoes until I met a man with no feet!' they said in unison and Mary crossed herself. One of the last plates Julia used was an image of the three children climbing over the lap of their long-suffering mother, which hung in pride of place on her museum wall.

'She was a good mother Mary, and you're the same, a natural Madonna.'

'If I am then I've learned from the best. Ma was fierce enough, and you too, Julia, but you were both good mothers and much kinder than you realised.'

Julia changed the subject, trying to ignore the deep flush that covered her face. But her heart sang. She had found some success in motherhood after all. Perhaps it was all one could hope, that some of the love thrown out might stick to the right people and help them to love in their turn.

On the way back from Galle, on the outskirts of the village that edged their plantation, was a secrets tree, a Bodhi tree with spreading branches and heart-shaped leaves. The villagers used it to whisper their secrets, make wishes, form pacts with whatever gods they worshipped. It was tied all over with tattered and faded scraps of fabric and writing bark. When she'd been to visit her dear friend, Julia often stopped at the tree, sometimes trying to decipher the symbols, mostly just enjoying the swish of the ribbons and threads and the spectacle of the tree itself. It reminded her of legends, like something Arthur's knights might have encountered, with an enchantress living in its trunk that might lead them to safety, or their doom. A fairytale tree.

The day Mary called her a mother, she decided to give it her own secret. From her pocket she took the star chart she had carried with her for most of her life. The ink was blurred and swirled from her strange baptism, the six stars streaked across the page and the edges torn where it had stuck to her wet skirts. She thought of Rohit, of diamonds and rosemallow flowers as she wrapped it round and round with a long strip of cloth and tied it tightly to a low branch. There. It was gone. A gift to the winds. No longer carried like a burden, or the weight of an ancestor.

Afterwards she felt so light and free that she half ran back up the hillside, crying out thanks and raising her arms to the purple-tinged sky, full of gathering storm clouds. Breath-hot winds ruffled her hair, she threw off her shawl and felt the first spit of warm rain tickle the skin of her arms. Thank you! The words screamed back to her, echoed by the thickened clouds. Thank you all of you! Which gods were hers now? She barely knew anymore, but she knew she was thankful they had given her a good life.

'Drink! Make you strong, big.' Llanku thrust a large bowl full of foul smelling, steaming liquid under her nose. Julia opened her eyes fully, for a moment unsure where she was. 'Five days sleeping! Time to drink.' She hauled herself up onto the pillows with effort, feeling weak and faint. Charles stepped forward and took the bowl gently.

'You caught a fever,' he explained. 'I don't know why you thought it was a good idea to dance on the hillside in a storm, but it obviously seemed like the right thing to do at the time. You were soaking wet and shivering when Eugene found you.'

'I don't remember.' A small shrine had been set on the box at the end of the bed, little mounds of rice and jasmine flowers, stuck with smouldering incense sticks. 'Was I? Did you think...'

'You've been very bad,' said Charles. His face was drawn. 'You were shouting and calling at first, then just rolling, sweating. You didn't seem to get better.'

'Mrs Julia will be getting better if she is drinking my tea.' Llanku danced from one foot to the other impatiently. Obediently she took hold of the bowl, enjoying its smooth warmth on her cold hands. It tasted as foul as it smelled.

'What's in this Llanku?' she tried hard not to pull a face, whatever it was made of had probably taken him days to find and a long time to make as he dried and pounded roots and leaves. He made teas for everything. All of them tasted so bad that the Camerons had soon learned not to complain of any ailment in his earshot.

'Secrets.' He tapped his left temple.

'Thank you,' said Charles. 'Come on, we should let Julia rest.' She waited until they had drawn back the main curtains to let in the sunlight and left the room before she put down the bowl, pulling the blankets around her shoulders, shivering slightly. Someone had left her portfolios by the bed. Two books lay next to them, some poetry and a novel by William Thackeray. It must have been Ewen; he had always been such a thoughtful child.

Lifting the heaviest of the portfolios, she leafed through its pages, thinking of her Glass House and the worlds she left inside it. Had the Circle ever found a use for it? Their letters didn't say. Sarah wrote only of conquests, of celebrities unknown out here, people she was never likely to meet. Emily wrote of the children; Alfred and Henry wrote of their work. Watts always made a point of relaying tales of her own fame. Sometimes it made her wistful. Though she enjoyed her newer portraits, the scrutiny of focus on these new island people, it was not the same. Generally, they were mistrustful of her camera and the humidity caused issues with the process that she could not understand; it left cracks and lines as though the images themselves were shattering and breaking apart.

In the pages of the book she saw the frantic and important work she had carried out at home. All the people in her life: the Madonnas, the kings and queens and angels, the Great Men. She had not made fortunes from her Art, but she had gained recognition and fame, created Beauty. 'I longed to arrest all the Beauty that came before me and at length the longing was satisfied,' she murmured to herself. 'I had, in the end, a life filled with Beauty.'

She leaned back against the pillows with her eyes half closed and watched the jewel-bright hummingbirds flutter in and out of the open window, feeding on the clustered blooms of the mango trees that grew by the side of the house. A sunbird hopped in, its thin beak picking through feathers that shone like mirrors. A single feather caught on the breeze and landed by her head. Picking it up to examine it she found it wasn't mirrored at all, just iridescent, ordinary without the company of others. The sunbird swooped across the window, joined by its clan in the canopy of trees, and in that brief moment Julia felt she witnessed the meaning of all things.

'Beautiful,' she breathed.

Acknowledgements

I have been fascinated by Julia's photography for many years and was prompted to write this account of her extraordinary life by two books about her art by Joy Melville (*Julia Margaret Cameron, Pioneer Photographer*, Sutton Publishing, 2004) and Jeff Rosen (*Julia Margaret Cameron's 'Fancy Subjects': Photographic Allegories of Victorian Identity and Empire*, Manchester University Press, 2016). I am grateful to the research of these authors. In building a picture of the woman and artist, my novel has taken a great deal of liberty with their careful facts and so I recommend those books to anyone wanting to know more about Julia's life and art, some of which can be found at https// www.jodycooksley.com.

Writing can be a solitary business and I would like to acknowledge and thank Jericho Writers for the unfailing encouragement to write. Especial thanks to Debi Alper and Emma Darwin for their powerful approach to self-editing and to Angela Young, Sola Odemuyiwa and Chris Lofts for their friendship and support.

Thank you also to the fantastic team at Cinnamon Press, particularly Jan and Rowan Fortune and Tracey Iceton, who are a pleasure to work with and who have all contributed to making a more readable book from my manuscript.

I am thankful for all the strong and special women in my life and particularly those who have supported and encouraged my writing journey: Jane Snell, Lisette Abrahams, Jacqui Seymour, Lilly Shimmell and Becky King.

Nothing would make any sense without my boys: to Matt, Ben and Ted thank you for the inspiration and for your constant love and humour.

LEAF BY LEAF